BEEN BLUED

BEEN BLUED

A Novel

Phyllis K. Twombly

Yes, these people know the author personally!

– Phyllis Twombly

iUniverse, Inc.
New York Lincoln Shanghai

Been Blued

iUniverse books may be ordered through booksellers or by contacting:

iUniverse
2021 Pine Lake Road, Suite 100
Lincoln, NE 68512
www.iuniverse.com
1-800-Authors (1-800-288-4677)

Because of the dynamic nature of the Internet, any Web addresses or links contained in this book may have changed since publication and may no longer be valid.

This is a work of fiction. All of the characters, names, incidents, organizations, and dialogue in this novel are either the products of the author's imagination or are used fictitiously.

ISBN: 978-0-595-44843-2 (pbk)
ISBN: 978-0-595-89164-1 (ebk)

Printed in the United States of America

www.ScifiAliens.com
(250) 219-8260

CHAPTER 1

▼

COVER STORY

Jerod opened his eyes. He was still in the reconfiguration chamber, still unable to see anything through the thick white gas. The only sound he could hear was his own breathing. Every previous configuration of the original Jerod had hated this, and he realized he did too. It would be a while until he was released, so he steeled himself for the wait. He felt the growth hormones kicking in. The correct aging seemed to be taking effect. He wondered if he'd be bald. Again.

Jerod sighed. All the lives he'd lived on Earth just couldn't compare to traveling the stars, no matter what cover story his buddy Coren came up with next.

He tried to remember his own appearance. He'd always had a secret fear of being unable to recognize his own face in the mirror. They tended to make him a bit short for a man, but muscular. Eye color seemed to be subjective, and if he didn't like it, he could pick another. As for age, he imagined they'd make him appear somewhere between forty and sixty. Age differences tended to matter less to the humans now. They'd started living a few decades longer, saying sixty was the new forty. Too bad they didn't have the same technology; they might be saying five hundred was the new two hundred. This much math was making him dizzy. Maybe it was too soon to think so hard after all the data and experience downloads.

He felt better as the genetic fog was replaced with atmospheric oxygen. He watched the gas recede and wondered if his people's hope would also fade away.

He looked over what he could see of his own body. His muscles felt familiar and comfortable, his skin smooth and taut. "Not bad," he muttered to himself.

He looked through the transparent walls of the chamber. Three men in white lab coats tended to banks of computers. An extremely old man in a black suit towered over him. The piercing blue eyes peering down over the top of black-framed glasses demanded his attention.

"How do you feel?" The voice sounded thick and muffled through the barrier.

The clear walls of the chamber around Jerod swooshed into the floor. He stepped forward and down, off the round reconfiguration platform.

"I feel fine, Coordinator. Upgrades and downloads from all preceding Jerod configurations were successful. Excess medical data was successfully purged. What's my next assignment?"

The Coordinator's expression remained unchanged. "Go get dressed. Nudity still frightens the humans."

Jerod tilted his head. Was the Coordinator developing a sense of humor? "Yes, of course, Coordinator."

One of the men in a lab coat was staring ahead, focusing on a stream of green letters and numbers. "That's sufficient," he mumbled. The stream stopped, suspended in the air. He waved his hand through it, allowing the data to absorb into his hand as he swiveled on his stool. "Wait up, Jerod. I've got your vocational download ready."

Jerod turned to see his best friend was looking well. He was taller than Jerod, by a good head and shoulders. His hair was barely receding, more at the edges than in the front. His nose was slightly longer than Jerod would have accepted, with a slight bump, but he had a solid jaw line. His blue-green eyes had a sparkle in them. His lips were still slightly oversized, in spite of the best genetic efforts.

"I see they still haven't got your lips right, Coren. Maybe the humans would have better luck with plastic surgery."

Coren absentmindedly ran his fingers over his lips. "And I still don't understand your fascination with my lips, Jerod. They're fine. At least the ladies seem to like them."

"Sure, sure, just not enough for you to have Been Blued." He regretted it the moment he said it. The hurt look on Coren's face was enough of a reprimand to cut him to the quick. His friend was actually blushing, something he hadn't seen in a long time. He knew it was up to him to restart the conversation. "I wonder what women really like."

"We're hoping your new persona will have better luck finding out. I've made you an actor, with reprehensible behavior. You're to play the roles, push the envelope on indecency with the leading ladies and try to seduce them."

"It won't work. You know we can't mate without having Been Blued."

"Of course I know that. But Darcy has this new theory that if we can get a woman aroused, she might be able to do something similar for one of us."

"He's not the one risking getting slapped around. I'm surprised you thought it was worth a try."

"We are desperate. Reconfiguration cloning will only take us so far. There are only a million of us left. My calculations project our extinction within three to five hundred years. Even less, if some awful cataclysm should strike this feeble planet, or if the humans detonate one of their nuclear weapons to start the last world war."

Jerod sighed. He looked around the lab. So much science and technology, and here he was, about to be some sleazy actor looking for an unsuspecting woman to seduce. "Okay, give me the download."

Coren touched his neck. A current went through both of them.

Jerod rubbed the spot. "You know I hate that."

"Yes, but it gives me such pleasure to see the spasm. It's either the computer download or you read a file five inches thick."

"Next time, I think I'll take the file."

Coren grinned. "I'm going to remember you said that. In fact, that gives me an idea for Jerod Sixteen."

"I'm not dead yet. Give Jerod Seventeen a chance, will you?"

"Of course."

Their conversation was interrupted by an angry voice. "Jerod, Coren, you're wasting time. Jerod's studio will be running late by the time he gets there. And like I said before, *go get some clothes on!* You'd think your new persona was a streaker."

"Yes, Sir." Jerod lowered his voice as he turned to leave. "As an actor, who knows?"

Coren laughed and slapped his friend's buttocks. "At least you have the physique for it. Any better and you wouldn't even have to hide your *thing.*"

"I play an alien," Jerod called back. "I might not have to, they might think it's part of the costume."

"With the possible exception of when the red swirls move about on their own," Coren mused. "Just how would you explain that?"

Jerod smiled. "Special effects?"

"Oh, wouldn't that be something? An alien with strange colors in his skin, who runs around exposing himself, sort of like you're doing now?"

Jerod gave him one last retort as he headed for the door. "Funny, I thought it was the *humans* who were afraid of nudity. And with you being a doctor and all."

"Never mess with the person in charge of your reconfigurations and downloads, Jerod," Coren called as the door closed.

"What a nut," he muttered to himself as he turned around and nearly bumped into the old man. "Coordinator! I'm sorry, I didn't see you there."

The old man grabbed onto him for support. "I think I need to be reconfigured, Coren. If you have a moment."

Coren motioned with his head to the other two men. They rushed over and helped support the old man. "Of course, Coordinator. Spencer, Perry, hold him steady. Computer, activate reconfiguration program for Coordinator Nine. Coordinator Ten is dying. Authorization Coren Thirteen; now, Computer, if you don't mind!"

A green stream of numbers, letters and images floated in the air between them. The old man wheezed out his last words. "Wish me luck, Coren?"

Coren sighed but nodded. "Better luck next configuration, Coordinator. Goodbye." He waved his hand above the old man's forehead and a spark leapt out.

The old man slumped. Spencer and Perry, brown-eyed brunettes who could pass for twins, eased his body to the floor, where it quickly disintegrated. Coren picked up the glasses, blew the dust off them, and placed them in his breast pocket. He stood in front of the computer. The green data stream hung in the air as he worked. The walls of the chamber Jerod had emerged from rose into place and filled with a white haze. Coren held his palm over his terminal. A spark flashed from his hand into the computer.

Spencer and Perry returned to their own consoles and went to work.

The computer began beeping wildly. Coren tried to work faster. "No, no, no! Not now, Computer, not now! Please! We can't afford to lose the Coordinator!" His fingers flew over the console. He relaxed as the computer settled down. "That's better. Enter data stream into subject's psyche."

The green data stream flowed into the reconfiguration chamber.

"Easy, Computer, take it easy, he's just a baby at this point. Okay, that's good. Now, age him to, oh let's say, twelve. No, make that thirteen."

"You know he doesn't like being thirteen," Spencer offered.

"That's okay," Coren responded. "He really hates being twelve. Either way, the extra time it gives him just might be worth it."

The computer began beeping again.

Coren tensed up. "This is *not* good. We can't afford to lose the Coordinator."

The walls of the reconfiguration chamber swooshed downward and a naked preteen stumbled towards him.

Coren's eyes grew wide. "Coordinator, you should know better than to interrupt your own reconfiguration."

"The computer needs me," the youth gasped. "Direct interface, it's the only way it can …" He placed his hands on the terminal. Before Coren could stop him, the Coordinator merged into the computer. "Keep me alive, Coren," a fading voice requested. The boy was gone, his physical body a pile of dust on the floor.

Coren redoubled his efforts on the computer. The beeps stopped, leaving an ominous silence in their wake. Coren looked at the other two. "Ideas?"

All three of them looked at each other in turn. Coren sighed and nodded. "It's agreed, then. Computer, initiate full shutdown and restart sequence. Defrag and clean all storage mediums in the process. Reinitialize all backups." He crossed his arms and sat down on his stool. "Get comfortable, Gentlemen, this will take a while."

Spencer and Terry retired to a sofa in the far corner.

"Computer, begin execution of directives now, Authorization Coren Thirteen."

The computer's lights went out. All lighting in the room went black.

The boy's voice pierced the darkness. "That's better. Thank you, Coren."

"Coordinator! I'm so pleased you made it. How do things look in the core?"

"Nasty. We've been putting this maintenance off far longer than we should have."

"Agreed. In space we'd have had time to do it. Here, on this planet, things tend to keep popping up."

"Now, now, can't keep blaming the Earthlings. They don't even know about us yet."

"I keep wondering about that. Their own UFO reports have gone way down since we eradicated the invaders. And yet very few of them have thought to wonder why." Coren tried to keep the conversation going, knowing the Coordinator needed to be slightly distracted to keep from being totally absorbed by the mainframe.

"Ah, yes, I was kind of wondering myself. They say cell phones are killing off the ghosts in England."

Coren laughed. "Cell phones? Is that the story our Europeans gave them?"

"Apparently. Hmm, I don't like the looks of this."

"What is it, what do you see?"

There was a pause that made Coren uncomfortable. "Coordinator? Are you still with us?"

"Yes. But we may need to acquire some human technology to complete this upgrade."

"What? You're joking!"

"I am. I've managed to develop a sense of humor."

A giant flash illuminated the room, making the ensuing blackness seem even darker.

The Coordinator's voice sounded strained. "That should do it. I hate that part. It feels weird, being part of the current. How long until you can get me a new body?"

The lights came back on. Coren looked at his computer terminal. "Normally, I'd say a few minutes, but we have to proceed with caution since you merged with the computer. You know your brain cells will have to be conditioned to accept your psyche. Allow for a few weeks, a month or two at the most. Meanwhile ..."

"I know, I know, try not to hang around any one part or program too long. What if I download a few national libraries, will that keep me safer?"

"It should. Is there anything else you want me to do while you're unavailable physically?"

"Actually, you can continue something I've been working on. Lately I've become concerned that our non-interference policy regarding human free will hasn't been adhered to rigorously enough. It's one thing to alter someone's memory to avoid our being detected, but I suspect it's happening all too often."

"I'll look into it, Coordinator. As you know, we've restricted that particular ability to several of our higher ranking men."

"It would be easier if they all shared Jerod's enthusiasm for life here on Earth."

"He was the first one to realize we should have a base of operations."

"So here we are, in the basement of his mansion, working two computer control rooms in hidden parts of this house, and buying up city property."

"We did name this town Martianville. If we hadn't controlled the council, it never would have passed. It was Jerod's vote that pushed it through."

"How do you suppose he'll do in this actor persona you've set up for him?"

Coren chuckled. "Knowing Jerod, the very girl he hopes will pick him will be the one to throw him out of character. Then we can get him back into his real work of medicine."

"You mean the whole actor persona is a prank?"

"You might call it a bit of revenge on Darcy's part. You see, Jerod accused Darcy of not having a sense of humor, so he asked me to be on the alert for the next time Jerod was reconfigured."

"I'm not laughing. We don't have time for things like this."

"I'm sorry, Coordinator. If I'd known you'd object, I never would have agreed to it."

"Perhaps we should encourage more telepathic communication among ourselves. Here on Earth we may have focused too heavily on verbal communication."

"It took us a while to learn the latest group of human languages. I remember treating a lot of sore vocal chords at first."

∗   ∗   ∗   ∗

Jerod was still attempting to snap the buttons on one sleeve of his shirt when the taxi pulled up. He closed the mansion door behind him and reached for the car door. The driver, a man with a dark complexion, a beard, and a turban, greeted him.

"Good morning, Mandeep. Please take me directly to the studio. Coren and Darcy are playing a little prank on me and I've decided to play along."

Mandeep smiled. "Always one step ahead of them, aren't you? Why play along?"

"It works to my advantage at the moment. I needed a break from the hospital. Not being able to help people with our technology was starting to get to me. I'm afraid I was getting close to giving human medicine a few unauthorized scientific 'breakthroughs.' This will allow me to get some perspective."

"How do you feel about being an actor?"

Jerod shrugged. "If I'm any good, there should be at least one female fan who falls in love with me."

Mandeep bit his lip. "Tell me again why we don't just take some human DNA for what we need."

Jerod's mouth fell open. "Because it's *wrong*, that's why. We will never resort to stealing DNA for our own purposes. Suppose you decided you never wanted a child. It would offend you deeply if someone suddenly presented an individual who was produced partly from your DNA. If we respect freedom of choice for humans, we have to wait until they're willing to help us."

"It would probably speed up the process if they knew about us."

"Before or after they dissect us?"

"You think they would?"

"If the roles were reversed, would we?"

"I prefer not to think that far. Do you really expect to find a potential mate among your new fans?"

"Let's say I have high hopes. Besides, I want more than just a mate for the purpose of reproducing. Our society needs to be able to rebuild itself and pass on what it knows to future generations. That requires family. I want a wife to share my life with, and when I find her, Coren will immediately take all our offspring and age them to young adulthood in the reconfiguration chambers."

"The way nature intended, you mean."

"Exactly."

"Do you think she'll develop the *thing?*"

"She might. You do realize you can call it a symbiont when we're talking among ourselves, right?"

Mandeep held up his hand to reveal red swirls circling through it. "I've got mine. Is it really true that 'Being Blued' will turn a man's face blue and download her memories into him?"

"That's what our archives tell us. It sounds like the experience draws on venal blood, instead of oxygenated blood."

"Here we are, the Monroe Studio. Am I supposed to pick up passengers today, or just run the car for our own people?"

Jerod looked at the black man in a suit, holding a blonde child in a pink jumpsuit. They were motioning towards the cab.

"They look alright. Go ahead and pick them up. Here's a twenty, you know how Mo gets when you don't collect."

Mandeep waited for Jerod to step out of the car, then pulled up to the man and the child. "Where to?" he asked once they were inside.

"Martianville Animal Shelter," the man instructed.

✳   ✳   ✳   ✳

The light blue walls of the shelter were plastered with posters on animal care and pictures of pets available for adoption. A red-haired woman with pale skin stroked the calico cat on the counter. Her voice was tired and tinged with sadness. "You might not recognize me the next time you see me, Kitty. The chemo will probably make my hair fall out. I wish I could take you with me, just to have someone to talk to."

The cat purred in response.

"You're the only kitty here that doesn't trigger my allergies. I guess it's because you're always getting washed too, the way you jump into the sink when I wash my hands. I'm going to miss that. Oh, look." She lifted the cat and pointed it in the direction of the window. "We might be able to adopt someone out."

A yellow taxi had just pulled in. The driver, a dark man in a turban, stayed in the car. His passengers, a young black man in a suit and a little blonde girl with curly hair, got out and came inside.

The shelter woman gave them her biggest smile. "Hello, my dears. How can we help you today?"

The man picked up the little girl. "My niece would like to adopt a puppy. I think she has her heart set on a poodle."

"Oh, and does she have her parents' consent?"

The girl giggled and nodded. She reached inside the man's jacket and pulled a letter out. The man leaned forward so she could hand it to the woman. The shelter woman looked it over, noticing the official seal. She smiled. "Of course. I think I know just the one." She winked at the man. "Wait here."

The girl put her head into the crook of the man's neck. "Thank you, Uncle Danny."

"Hey, don't thank me yet. A puppy can be a lot of work."

The shelter woman came back into the room with a gray bundle wriggling in her arms. "I think this little pup is just what you're looking for. She's housebroken and already has her first set of shots. Oh, and she adores little girls."

The man put the girl down as the woman set the dog on the floor. Girl and pup got tangled up with each other. The adults laughed.

"Have you got a name picked out yet?"

The man was about to say something when the girl spoke up. "I want my best friend to help me name her!"

The shelter woman checked the paper again. "All right. I think we can make an exception in this case. Just make sure they call us once a name has been decided on."

The man picked out a collar and leash from the rack beside the counter. "I think we'd better put these on the tab, too."

"Of course." The woman helped them get the collar on the excited puppy. She watched from the window as they got into the taxi. She stroked the cat in her arms and burst into tears.

CHAPTER 2

▼

THE STUDIO

An old man with deeply wrinkled skin, receding white hair, and bulging eyes was sitting in a canvas chair and chewing the end of an unlit cigar. His rumpled gray suit bore coffee stains and ash burns. The joints in his leathery hands appeared almost pointed. He looks like a smaller version of Winston Churchill, if the British version had ever let himself go, Jerod thought.

The shaky, high-pitched voice grated on one's nerves when he spoke. "About time the not so great Jerod Seventeen graced my humble set," he whined. "Think you're so important you can waste our budget on being late, eh?"

Jerod detected an accent and noted the fellow was probably from Canada. "That's the way we Americans do things, especially when confronted with a DeMille wannabe from up north."

The old man laughed, then coughed. It sounded like he was choking on his own phlegm. Jerod rolled his eyes. It would be at least three minutes before the old man would be able to speak again. If only he was still a doctor, he might be able to help him. Unfortunately, his medical training had been purged. Jerod shrugged mentally as he thumbed through the pages of his script. He felt a tug on his sleeve.

A young woman in a navy scrub top and loose matching pants seemed to be sizing him up. Her green eyes and blond hair were shining in the lights. She was slightly taller than him. He checked her shoes to see if she was wearing heels.

Instead he saw plain black canvas shoes. Remembering his cover story, he took his time looking all the way up her body, a slight smile on his face.

"Oh, hello. Are you a fan, Sweetie?"

She tilted her head and cocked an eyebrow. "I'm from makeup. It's time to get you into costume."

"Of course." He tried to pinch her rear, but she was too quick.

"Try that again, and you'll find yourself flat on the floor. Your reputation precedes you, and all the ladies on this set have been taught self defense."

He tried to look disappointed, in spite of laughing to himself. Modern females were so much more interesting than previous generations.

"I'll try to behave. But no promises."

She spun around and grabbed him. He found himself struggling to breath as her tongue probed deep into his throat. It wasn't anywhere near as pleasant as he'd expected.

Just as suddenly, she let go, leaving him off balance. "How do *you* like it?" she hissed.

He recovered quickly and wiped the back of his hand across his mouth. "I like it a lot. How do I get more?"

She scowled. For a moment he thought she might slap him. "Men like you …"

"Learn to keep a respectful distance from women like you." He tried to look harmless. "Does that satisfy your concerns, Miss, uh? I'm sorry, I don't know your name." He offered her his hand.

Her eyes narrowed as she scrutinized his face. At length she relaxed and shook his hand. "Miss Breton. All right. As long as you behave, we'll be able to work together. Just keep one thing in mind. My uncle's a lawyer who specializes in harassment cases."

"Really? I wonder what he'd say about that kiss?"

"He'd no doubt be angry that I was manipulated by reverse psychology into giving it to you."

Jerod lifted his eyebrows. "I see. You are quick."

"And don't you forget it. I can make the costume go on easy, or I can make it extremely uncomfortable."

He shrugged. "Why don't we go for easy today?"

She led him down a hallway that bore gory posters advertising various sci-fi horror flicks. She opened a door into a brightly lit room full of mirrors, chairs, makeup counters and wardrobe trunks. A large black box in the center of the room bore a sticker with the letters JS.

"I find it easier to get an actor into a costume like this if we start in the middle of the room. Take your clothes off."

"So soon? Alright, alright," he responded to her withering look. "I'll behave. You have to remember, when so many women have had their way with you, being sexy is a hard habit to break." He began unbuttoning his shirt.

"More sleazy than sexy. I have a sneaking suspicion even your creepy side isn't real."

He put his shirt aside and started to undo his belt. "What makes you say that?"

"Women's intuition. Plus, you didn't respond normally when I kissed you. Either you were totally taken aback, or …"

"Or?"

"Or you're gay." She shot him a smirk.

Jerod stepped out of his shoes and dropped his pants. "My Dear, I wouldn't know how to be gay."

She handed him a pair of tights in a package. "Meet your new underwear. From now on, wear these instead when you come to the set. They're designed to reduce chafing. You'll have to remove your briefs. I can leave the room if you're self-conscious."

He took the package, careful to touch only her fingertips. "That won't be necessary. Just try not to stare."

She shook her head. "I have too much to do, unpacking your costume. This is the first time it's coming out of the box."

Jerod struggled to get the tights on. "Are you sure these are the right size?"

She laughed, a muffled sound from the other side of the box. "Now you know what putting on pantyhose is like. Yes, they're the right size. Quit squawking and get on with it. Oh, those idiots, they forgot the vest."

"Here." She got up and handed him an ugly, mottled blue and green set of beastly legs ending in large, clawed feet. "These go on like really, really long socks. Put this piece on over top, but be careful not to rip it with your new claws."

Jerod looked at the piece in question. It appeared to have hooks to fit into the top of loops inside the legs. "What holds this up, an erection? Sorry, sorry, habit …"

She continued to scowl. "The *vest*, which they *forgot*, was supposed to hold them up." She sighed and pushed herself up by balancing on the chest. "Good thing I'm always on the ball. I've got some extra suspenders that'll do the trick for now. Just hold that until I can hook you up."

Jerod tried lifting his new monster leg. "So this is what it's like to be a swamp monster. Kind of awkward, it'd be hard to run. No wonder they're extinct."

Miss Breton was clipping a black pair of suspenders to the top of his bottoms. "If you want to meet a real monster, I can bring the frilled lizard tomorrow. He's quite friendly. I almost have him trained out of biting."

"Almost. That gives me confidence."

"Oh, it's just love nips, he's just a baby."

"Maybe we can compare legs."

"His are nicer."

"Now there's something every actor wants to hear."

She stood back from him. "I think we can work with this. How do you feel about being green for a few days?"

"An environmentally friendly monster?"

"No, no, look, just hold still. And you might want to cover your face."

Before he could object, she grabbed a couple of cans of body paint and started spraying madly. He covered his face and tried not to choke on the fumes and excess spray that got through. He shuddered with relief when she started on his back.

"Try not to move, no, wait a minute. Do that again if you can."

"Do what again?"

She peered around his side. "That quiver that went through your spine. It gave the paint an interesting effect."

"At this point I'd shake like a dog if you'll promise to make this go quicker."

He did his best to call up a muscle spasm.

"Perfect, but not quite that hard. Again. Wonderful. Now, a little blood smear here and there, and then we can do something about your face."

"I do get it back afterwards, right?"

"A sense of humor. Keep that, you're going to need it. Now *sit!*"

Jerod sat down and grimaced at what he saw in the mirror. The monster part was definitely working. Miss Breton scooped a glob of purple gel from a small tub on the counter and went to work on the little hair he still had.

A knock on the door made them both turn. "Come in," Miss Breton responded.

A slight brunette teen, with large green eyes, was holding a cage. Her blue jumpsuit was tight enough to show off her developing figure. "Sorry, Mom, Dad came to pick me up early and Tony can't watch your lizard anymore." She put the cage down with a slight jolt. The lizard hissed at her. "I gotta go, Dad's waiting and you know how he gets."

"Yes, Nikki. That's why *I* have custody. Go ahead, have fun, and don't forget, I'll know if you skip school Monday."

The girl half turned back, her hands clasped together, her head tilted, an affected lilt in her voice. "Oh, yeah, nice meeting you Mr. Seventeen. It'll make all my dreams come true if you give my Mommy an autographed picture for me to frame and put beside my bed, where I can dream about you *all night long.* 'Bye, 'bye." She did a slight curtsy before closing the door.

Jerod looked at the cage, then at Miss Breton. "Your daughter has learned well."

She picked up a towel and wiped the gel off her hands. "What do you mean by that?"

"Maybe I shouldn't tell you. It can only worsen our already tenuous working relationship."

She leaned back, her hands on her hips. "Now I really have to know."

"Let's see, she brought your lizard to you, forcing you to deal with it instead of her, a nice way to manipulate the situation, and …"

"And?"

"And she took the opportunity to remind you of something you see as a flaw in your ex, with the phrase, 'you know how he gets,' and …"

"And?"

"And she took the opportunity to expose your contempt of actors with false idol worship towards me. I believe that used to be called, 'damning with faint praise.'"

Miss Breton stared at him for a moment, then laughed. "You're something else, you know that? Here you present yourself as some shallow jerk without a clue, but you do have a handle on things, don't you? You got my whole family situation analyzed in under two minutes."

He looked at the door. "I wish I had a child."

"Yeah? I can sell you that one if you want."

"You don't know how lucky you are. I've always wanted to be a father."

"You mean, with all your fooling around, all those women, not one of them …"

He looked up at her, almost pleading with his eyes. "Not even one."

"Wow." She put a hand on his shoulder and looked at the mirror. *"Wow!"*

The lizard hissed. Miss Breton went to the cage. "Where are my manners? Jerod, meet Taz." She opened the cage. "Taz, come out and meet Jerod Seventeen."

The lizard looked at its open door and flicked its tongue. Without further hesitation it scampered across the room on its hind legs, climbed up Jerod's legs and chest and perched itself on his shoulder. It looked back at her and frilled its gills.

"That's amazing. Taz doesn't like, you know, *men*. No offense."

"None taken. Perhaps he likes my legs, or maybe he just recognizes one of his own kind." Jerod offered his hand to the creature on his shoulder.

Taz opened his mouth, as if to bite, then paused. Instead, his tongue flicked out a few times, brushing Jerod's finger.

"I have a crazy idea. If Taz will stay on your shoulder, we should have the publicity shot taken with him. The publicity guys can airbrush your monster head in later. What do you think?"

"I like it. But it's your idea, shouldn't you suggest it to the director?"

She snorted. "That old fart? He's too sexist to listen to any idea from a 'lowly' woman. But he might accept it coming from you."

Jerod tilted his head, and Taz followed suit. "On one condition. Once the movie's made, we make it known that the picture was *your* idea. Maybe this director won't appreciate it, but others will. They're not all stupidly sexist."

Miss Breton bit her lip. Jerod wondered if she was about to start crying.

"I'm sorry, I didn't mean to hit a sore spot."

She gasped for air. Taz ran down Jerod and scampered to a drawer near the floor. With a claw, he opened it, jumped in, and turned around. He grabbed something in his mouth and raced back to Miss Breton with it. He put his front claws on her knee, allowing her to take it without bending down too far. Then he scrambled back to his spot on Jerod's shoulder.

She made quick use of the inhaler and brought her breathing back under control.

Jerod watched in disbelief. "Are you okay?"

She nodded and continued to work on her breathing.

"I didn't know a lizard could be trained to do something like that."

Miss Breton looked puzzled. "He isn't. He's never done it before. I don't know why he did now, but I'm sure grateful. You wouldn't have known where my inhaler was."

"Anything else I should know that might become an emergency?"

"No. I wasn't even going to tell you about this."

He took her hand. "Now look, let's put all joking and ego aside for a moment. You're right, the whole sleazy, macho man persona is a *role* for me, not who I am or who I want to be. I do have that reputation to keep, but I'm not sexist and I'm not inclined to seduce every woman I meet. I'm just a regular guy trying to earn a living doing something I love.

"So when it comes to things that matter, like being able to save a life, I'm going to do whatever it takes. Don't pull the tough chick routine on me when I can help you."

He settled back in the chair. "Besides, you seem like a nice lady with her head on straight. If you'd have me as a friend, I'd like that. Sometimes it will mean continuing this phony little feud we seem to have started for the sake of appearance, but if you think you can handle it ..."

She put her other hand over his mouth. "You actors do get going when you think you've got a role. But if you mean it, that you respect me and want to be friends, I think I can handle copping a 'tude for the camera.

"I always have an extra inhaler in my purse. I wonder how Taz knew there was one in the drawer down there."

Jerod winked at the lizard. "We monsters know everything. Except maybe that avoiding extinction thing."

Taz hissed.

Miss Breton shook her head. "You look like two of a kind. But don't worry, I doubt either of you is about to become extinct in the near future."

Jerod considered asking if she'd like to help make sure, but thought better of it. "Should I really give Nikki a photo?"

Miss Breton shrugged. "Only if you want to. I think she prefers younger men. No offence."

"None taken."

CHAPTER 3

▼

KELLY

The red-haired airline agent adjusted his jacket. He pushed his thick-framed glasses a bit further up his nose. His garish, yellow lanyard clashed horribly with the navy uniform. He tapped a bony finger on his keyboard, mostly as a way to pretend he was actually doing something for the customer.

He tried to sound tired; something he figured would either calm or irritate the young lady. Working the job these days, a person couldn't win.

The big brown eyes were demanding he look up. He wished he could avoid them, but didn't want to look shifty. He tried to sound apologetic.

"I'm sorry, Miss Ravell. With the weather from Riverdale, and your flight being delayed, you've missed connections for most of the day. I suggest you explore the town. There's a lot to see here, we're sort of the second Hollywood for horror and science fiction. Maybe that's why the town is called, 'Martian-ville.'"

Kelly ran her long tapered fingers through her short sandy hair. "No connections at all?"

"None that would do anything but delay you even more. If you come back tonight around 10:30 p.m. there might be something." He paused. "Do you need anything from your suitcase? It would speed things up if you could leave it here, then we wouldn't need to put it through security again."

Kelly thought for a moment. "No, anything I might need is in my purse or on my cell phone."

"Oh, good. Can I have the number in case we need to contact you?"

"Just a second. I haven't memorized it yet." She pulled it out of her purse and flipped it open. "Not again. I just charged this thing yesterday and it's dead. No, wait, it's working. No, it's dead. This thing is going straight back to the store when I get home!"

He pointed at a sign. "You might have better luck outside the terminal. We have too many things transmitting for most phones to work."

She looked where he was pointing. The sign read, 'Cell phone And Laptop Reception May Be Minimal Inside Buildings.'

She closed the device and tucked it back in her purse. "So, I don't suppose you have an information package with things to do here?"

"No, but the Information counter does. It's one floor down, just before the shopping area."

Kelly smiled at him. "Thanks for your help, the bit you could give. I know this wasn't your fault and a lot of people have probably been grouchy today."

"Thank *you*, Miss Ravell. Nice people like you do get restaurant discounts and studio pass vouchers. I hope it helps you pass the time." He handed her a fat package of visitor coupons. "Have a nice day."

Kelly thanked him and headed down the stairs towards the Information counter. Seeing the long lineup, she shrugged and walked outside. She picked a taxi from those waiting at the curb and got in. The first coupon in the envelope was for the studio.

A dark skinned, bearded man with a turban turned around and eyed her through the security grating. "Where to, Miss?"

She tilted her head. "Is there a café near this, uh, 'Monroe Studio?'" She held up the coupon.

"There is. My cousin, Mo, runs it. I'll take you straight there. He makes the best kebabs and the best coffee in the whole city. Say hello for me and he will give you friendly discount. Please fasten your seat belt. It is now state law. And no smoking, please."

The car started to move before the man finished speaking. Kelly leaned back to grab the harness strap. She clicked it into place. She leaned forward enough to read his name on the card posted on the security screen.

"Thank you, Mandeep. I'll be sure to mention you by name."

"Don't bother. All my male relatives who drive taxi are also named Mandeep; a silly quirk of my father's. Silly man, but a good father. Eighteen children, all male. Except for my sister. I keep forgetting about her."

"Because she's female?"

He laughed. "No. Because she was only born last month."

Kelly knew she'd regret asking, but went ahead anyway. "Does your father have more than one wife?"

He laughed again. "No. But this country has something called 'a paternity suit.' He loses, every time. And every time, my mother threatens to leave him, so he swears he will be good. But I think it is hopeless."

Kelly tried to hold her laughter in.

"It is okay to laugh. We find it funny. Except for my mother. Good thing she's rich."

"How does that help?"

"Every time my father introduces another child, she adopts it as her very own. She's a wonderful mother."

"What about the other women?"

His eyes in the rear view mirror looked surprised. "We do not adopt the women my father fools around with."

"No, I mean, don't they keep their babies?"

"No. So far the babies all look like my father, so the mothers don't want them. Besides, babies interfere with their profession."

Kelly thought she caught a wink and decided she knew quite enough. "So, what all is on these kebabs your cousin makes?"

He roared with laughter, so hard she thought he might lose control of the vehicle. "You Americans. How much did you believe of what I just told you?"

She felt her cheeks flush. "All of it."

"I am sorry, but you looked so serious when you got in, I thought maybe you just needed to have someone tease you a bit."

"It was kind of funny. And you're right; I was getting way too serious over a delayed flight. Life is too short for that kind of stress.

"But I hope the part about the café was true."

He smiled broadly. "And the part about the discount."

She smiled back. "What about the studio? Is it really worth seeing?"

He shrugged. "It's easier to get into than the expensive, better known studios. But it's also very laid back. If you're a writer with a manuscript, they'll actually take a look at it. Not like Hollywood. If a writer has talent, this studio will give him a chance."

"We can all use another chance."

"Indeed. Here we are, my cousin's café, 'The American Refill.'" He lowered his voice. "Some of the actors just call it, 'The Fill,' something my cousin hates. Try to avoid that."

"Thanks for the warning. What do I owe you?"

He turned around. "Nothing. Call it my random act of kindness for the day."

"I've been treated so well since I got here, I might be tempted to move to this city."

"I hope you do. Martianville has a lot to offer, and I've got the feeling you do too. Have a nice day."

She got out and thanked him again before closing the door. He waited until she began crossing the patio before grabbing the car's radio mike. "This is Mandeep. Come in, Mo."

"This is Mo," a cheery voice responded.

"There's a nice one headed your way. Be good to her. I have a good feeling about her."

"Did you give another one a free ride? You know that's against the rules."

"You are as bad as the DMV. Lighten up."

A sigh escaped the speaker. "Okay. Mo, out."

*   *   *   *

The American Refill was splashed with varying combinations of red, white and blue on the patio deck, table and chair sets and windowsills. Small green vases on each table bore miniature flags instead of flowers.

Kelly's eyes took a moment to adjust to the dimmer light inside. The ceiling was red, the walls were white and the floor was a navy blue with large white stars. Tables and chairs were the same as those out on the patio. An old jukebox in the corner had been repainted to match, with telltale spots of its original colors peaking out from under faded paint. On the walls, neon signs from a bygone era advertised cola and other products. Booth seating had been replaced with more table and chair sets. In spite of the generally faded appearance, the entire café was squeaky clean.

Another dark skinned man with a neat white mustache eyed her with slight interest. His shoulder length hair was completely white, and his face deeply lined with the wrinkles of age, but his brown eyes were keen and bright. His apron looked as old as he did, but it was spotless. He resembles Mandeep, probably the cousin, Kelly thought.

He spoke with what sounded like a Midwest accent, in a pleasantly deep voice. "May I help you, Miss?"

"I'd like a coffee, please. And I hear your kebabs are good."

He laughed as he poured out a cup from the machine, possibly the newest piece of equipment in the place. "Oh, that Mandeep. He's been telling stories again."

He turned around to give her the cup. "We only serve kebabs on special occasions. Otherwise, it's burgers and fries, milkshakes, that sort of thing. Can I get you a burger, no, let me guess; a cheeseburger, extra tomato, and mashed potatoes instead of fries."

"That's amazing."

"Not really. I noticed you look very fit. That's what most of our healthier customers order."

"Thanks for the compliment."

"Sit anywhere you like. The sun gets a bit extreme this time of day. I'd suggest a table on the left just outside the door, there's good shade there. I'll find you when your food is ready."

*   *   *   *

"How was everything?" he asked as he poured a second cup of coffee. Kelly had picked a table in the shade. Other diners had filled up most of the other tables and kept the volume to a dull roar.

"It was good, thank you. My compliments to the chef."

"Can I get you anything else?"

"I'm good, thanks. Are you the only person working on the floor today?"

"Oh no, we merely assign one person to serve outside and two or three to work inside." He bent down, clasped his hands together and whispered to her. "I'm glad you chose to sit outside. Most of the other diners out here are from 'The Monroe Studio,' down the street. Have you ever heard of Jerod Seventeen? That's him, on the outermost table. I hear he might be looking to settle down."

Kelly glanced at the fellow, then gave Mo a half smile and whispered back. "Why tell me?"

He pulled back a bit, shrugged and moved his hands slightly apart. "Who knows? A nice single lady like you might be looking for a challenge, someone to tame; I think he just needs a confident woman like yourself."

Kelly felt strangely comfortable with the old man's suggestion. She realized he was hinting at a possible introduction. "So who else is here?"

Mo looked surprised but recovered quickly. "See the fellow at the table behind me? That's Sid Loma. He's, oh, what is the word, you know, of two cheeks."

"You mean, two-faced?"

"Yes, that's it. The rest of these people …" He shook his hands, palms down. "You probably don't want to know, not personally. But if you're a good writer, looking for a place to start …"

"No, I'm just a traveler with bad flight connections."

"Oh. That's too bad. They are always complaining that they can't find good writers. But they'll be happy to see you if you want to explore the set."

*   *   *   *

Jerod looked up from his table. There was the usual mix of people he knew and those who just seemed to show up at the café. He wondered how many of them were aware of his fledgling career as an actor. Mo had certainly been doing his part, pointing him out to every single woman who showed up. Barely a few weeks into his new life and he felt like he'd met every single human female in the Midwest.

Still, there was a part of him that couldn't quit thinking about Miss Breton. Their exchanges on the set had been brief, but definitely friendlier since that first day.

The daughter was intriguing, with her bravado and childish ignorance. She dressed younger than her real age, something that puzzled him. Why would an eighteen year old dress and act like she was barely thirteen? He wondered what his own children might be like, if he ever got the chance.

It was strange, the way thoughts of the mother quickly turned into thoughts of the daughter. They were another man's family, Jerod reminded himself, a human family. There were times when being an alien definitely had its disadvantages.

Then there was the divorce. While they *were* desperate, he doubted the Coordinator would accept the idea of someone from a broken human relationship as a suitable mate. Their own females had always mated for life. Human stepchildren? Would that be an answer? Mo asking if he wanted anything else interrupted his musings.

"Just the usual. A wife, children, you know, all the things we'll never have."

Mo chose to counter the dismal comments with some of his favorite sayings. "Never give up hope. And never give up on friendship. I proofread your report. Your spelling in English is *still* horrible; you really should do something about that. But I agree with your point of view, that if friendship is the best we can do, maybe that counts as family.

"By the way, can I introduce you to someone? There's a very nice young woman sitting just over there."

Jerod looked at the spot on his wrist where his watch should be. He'd taken it off earlier, after the strap pinched his wrist for the third time. He grabbed Mo's wrist instead to check the time. "No, I have to get back to the set. You know how he gets."

Mo looked so disappointed that Jerod almost reconsidered. "Maybe next time. I doubt I'll be missing out on 'the one.'"

"But can you afford to take that risk? Isn't your current mission to find a mate by any means possible?"

Jerod stood up. "Until that last comment, you almost had me. Perhaps, if I was supposed to succeed in this mission, they would have had the foresight to give me a full head of hair. Do you know what value human women place on a man's hair? There's only a small percentage that prefer bald men."

"Small, but lucky? It's very human looking." Mo sighed as he watched his friend go. Without moving his head, he rolled his eyes in Kelly's direction. An obscure telepathic suggestion might be in keeping with the day's unfolding events. He went back inside and waited for her to come in with her bill.

*   *   *   *

Kelly toyed with her coffee cup. Two cups was her daily limit, but with the incredible flavor of what they were serving here, she'd just finished her third. She picked up the bill, wondering yet again if *Please Pay Server* meant any server, or the one who had waited on her. It didn't look like the old man was coming back out, so she picked up her purse and went inside.

Mo smiled as he watched her approach the cash register station, a large, rectangular counter with an antique register. "Was everything satisfactory, Miss?"

His tone was soothing, suddenly almost seductive. Kelly felt herself trusting him completely. Such a nice old man, she thought.

"Do you find Jerod Seventeen attractive, possibly enough to consider him husband material?"

Kelly tilted her head. "Of course I do, but that's an odd thing to ask."

Mo brought the telepathic connection up a level. "You will find Jerod Seventeen wandering about the set. You will find a reason to kiss him. Then you will decide whether to select him as your mate. Do you understand?"

Kelly nodded. Mo eased off mentally as he gripped her shoulder with a strong hand.

"Oh, goodness, I suddenly felt weak."

Mo let go as she regained her balance. "It's the difference between the air conditioning and the temperature outside. You'll feel fine once you're back in the fresh air."

"Do you take credit cards?"

"Don't you remember? You just paid your bill." He held up a receipt, showing she had paid cash.

"That's right. I paid cash. Oh, I'm sorry, I forgot the tip."

"Never mind. Your charming company was reward enough." He winked and released her mind completely.

*   *   *   *

Mo waited for her to leave, then picked up the CB mike. "Mo to Mandeep. Come in Mandeep."

Mandeep put down the paper he'd been reading and touched the button on the CB. "Mandeep here. Go ahead, Mo."

"You were right. She really is special. I tried to introduce him to her, but he took off."

"He took off? That's strange."

"It's a good sign. He's subconsciously avoiding her. I sent her to him with a telepathic suggestion to kiss him."

Mandeep snorted. "I tried that one time. He wouldn't speak to me for three months."

"Yes, but you sent him a woman with an ugly nature and she slapped him very hard. This time will be different. I can feel it. She has a far more compatible nature."

"I hope you're right."

Mo grinned. "I'm always right. That's my role. Remember?"

CHAPTER 4

▼

THE FALL

Kelly showed the uniformed guard at the gate her brochure. In spite of dark sunglasses, the beefy man's face lit up when he saw the paper. His suntanned complexion glistened as he spoke in a California accent.

"Go right in, Miss. I'm sorry we don't have any kind of guided tour today, since there's no filming going on, but you're more than welcome to look around. Just be sure to knock first on any of the doors marked 'Wardrobe' or 'Makeup.' Feel free to take pictures." He smirked. "Unless you find someone half-naked. Then take *lots* of pictures."

He winked and moved the yellow and black striped sawhorse from the entrance to give her space to enter.

Kelly read his nametag. "Thank you, Chuck. I don't need a visitor pass or anything?"

"No, Ma'am. If anyone had thought you were dangerous they wouldn't have given you a brochure. In a way, you've already been security screened."

"That's a very laid back way of doing things, don't you think?"

He shrugged. "Maybe where you come from." He waved his arm, ushering her in. Apparently the conversation was at an end.

Still a bit puzzled over the encounter, Kelly proceeded to cross a large, empty parking lot. The main building was huge, with only a few windows. The door was propped open with another sawhorse, in spite of a sign advising that this door was to be kept shut. Careful not to dislodge it, she stepped inside and stopped. It took her eyes a moment to adjust to the dim indoor lighting.

She saw a row of doors to one side, several of which were designated as offices. Right in front of her was a long corridor, its hallways plastered with movie posters. She strolled down it.

*   *   *   *

Darcy settled back in a corner of the rafters. His light brown complexion and green eyes went well with the black he usually wore. Dress suits, casual or workout wear, it was all the same. He felt as dark and foreboding as his clothes. He was a tall man when he was standing, but not a handsome one, according to what *they* thought. Genetic enhancements had made him stronger than any dozen of them put together. His assignments usually involved engaging the more dangerous aspects of life on this planet of humans. He was down to three possible reconfigurations, and even the substance inside his skin seemed to sense their time was running out.

He held up his hand, looked at it, bid the thing to acknowledge him. Green swirls raced about angrily, causing a noticeable rippling effect in his palm. Green. Not red. He'd had to work to hide that. Ancient rumors about vegetarian diets corrupting the damned thing might still be taken seriously. It was his own conviction that his appeared green because of his naturally darker skin color, not his diet. Surely, there was nothing evil about that.

Still, he couldn't get past the fact that some days he just wanted to hurt the rest of them for dragging everyone back here. It was bad enough they couldn't reproduce. But he'd rather be exploring space, meeting new aliens, maybe finding the means to procreate that way.

He spotted Jerod wandering about below. Jerod Seventeen, their youngest, 'the man with the most life left.' The rest of them were down to about a dozen reconfigurations. Darcy had made the latest incident, in which Jerod Eighteen lost his life, look like an accident initiated by cheap human technology. It shouldn't be too difficult to do something similar here.

He projected the path Jerod was wandering. It should take him right under a set of spotlights. Perfect. Some idiot was wasting electricity, leaving all the lighting on just in case some dumb human wanted to visit the studio, take pictures, or drop off a script. Creative writing was something the humans were much better at, not that it mattered. His own opinion was that they'd never find earthbound humans useful for mating; so looking for one with good writing and organizational skills was foolish. None of the female lawyers, bankers or Chief Executive Officers had been suitable, so what use would a writer be to them?

He noticed the female wandering below, probably another tourist. She'd be of no consequence. He pulled out a small transmitter, his own creation, and aimed it at the metal of the stands supporting several banks of spotlights. Silent and invisible, the device sent a beam that quickly ate away layers of metal. Several of the stands would most likely let go at about the right time. They might fall on someone else entirely. There could be a huge loss of life, all of it human. Jerod might escape unscathed. It was an acceptable risk.

His objective for the day accomplished, Darcy quietly rose to his feet and silently stole away into the darkness. He didn't even notice the device slipping out of his pocket. It broke into pieces on the floor below.

*   *   *   *

Jerod knew he didn't need to be at the set today, but it had been a convenient excuse. He preferred to come back here than to suffer through yet another of Mo's introductions. The old man meant well, and went out of his way to promote whatever profession Jerod was in, but some days Jerod didn't feel like meeting every single woman to wander into the café.

This was the day Miss Breton had to take Nikki to band practice, followed by swimming, then to the mall, which would apparently take up the rest of the day. No makeup artist, no costume, no weird underwear. No costume also meant no filming, not even a rehearsal. Today he could just roam the set and let his mind wander. In space there'd been more times like this, to just relax and think things over.

Coren and Darcy had both been unimpressed with his report on a single mother and the lizard she wrangled for the set. They advised him to look elsewhere rather than waste time on a friendship with no hope of reproduction. Here he was, looking elsewhere. Or, as Mo liked to admonish, wasting time, not really looking for a lover at all.

In spite of the cover story he'd absorbed four days ago, he felt completely obscure. A few fans had screamed their pleasure at the previous day's filming. All of them teenage boys on a field trip, all 'nerds.' Not one young lady among them. Worse, the script only called for one actress, someone they hadn't even cast yet. Perhaps they'd erred in making him an actor in the horror genre. The more he mused on it, the more it made sense.

The only thing to do now was to have Coren rewrite the whole acting background, look for more of a 'boy gets girl' genre. Inwardly he groaned. It would mean assimilating another download, and adjusting his attitude to whatever it specified.

Jerod looked up at the sound of another groan, something metallic. Too late, he realized a bank of hot spotlights was about to crash down on him. He closed his eyes and cringed. He gasped as a woman's smooth, strong hands grabbed his arms and yanked him aside. His own reaction spun them both around, causing them to tumble to the ground.

A terrible crash was immediately followed by the jarring sounds of breaking glass. The surge of electricity caused a massive white flash. Other banks of spotlights on the same circuit exploded, showering shards of glass, plastic, and metal everywhere. Everything went silent and black as the power failed. Back up generators quickly hummed to life, giving the entire set a ghostly, half-lit appearance.

Flat on his back, Jerod realized there was now a human woman lying on top of him. He opened his eyes. He'd seen her before, at the café, and wondered if she was the one Mo wanted to introduce. Maybe he should have agreed to meet her after all. She seemed prettier than he remembered. She was also surprising light, a wonderful combination of warm, soft flesh and firm muscle. It dawned on him that his arms were tightly wrapped around her. He loosened his grip, causing glass fragments to fall and break on the floor.

The human looked as surprised as he felt. Her brown eyes and sandy hair glistened. Or was it the dimmer lighting that seemed to make her glow? Funny. He should know the difference but he couldn't focus right now.

She was saying something, this fascinating human female, asking if he was okay. He'd be expected to respond. He tried to think of something a slightly obscene actor might say. Why couldn't he think clearly? And why was he gasping for air? He cleared his throat and tried to slow his breathing and pulse.

"I'm fine. But I suppose, Sweetie, now that you've got me where you want me, you'll *have* to have your way with me." He winked and grinned at her.

She patted his chest. "Not until we're married," she retorted. Her confidence was disconcerting. Worse, she was now getting up, taking several pleasant new sensations away from him. More shards fell off of her, their tinkling adding to his confusion. His uncertainty over what to do next was resolved as she offered a hand to help him up.

He cleared his throat again as he stood up, still holding her hand. "My name is Jerod Seventeen."

"I'm Kelly. Kelly Ravell. I'm pleased to meet you. Sorry to have knocked you off your feet like that, but …"

"It's nice to know the name of the lady who saved my life. I thought I'd had it." He glanced at the shards of glass and lumps of twisted metal.

Kelly nodded. "I saw the supports start to bend, but I thought I just might be close enough to reach you."

Jerod tentatively slipped his arms around her and searched her face for signs of resistance. "I'm so glad you were. I want to thank you, personally." He pulled her close and leaned forward. "Very personally." It surprised him to feel her heart beating almost as hard as his own.

Her lips found his as she closed her eyes. Her arms and hands caressed his shoulders and back.

Jerod tried to respond in kind. It was sweet, and friendly, and exhilarating, nothing like the kiss from Miss Breton. Wanting it to last forever, he found himself wishing he knew what to do next. Thoughts, feeling and images flooded into his mind. He realized this woman's entire history had been imprinted on his mind, something only the symbiont was supposed to be able to do. A faint hope rose to the surface of his psyche.

Kelly opened her eyes. She found her hands had worked their way up Jerod's neck and now cradled his face. The sides of his cheeks were fading shades of blue.

"That's odd. It must have been a trick of the light. You looked blue for a moment."

He tried to hide his excitement. "Blue? Really? I mean, of course it must have been this dim lighting." He tried to laugh but it caught in his throat and came out more like a cough.

Kelly started to pull away. "I'm sorry. This was really, uh, forward of me. I don't usually, I mean … I don't know what I mean. I should get going."

A sense of panic stabbed his brain as she began to slip from his grasp. *"No!* I mean, no. It was entirely my fault. I'm sorry. I didn't mean to offend you. Please don't rush off."

"I do have to leave, I'm already running late. But if my flight gets delayed another day, maybe we can meet for coffee tomorrow."

Jerod nodded. "Coffee. Tomorrow. I'll see you then. I mean, if you're still delayed. I mean, if your flight is still delayed …" His voice trailed off as she hurried away.

He stood staring in her direction for some time after she was gone. Suddenly he felt himself inhale sharply. With a start, he realized he'd stopped breathing until now.

He gazed happily at the palm of his right hand. "That flight will never leave, will it?" Red swirls circled playfully just beneath his skin.

*   *   *   *

Kelly rushed off, wondering how she could have lost control like that. She rubbed her forehead. A vague memory bubbled just beneath the surface of her conscious thought as she struggled to pinpoint it. Her eyes narrowed. "Mo!" she muttered.

Her anger stoked at the thought of having been manipulated, she stormed out of the studio, practically snarled at the security guard at the gate, and speed-walked back to the café. Her fury was only slighted abated by the effort of navigating four long city blocks. Her eyes narrowed again as she spotted her target.

"You!" The word caused startled diners to look up. Mo turned in her direction. Instinct told him that the address was aimed in his direction, as was the nicely manicured finger.

He gave her a friendly look of recognition. "Ah, Miss, you have come back. What else can we do for you?"

His calm response only made her angrier. "I need to talk to you, in private!" she snapped.

He nodded. "I thought you might. Please, come this way." He extended his arm towards the interior of the café.

She stormed past him and looked around. There were no other customers inside. He followed her and pulled out a chair at a far table.

"Please, have a seat."

Her nostrils flared. It was cooler here and she was now finding it difficult to maintain her anger. She plopped herself down and glared as he took the chair opposite.

"You gave me a post hypnotic suggestion, didn't you?"

He waved his hand in the air. "I did nothing of the sort. That would be barbaric. I did give you a telepathic suggestion, as we are far more sophisticated."

"Call it what you want, you had no *right* to take away my freedom of choice like that."

He leaned forward with a fierce look that frightened her a little. "I had *every* right to do what I did. We saved this little planet of yours on more than one occasion and we're about to become extinct if we can't find human females to mate with. Now if you responded to my telepathic suggestion it was merely because on some level you *wanted* to. All we can do is hope such a suggestion will find resonance within the person. Otherwise the human psyche will totally override it."

He blinked and the fierce look was replaced by an expression of amusement. "So, if you managed to discover what I did, you must have kissed him. How did that go?"

He stroked his fingers over the back of her right hand. Kelly felt like she was reliving the incident. She poured out the whole story.

Mo listened intently. "Now be honest with me. Do you feel your free will has been violated?"

"No. You may have manipulated circumstances, but I wanted to do what I did."

"What would you like to do next?"

"I don't know."

"Do you trust me?"

"Yes. But things are moving too fast for me."

"Then I'll slow them down a bit. You can let me take care of some of those details. You don't have to remember everything right now." He touched the back of his hand to her cheek.

She closed her eyes.

*　　*　　*　　*

The next thing Kelly knew, Mo was refilling her cup of coffee, a smile on his face. Other diners, mostly men, she noted, were enjoying their meals, keeping a subtle buzz of conversation going. Everyone she made eye contact with gave her a little smile.

Mo strode up to her table, a nearly full coffee pot in his hand. "Did you enjoy the studio, Miss? Was there a tour today, or did they just let you wander around? They'll do that if there's no filming going on."

Kelly took a sip of the coffee. It was even tastier than she remembered. "I just wandered around. Oh, and I met your friend, Jerod Seventeen. In fact, I might have saved his life."

"Really?" He looked around conspiratorially and sat down at her table. "Tell me what happened!"

"A spotlight support gave way. Metal fatigue, I guess. I managed to yank him out of harm's way."

Mo stood up and patted her shoulder. "I bet he was grateful."

"He sure was. He kissed me to thank me. It was so sweet. Funny thing, though, I don't remember leaving the studio or coming in here."

He laughed. "That must have been some kiss. You did look a bit out of it when you came in." He swirled the coffee pot in his hand. "That's why I brought you my own special blend. It brings one back down to Earth." The sparkle in his eye suggested more than he was saying.

Kelly took another sip. "Tell me, why is everyone so friendly here? I've traveled a lot to research my thesis and it's rare to find so much hospitality in a bigger city. It seems to be everyone, not just customer service people."

Mo considered just how much to tell her. He decided to make a joke of it. He grinned. "This is Martianville. We must all be aliens who have come to teach people on this planet to live together in peace and harmony."

Kelly choked on her coffee. Mo tapped her back gently and the spasms stopped. "Yeah, yeah, I'm sure that's it. Really, Mo, you have the wildest sense of humor. Still …" Her eyes narrowed slightly.

He wondered if she'd be able to shake off the memory block. She had a strong mind for a human. "What is it?"

"I've finished my training and I've been wondering how to put it into practice. I know I can't change the whole world, but maybe in a city like this there'd be enough like-minded people to form some sort of organization. I had been thinking of moving to the east coast, closer to international destinations. The first thing I'd like to do is find a way to improve the coordination between relief organizations. From what I've learned, there's a lot of overlapping that diverts funds away from the actual charity work."

"You have big plans."

She shook her head. "Just important ones. I know you can't stop a lot of bad things from happening, but if each person did the good they were capable of …"

"The world would be a much better place," he finished for her.

She took another sip. "Yes. It would."

"Would you like more coffee?"

She looked at her watch. "No, I really should get going. I'd like to contact my sister and see a few more places before going back to the airport."

"Would you like me to call you a cab?"

She stood up and pushed her chair in. "No, I need some exercise. It helps if a person stays active when traveling, and here I've just been leisurely strolling about."

"While saving actors from the harsh glare of the spotlight," he teased.

She laughed, and then paused. Something seemed different. She couldn't pin it down, so she shrugged and went to pay the bill. Mo eyed her carefully as she dug in her purse for her wallet. She was definitely close to breaking through the memory block. It was risky, letting her leave in this state, but he was more concerned about the potential for brain damage. Jerod, Coren and Athens were the ones more skilled at interfacing directly with human minds.

"Are you all right?" Kelly asked him. "You seem a million miles away."

Mo smiled. "That's not that far by some definitions."

She shrugged and handed him a twenty-dollar bill. "Judging by the cost, it's twice as far if you take the plane," she joked. "Especially when they lose all your stuff."

*　　*　　*　　*

Alison Owen ran a tiny hand through her long, red curls. Her best friend, blonde Amber Wembley, was sitting in the wading pool. They splashed each other with gusto. Both girls giggled as Kiko, Amber's miniature poodle, shook her gray fur for all she was worth, spraying them with more water. Amber grabbed the dog and placed it in the pool. It looked at her, snorted, and sat down in the water. The girls continued to laugh and splash about.

A young man with a malevolent sneer watched them from a black van parked across the street. Dark sunglasses hid his enlarged retinas. The black-haired teen in the back of the van stirred.

He glanced at her over the top of the sunglasses. "Go back to sleep, tramp. You'll need all the rest you can get. You have a couple of new ones to train tonight."

He tossed the last of his cigarette through the open window. He pulled a handgun with a silencer from under his seat, took aim and shot the poodle. The girls screamed. He got out and ran over to them.

"What's wrong, Sweetie Pie?"

Alison pointed at the quickly growing bloodstain in the water. Amber was still screaming.

"Kiko's been hurt! Can you help her?"

He scooped the animal out of the pool. "Come on, girls, we've got to get your dog to the vet."

He ran to the van and held the door open. As soon as both children were inside, he threw the dog's body into the street.

The girls shrieked. The black-haired teenager in the back woke up. She hated this, but she knew the drill. She gave them an open bottle of pop. "Shut up and drink! Both of you!" she demanded.

Wide eyed, the girls stared into the mascara-obscured eyes and obeyed. After a moment they both fell unconscious. She checked their pulses and scowled at the driver. "You're despicable, Lyle."

"Just do your job, you whore." He started the van and drove off.

CHAPTER 5

▼

THE CONFERENCE

Jerod didn't even notice the silence when he walked into the conference room. About a hundred men, seemingly from various racial and ethnic backgrounds, had crowded in. Most of them chose to stand, in spite of the abundance of chairs and tables. All eyes were on Jerod.

Coren happened to be closest to him. "Is it true, Jerod? The rumor that you've Been Blued?"

He shrugged, pretending to appear indifferent. "I don't know, Coren. You hear about stuff like that, but does it really happen anymore?"

"The test! We need to administer the test!" Coren shouted.

Echoes of "the test, the test," rose throughout the room.

Jerod took off his jacket, placed it over the back of the chair and sat down. He leaned back. Let the test begin. He was happy to let them know how he felt. Then they'd have incentive for delaying Kelly's flight.

Coren scowled at Jerod, then squinted. "Computer, run a level one scan of Jerod Seventeen for signs of having Been Blued. Allow all units present to confirm or deny. Authorization, Coren Thirteen."

Jerod closed his eyes and offered no resistance to the computer's intrusion. His body jerked slightly as a visible blue current sparked through him. A green word, full of alien symbols, appeared in the air before him.

Coren stared at it. "Blue," he muttered. Soon all the other men nodded in agreement. A collective sigh of contentment went up as they gazed at the ancient script. It turned into a swirl of energy that melted into Jerod's forehead.

He opened his eyes and leaned forward, resting his elbows on the table in front of him. "So what do you say, Gentlemen?"

Coren reached over to shake his hand. "Congratulations, Jerod Seventeen. You've Been Blued.

"That hasn't happened in over five centuries. Now before we execute the plan, we need to see how far you can take things with the young lady, see about a pregnancy."

Jerod straightened up in his chair. "We might have a little problem there."

Coren and the others gave him blank looks. "But all indications were that if we were relatively handsome and observed their cultural and personal boundaries, the females of this planet would be extremely responsive to us."

"It's not that, she's very responsive towards mating under the proper conditions. It's the reproducing she doesn't want."

"That *is* a problem," the Coordinator's young, disembodied voice boomed out.

Jerod looked up. "Kelly has a valid reason for not wanting a pregnancy, Coordinator. She was badly injured in a car accident a decade ago. She spent a year in a coma and another five in rehabilitation. She might not survive a pregnancy. We have no right to ask her to sacrifice herself for us, even if it would mean the continuation of our species. Besides, it does us little good to lose our first prospective mother in five hundred years to a single birth."

Silence followed until Jerod spoke again. "Look, there are other methods. All we really need are the reproductive cells from mating, and the ship's laboratory. Why don't we use some of the reconfiguration chambers as incubators as well? It would speed things up, since we'd be able to have several children at once instead of just one. We were planning on aging the first several generations to adulthood anyway."

There was a pause before the Coordinator spoke again. "Incubators weren't part of the plan. Then again, nothing else has held much promise for us. Very well; but you must discover her potential for leadership."

Jerod tried to remain calm. "She's a person of faith, but she's always wondered if there were other intelligent species. *She's* very intelligent. I'd say she has extreme potential."

"Enough! Having Been Blued is already affecting your judgment. You've never lost control like this before, none of the previous Jerods ever behaved like this. Hey, where do you think *you're* going?"

Jerod was halfway out the door. "My symbiont tells me that Kelly's hurt her ankle. She's lost and trying not to be frightened. She needs me." He finished pulling on his jacket and was gone.

The men looked at each other as the door closed. Coren turned to Spencer. "Telepathic and spiritual bonding already, that went faster than when we had our own females. I hope I can find a human who will cause me to have Been Blued."

Spencer smiled awkwardly. "We all do."

"Gentlemen," the voice chided, "you have work to do. Jerod should be bringing Kelly to the Martianville Memorial Hospital within the hour. Coren, you're filling in for Doctor Athens tonight, so you'll be responsible for fixing Kelly's ankle.

"Then there's the issue of her flight. Let's not be too extreme, we don't want to frighten the humans. Suggestions?"

Coren snapped his fingers. "She would have tried to reschedule when her flight was delayed. Let's lose her reservation altogether. Blame it on the computer, the humans always buy that one."

"Agreed," the voice responded. "Computer fallibility has been a reliable scapegoat. In fact, if our own mainframe hadn't been slightly neglected … isn't anybody listening to me?"

Coren watched the rest of the men leave the room. "I'm still here, Coordinator. Don't worry, they're all rushing off to make the necessary arrangements."

"I guess this is pretty exciting. I wonder if it will turn out to be an isolated incident or if we'll finally be able to look forward to a new generation."

"Only time will tell, Coordinator. If we could just figure out why Jerod has Been Blued, it could secure our future."

"It's been my top priority since it happened. If I can't figure it out while linked to the mainframe, we're left with nothing but guesses."

"Don't think too hard, Coordinator. You've been stuck to the mainframe before. Remember how difficult it was to scrape your psyche out of there the last time?"

"How's my new body coming?"

"You'll be pleased to know the conditioning is going well. How do *you* feel?"

"Oh, to be a kid again." The comment was followed by a childish laugh, which broke into a harsh rasp. There was a pause. "I think my voice just broke."

Coren grabbed his own jacket from the back of another chair. "Hang in there, Coordinator. I've got to get to the hospital and see about Kelly's ankle. Any thoughts?"

"Make sure she's healthy. The humans' medical knowledge is still a bit sub-standard. Do anything required to bring her up to ours."

"What about our non-interference policy on their health, restricting ourselves to no more than their own doctors would do?"

"Consider this woman a special case. The policy does not apply to her. You have a free hand to ensure she meets our criteria."

Coren felt a rush of adrenaline as he reached for the door. "Finally, a challenge. It's been difficult to restrain myself with the humans, there's so much wrong with so many of them. Thank you."

*   *   *   *

The black van careened around a corner. The teen in the back, trying to put on makeup, fell off her bucket seat. "Damn it, Lyle, if you keep driving like this, they'll wake up. Are you stoned again?"

He glared at her, narrowly missing two parked cars. "No. I'm starved. Here's a twenty. Go get pizza." The van squealed to a stop at a convenience store. "And don't try to be funny and bring it back frozen again. You got nine minutes."

She tumbled out and went inside. Lyle turned and looked at the two sleeping girls. Maybe about seven or eight, he guessed … years to go before they hit puberty. But some men liked that, no risk of pregnancy, a tradeoff for undeveloped body parts. He shrugged. It wasn't his thing, but it made him money. He couldn't even remember what had happened to the last two.

Or could he? He hated anything that made him feel less than all knowing. The drugs had made everything knowable. He strained his mind. Vague images of accidental drowning came to his mind, a hot tub, and a client who paid extra for hiding the bodies. That was it, the two girls before this had drowned when the stupid john made the water in the hot tub too deep for them.

Lyle looked back. "Don't worry, nothing bad will happen to you two, I'll see to that. There will be nothing but real gentlemen for you two; fine, *rich* gentlemen."

The smell of hot pizza brought him out of his reverie. "About time, Hallie!" He checked his watch. "With three seconds to spare."

"Stuff it, you pig. I had three *minutes* to spare. There was no-one else in there, so I didn't have to wait." She looked at the sleeping girls in the back, still in their bathing suits. Her expression softened. "We don't have to do this you know, we could just drop them somewhere."

He eyed her with disgust, talking through half-chewed cheese and pepperoni. "And have them miss their debut, the most important night of their lives? I'll find you a nice old guy who looks repressed. Then you can teach him a thing or two and show them how it's done. You remember how it's done, don't you?"

She spit out the pizza in her mouth. "I hope some cop shoots your brains out!"

He wiped one hand on his jeans before running it through her hair. "That's no way to talk to your sugar daddy." He tightened his grip on the hair in his hand and yanked hard.

Her head smacked against the van's metal frame.

"Oh, jeez, I'm sorry. I didn't mean to ... Are you okay?"

Hallie blinked hard and touched the spot. She showed him a smear of blood on her fingers. "I think you'd better get me to the hospital. I've had a concussion once before ..."

"Okay, okay, just stay awake. I'll look after you. Don't worry. I always look after you. Didn't I promise to always look after you?" He turned the key and the van roared to life.

"Shut up and drive," she moaned.

CHAPTER 6

▼

TRUE BLUE

Jerod realized he was stepping out of his black limo with no memory of getting in or giving the driver directions. It didn't matter. Kelly was trying to prop herself up against a lamppost, biting her lip, tears spilling down her red cheeks. Her left foot was suspended at an odd angle. She melted into Jerod's arms the moment he reached for her.

"There, there now. I've got you," he solaced to the sobbing head buried in his chest. So this would be compassion, maybe empathy? He'd sort it all out later, in time for his report.

"Did you hurt your ankle?" he heard himself ask.

Kelly stopped trembling. "Uh, huh," came the muffled response.

"Now don't you worry about a thing. Martianville Memorial has the best doctors money can buy."

Kelly lifted her head. "Oh. I'm sorry; I forgot to buy travel insurance. I'll pay you back." Her face was pale but her voice was steady.

He placed a finger under her chin and gazed into her eyes. "The money doesn't matter. I'll look after you. I promise." He'd almost forgotten, the way human eye color could vary in different lighting. Filled with pain, hers were a darker brown than before.

He gripped her around the waist and helped her into the car. She let out a gasp as she slumped against the seat. He sat as close as he dared, then took her head in his hands. Her eyes were losing focus. Jerod realized she was going into shock. He pressed two fingers against her forehead. The resulting mindlink, allowing his brain to sustain hers, would keep her out of danger until they reached the hospital.

The driver lowered the dividing window. Green eyes flashed from below the rim of a chauffeur's cap. "Have you gone insane? She could wake up knowing everything about us."

"She'll find out sooner or later. This way she'll know I'm telling her the truth. She's falling in love with me already, in spite of current human modesty. I'm going to let her explore my mind, so she can see her trust won't be betrayed."

The driver scowled. "I hope you know what you're doing."

Jerod shot him a look. "After hundreds of years without mates, Andrew, none of *us* knows what to do. We have to rely on these humans for help. We've earned it, in spite of the Coordinator's desire to keep that little secret. Never forget, we saved this planet a few times. Someday we should tell them that."

"Right. And just before they dissect us, we can tell them all about the aliens we've encountered and the scientific breakthroughs we've made and how we're no longer really human because we …"

Jerod held up his other hand. "We're still human enough to come back to Earth when we need to, still human enough to appreciate … Oh."

"What happened?"

"Kelly just discovered my mind within hers. She's, uh, she's pleasantly surprised. I didn't expect that. Most humans require a bit of overriding to prevent them from kicking me out."

"You be careful! These humans haven't even figured out world peace yet."

"Kelly has. I bet she is ready for leadership."

"We've arrived at the hospital. Coren's waiting for you. Take her directly to room 14B. And for the love of space, break that mindlink before Coren accuses you of meddling with her free will."

The limo stopped near an emergency entrance.

Jerod pulled his hands away from Kelly's face and opened the door. He got out and reached back in to pick her up. "Room 14A, got it."

"No, *14B,*" Andrew scolded.

*   *   *   *

Jerod carried Kelly into the hospital, past the nurses' station and down the hall to the elevator. "We called ahead," he answered to their protests.

The nurses looked at each other. "That's highly irregular," said the younger one in pink scrubs.

The nurse in green shrugged. "Probably another one of Dr. Coren's charity cases. *He's* very irregular."

At the mention of Coren's name the first nurse blushed. "But *very* handsome."

The second nurse nodded. "In a dangerous sort of way. You're too young to get involved with a man like that. Trust me." She pushed her glasses higher up her face. "I've been burned enough to know."

The elevator opened and Jerod waited for the three orderlies to step out. Another one stepped inside after him. Seeing Jerod's arms were full, he asked what floor.

"Fourteen," responded Jerod.

Confound him, the man punched the buttons for floors two, five, eight, and fourteen.

Jerod tapped his foot on the floor. The elevator went straight to the fourteenth floor without stopping. As he stepped out, he chuckled while the orderly frowned and jabbed more buttons.

"Here we are, room 14A," Jerod said to no one in particular. Holding Kelly as best he could with one arm, he threw it open to be greeted by a hysterical scream.

Jerod squinted. "Right, room *14B*. Sorry about that, Ma'am! But you look great, the diet's really working for you!" He closed the door and crossed the hall.

Coren yanked open the door and tugged Kelly to the examining table. The two men shifted her onto it. Jerod kicked the door shut behind him.

"Jerod, what did you do? She's gone into shock."

"I think her ankle's broken. I couldn't keep her awake, so I linked …"

"No, I don't want to hear it. I think having Been Blued has made you lose all your senses. I can wipe her memory just before I wake her."

"No!"

Coren's eyebrows went up. He looked at the grip Jerod suddenly had on his arm. He tilted his head. "I beg your pardon? What do you mean, 'No?'"

"She needs to know everything about me, I mean, about us. You're the one who's always insisting the humans be allowed to make their own choices. How can she choose what she doesn't know?"

Coren scowled. "All right. But we can't go halfway then. If we put all the data into her subconscious, it will help her brain to process it. Once she makes that adjustment, she'll understand everything. It won't be gradual. You'll have to be physically beside her when it happens, in case she doesn't choose to be with us and you have to wipe her memory."

"What? How could she choose to leave me? I mean, us?"

"Like you said, I believe in autonomy for the humans. Look, if you think you're falling in love, you'd better realize you're risking loss. It's in all their literature. Sometimes love just isn't enough."

Jerod felt his breath catch. "I don't think I could handle it if she rejected me. It never occurred to me that she might not love me back."

Coren looked his friend over. He hated it when Jerod looked pathetic. He patted his shoulder. "Well, I suspect she does like you. Look at how quickly she got into the limo, after only knowing you such a short time. A human as strong-willed as this one might have insisted on waiting for an ambulance.

"Look, I need to get to work before she slips into a coma. She'll be very suspicious if she wakes up to find you in the room. Just wait out in the hall."

Jerod stepped outside. He looked around, and then strolled down the hall. He sat down on a bench near the window. He stared out at the emerging stars and the city lights.

"Hiya, Cutie!" a falsetto voice greeted him.

He looked up. A pretty girl with too much makeup and a very tight skirt was addressing him. Her low cut top seemed to be a few sizes too small. He guessed her age to be sixteen, maybe seventeen.

"Oh. Hello."

A few feet away, a twenty-something punk in jeans and a black leather jacket slicked his hand through his hair. His nose was sharp and overly long. The cold look in his eyes suggested the girl was working for him.

Her hair had been dyed black, but there were blonde roots peeking out. Needle tracks ran the length of her bare arms. Her voice was artificially cheerful, tinged with weariness and pain. "I just wanted you to know, I'm here if you need..."

She bent down and whispered in his ear, tickling his neck with her fake feather boa. A tear from her eyes fell onto his face.

Jerod jumped to his feet, grabbed her arm and squeezed the side of her neck. "Now you listen! You're gonna wash this trash off your face, use that two hundred and twelve bucks in your purse to buy a good meal, some nice slacks and a decent blouse and get yourself on a bus back to your momma! You will never do drugs or the streets again! You got that, Hallie-Mae Wilson?"

The young woman gasped. Red streaks raced through her neck. She turned around and stormed down the hall. The young man in the leather jacket tried to grab her arm but she shoved him away and continued to the elevator.

Before he could recover, Jerod grabbed the fellow's collar and squeezed his neck the same way. "Oh, 'Mr. Big Time Pimp Lyle,' huh? How does it feel to be helpless? You like that, Punk? Do You? No more! You're going to take those two little girls you kidnapped and drugged tonight and return them to their parents. No raping, and no pimping! Then you're going to turn yourself in at the nearest cop shop and *beg* them to get you into rehab. You're going to spend the rest of your life helping young women instead of trying to destroy them! Hit the stairs! *Go!*"

The young man turned, ran to the stairwell and raced down.

Jerod felt his anger subside. He rubbed his chin in bewilderment. "What on Earth did I just do?" he asked himself. He grinned. "Repressed? Ha! Kelly would be so proud of me." He turned and sat down again. The stars looked a little brighter.

*   *   *   *

Coren flipped open a handheld computer. It emitted a small red beam of light over Kelly's ankle. "Broken," he observed. "Can't have that." He pressed a button and the light switched to green. He frowned and moved the device in short, quick strokes. "It's been a long time since I did this. Oops. Never mind, Doctor, that tendon should feel sore, she'd wonder about it if there was no pain at all. As for DNA, she's pretty close to perfect. No sign of the Diabetic or Alzheimer's precursors the humans are currently so worried about. Looks like the past twelve generations of her family behaved themselves. You'd almost think she was one of us." He slipped the device into his coat pocket. "Disappointing, in a way. All my knowledge and the best I get to do for her is fix the ankle, heal some scar tissue and update her vaccinations."

He stroked her forehead. "Let's have a look at this personality." He frowned for a second, delving into her mind. "You really are a sweetheart, aren't you? What's a nice girl like you doing on a planet like this? Maybe we can fix that. Do me a favor, okay? Love Jerod back. Please? He's crazy about you. And I think the rest of us need you to love him, too, if only to prove we might have a future." He stroked her forehead one last time before frowning again. "Wake up!" he demanded.

He picked up a file as she sat up. "Now, Miss Ravell, I see from your files that you dislike seeing doctors. Any reason for that, or should I take it personally?"

Kelly shook her head. "What? Where am I? I don't remember coming in here."

Coren waved his hand. "Of course you don't, you passed out from the pain. The sprain's been taken care of, and I saw you were overdue for a tetanus booster, so that's been taken care of too."

"But how did I ...?"

"Your boyfriend brought you in."

"Boyfriend? Oh, you must mean Jerod. He's not my boyfriend."

Coren raised an eyebrow, a slight scowl on his face. "Speaking of that, I don't see anything on your chart about sexual history."

Kelly's jaw dropped. "I don't have one. My faith forbids sex before marriage!"

"Really? I doubt that."

"You can doubt what you like, Doctor, and I'll believe what I choose!"

Coren closed the file and crossed his arms in front of his chest. "Do you believe in the medical profession?"

"Of course. We're not barbarians, you know."

"Then why have you been neglecting core mainten ...?" He shook his head at the error. This human was easily matching both his wits and his bravado. It was unsettling, in a pleasant sort of way. "Why have you been neglecting yearly checkups? And they should have told you back in high school to get a tetanus booster every decade afterwards."

"They did. I just forgot, that's all. Besides, I'm strong and healthy. Why should I tie up medical resources with unnecessary checkups that will just confirm it?"

"Strong and healthy? I'll be the judge of that. Now look, if you ever want to have a baby ..." Coren started to pace.

"I don't."

"Medical science has progressed to the point ..."

"I told you, I don't."

"That it would entirely safe for you to conceive and deliver a child."

"Weren't you listening? I don't *want* a baby. Not ten years ago, not today, and not tomorrow. The scar tissue doesn't matter."

Coren stopped and stared at her. His voice softened. "Just something to think about. You know, if you ever change your mind, we can help.

"As for the fellow who brought you in, he seems very kind. A nice young lady like you, you could do worse, you know." He leaned back against the examining table and grinned.

"You're a very strange man, Doctor."

Coren straightened up, a wry look on his face. "I suppose I am. We're done here, you can go."

"What about my ankle?"

"Your ankle? Oh, right, your ankle. It was just a sprain. Take it easy and you'll be fine. No mountain climbing or running marathons for a while. Swimming is still okay. Now off you go, your boyfriend's waiting for you."

Kelly felt herself being hustled out the door. She had a sudden urge to leave the room, even as she wondered how the man knew about her hobbies. After closing the door she opened it and looked back in.

"Doctor?" The room was empty, unless he'd hidden in a closet. Somehow the thought suddenly made sense, so she closed the door again, shook her head and turned around.

Jerod managed to restrain himself enough to walk calmly. "How did it go? Can you walk? Would you like a wheelchair?"

"No, apparently it was just a sprain. The doctor said I should just take it easy, no running, and no mountain climbing. Funny thing, he said swimming was okay. I wonder how he knew about my interests."

"Maybe he just guessed. You do look very healthy."

"That sounds like a compliment."

"Of course it is. Do you like compliments?"

"Of course I do."

Jerod gave her his arm and started for the elevator. "Then stick with me and you'll never run out of them."

"Sounds like an offer too good to refuse. Wait a minute, what time is it?"

Jerod checked his watch. "It's almost ten-thirty."

Kelly gasped. "I have to get to the airport, call my sister, find my luggage …"

"Okay. Don't panic. The airport's only ten minutes from here."

Kelly pulled her cell phone from her purse. "Wouldn't you know it? Dead. This phone's been nothing but problems from the moment I bought it."

"You can use mine. It's in the limo."

The elevator opened. The two of them stepped inside. Jerod pushed the button for the main floor. Kelly leaned against him, and then pulled away.

"I'm sorry. All of a sudden I'm exhausted."

"That's all right. It was nice."

She smiled. "Only nice?"

"Very nice." He kissed her cheek.

"You're so sweet. Not at all like the reviews I've read."

Jerod chuckled. "Hacks! Not a decent writer among them. How could they capture the real me?"

Kelly laughed. "Maybe that's my job."

Sheer terror gripped Jerod. They'd always feared the humans might suspect, capture, and even torture them. A cold shiver raced up his spine.

Kelly caught her breath. She pulled his face to hers and planted her lips firmly on his.

Jerod's fear evaporated. She was responding to his tremor, a thought that pleased him and brought a whole new sensation to his brain.

The elevator door opened. People were filing in, surrounding them. He didn't care. A few cleared their throats. Others giggled. The elevator started up, and then stopped. The doors opened again.

"Ground floor," someone announced.

Kelly pulled away. Jerod discovered he was slightly out of breath. His heart was pounding. Kelly seemed to be handling things much better, a slight smile on her face.

"This is our stop," was all she said.

He followed her out amid wolf whistles and suggestive comments.

$$* \qquad * \qquad * \qquad *$$

Back in the limo, Kelly settled back and tugged on the seatbelt. "You know, you act like being kissed is brand new to you. I would have expected an actor like yourself would have had a lot of experience with women."

Following her lead, Jerod put on his seatbelt. "Like I said, those writers don't know the real me." He tapped on the panel of the privacy glass and the car eased into gear.

"'The Real You.' How do I know if this is the real you? You're an actor, how do I know you're not just acting?"

"Do you *want* me to act differently? I can act any way you want."

Kelly's face turned red. "No, uh, this is, this is fine. I'm not sure what *this* is, but so far, it's fine."

"Only fine?"

She bit her lip. "Any finer and I might have to kiss you again. It's getting to be a bad habit."

"Why do you say that?"

"Because I'm about to get on a plane and leave. I may never see you again."

"Why do you have to leave? Why can't you stay here? With me?"

"Maybe I'd like to. But I've worked hard to get the education and training I need to make a difference in the world."

"What about making a difference in my world?"

"Can you tell me that your world is going to be more than just you and me?"

"I can guarantee it. Stay with me and you'll make a difference in ways you can't even imagine."

"But there are so many people counting on me right now."

"I'm counting on you."

"Then I guess I start making a difference in the world by letting you down. Maybe if we'd met in other circumstances ..."

"Don't count me out yet. A good friend of mine once said the whole world can change in a second." He reached towards a small set of drawers opposite the seats. For a second Kelly wondered if he was about to serve champagne. Instead, he pulled out a cell phone. "You needed to call your sister." He offered her the device. "I'll try not to listen in."

She took the phone and dialed. "That's all right. I've got nothing to hide. That's odd. Her number's busy. She's never on the phone this late."

Jerod closed his eyes for a moment. He smiled when he opened them. "Katy's fine."

Kelly handed him back the phone. "I hope so. Hey, how did you know her name?"

Jerod shrugged. "Lucky guess. A lot of parents give their children similar names. Especially daughters."

Kelly frowned slightly. Something was telling her this man knew too much. The same something was telling her it was all right, that it would all work out.

Jerod looked out the window. "I've always loved planes. They're so amazing. All that weight and they still soar like a bird."

Kelly looked at the terminal designation, 11D. It was the right one, oddly enough, as if the driver had known exactly where to go.

"I'll go with you," Jerod offered. "Sometimes a woman traveling alone gets better treatment if it looks like there's a man with her."

"Tell me about it. Sometimes I've had to be downright aggressive to get good service."

Jerod offered his hand and helped her out of the car. He crooked his elbow and lightly placed her hand into it. "That should convince them," he said.

Kelly resisted the urge to giggle. She couldn't deny being with Jerod was much more fun than being alone.

*   *   *   *

"Yes, Sir, Ma'am, can I help you?" The airline agent, a pale man with graying hair, looked extremely weary.

"I had to reschedule a flight. My plane from Springfield was late because of bad weather and I missed the connector to Riverdale."

"Name?"

"Kelly. Kelly Ravell."

The agent tapped his keyboard and gazed at the computer screen. "Ravell, Ravell … Ravelli? No, no, that's a Sam Ravelli. You're not using Sam instead of Samantha?"

"No, I told you. *Kelly*. Two 'L's, with a 'Y.' It's not short for anything."

"Right, right, Kelly Ravelli, I mean, Ravell. Sorry, Miss, it's been a long night and I've worked two shifts already. It looks like there's no record of you flying with us. Don't worry; sometimes the computer loses people on us. Do you still have your last boarding pass?"

Kelly opened her purse and produced the paper.

The agent took it, looked it over, and tapped the keyboard again. "Yup, there it is. I mean, there it isn't. We lost all files on Springfield flights for the past week due to a glitch in the main computer. I'm terribly sorry, your money will be refunded and we'll offer you a travel voucher anywhere in North America, valid for up to three years. If we're still in business by then, the way things have been going. I'd offer you a hotel voucher, but all hotels in the city have been booked due to the mix-up."

It pained Jerod to see Kelly's angst. "Don't worry. My place has several guest rooms. We'll get this all straightened out tomorrow."

He turned his attention to the agent. "I don't suppose you'd have Miss Ravell's luggage handy?"

The agent pointed to another desk. "All luggage from the Springfield flights has been sorted alphabetically. She'll need to show photo identification to claim it."

*   *   *   *

Back in the limo Kelly felt herself getting sleepy. If she were certain she could trust this man, it would be all right to fall asleep. If not …

Her eyes closed.

The privacy glass rolled down. Andrew's piercing glare filled the rear view window. "What now?"

Jerod smiled. "She's getting closer. I can feel it. I'll try to arrange supper with her sister tomorrow night."

Andrew scowled. "You do know we've stranded nearly a fifth of the State just to keep her here."

"What's a few days of travel delays for a few thousand humans when we're talking about the entire future of our people?"

"You know the Coordinator's views on messing with the humans."

"We prevented an alien invasion of this planet because of the Coordinator's views, with no small sacrifice to us. I'd say we have every right to inconvenience people when it's this important."

Andrew hated it when Jerod was right, which was most of the time. "All right. You'll need a driver. I'll make myself available for tomorrow. Meanwhile, what do we do with your sleepy friend?"

Jerod chuckled. "Take her home. Put her to bed. Wake her with a kiss."

CHAPTER 7

▼

BETWEEN FRIENDS

Jerod stood waiting for the maid to tell him she'd tucked Kelly into bed. "Thank you, Janet."

The agency had all its maids in French uniforms, something that usually made him uncomfortable; he found it attractive and repulsive at the same time. Tonight it didn't bother him at all. Besides, having a maid saved him from having to undress an unconscious woman who might wake up and get the wrong idea.

"Have the agency send extra help in the morning, a maid to tend the young lady, a butler and a chef. You know the people I like."

Janet pulled a small notebook from her apron pocket. "Very good, Sir. Anything else?"

Jerod looked straight into her eyes. "What's your human impression of Kelly?"

"Sir?"

He kept her gaze. "What does your intuition tell you about her?"

"She seems very kind, the sort of person who'd risk her life to help anyone in trouble."

"How does she think of me? What would be the chances of a potential mating?"

"Very high. Better than anyone else you've asked me about."

"As usual, you will forget the questions about your intuition."

"Yes, Sir. An extra maid, a butler and a chef. They'll be here before 6 a.m."

"Thank you, Janet. You may go for the evening."

"Yes, Sir. Thank you. Good evening, Sir." She went to the closet and gathered her things.

*   *   *   *

Jerod was halfway up the winding staircase before Janet shut the door. He allowed himself a quick look into the guest room. Kelly was sound asleep, so motionless that he listened for the sound of her breathing. Her suitcase and purse rested on a loveseat.

Jerod realized he was staring. He closed the door and retreated down the stairs. He went to the library and closed the doors behind him.

Coren was smiling up at him from behind the massive oak desk situated at the back of the room. A gray leather sofa was to the left, a few matching chairs to the right. Shelves filled with books and statues lined the walls.

"Good news, Jerod. Your little human has never mated before. In all probability, she's never even seen a naked human male. That means you might not even have to hide your thing."

Jerod frowned. "My ... *thing?*"

"Yeah, you know, your *thing*. You do remember it, don't you?"

"Oh. *Oh!* My *thing!* You don't have to worry about that, it fell off when she kissed me."

Coren's mouth fell open. Seeing the spark in his friend's eyes made him scowl. "Eighty-three configurations of the original, and you still retain that awful sense of humor."

The smile almost disappeared from Jerod's face. "Eighty-seven configurations of Coren and you still have trouble knowing when I'm joking."

Coren bit his lip. "There's bad news as well. I'm afraid you might be the last of the Jerods. Having Been Blued has begun to return you to a less static state. We may not be able to reconfigure you again. You're becoming too human."

Jerod stared into space for a moment. "It's worth it. You know, I think I finally understand something that we forgot thousands of years ago. We've been trying to preserve ourselves for so long that we lost the concept of love."

"What's love got to do with it?"

"Everything. From the moment Kelly first grabbed me, everything changed. It wasn't just Being Blued. She transformed my whole frame of reference in a split second. I can see everything we lost, from the time we left this planet to the moment we saved it. We've used stopgap measures to prolong our existence and in one last ditch effort to stay alive, we came home. Home means being around family. We orphaned ourselves when we left, by leaving everyone else behind. Maybe it's time we all became human again."

Coren folded his arms and leaned back. "Watch it, Jerod. Talk like that nearly got you killed back at the studio. Some of us have accepted the status quo and others can't wait to leave. They might not want to stay here to 'become human,' as you put it."

"Were you able to put the device back together?"

"That was the easy part. Figuring out what it's for is another matter. Here, see what you think." Coren pulled Darcy's device out of a desk drawer.

Jerod took it, looked it over, and tried to activate it. "Sorry, I got nothing. Whoever made this thing didn't make it Martian friendly." He handed it back to Coren. "What do you suppose it was?"

Coren put it back in the drawer. "Some sort of multipurpose tool. We think it was used to weaken the metal supports for the spotlights. Kind of a hit and miss effort, so it was obviously someone who didn't care if it killed you or a human. And with the resulting explosions, it could have taken out several victims. Diabolical, when you think about it."

"You think some of the humans know about us?"

"I doubt it. I think this was one of our own. Like I said, not everyone's happy about being here instead of out in space. Others have been pushing the boundaries of human free will. In fact, you'll be lucky if your little stunt with that kidnapper tonight doesn't get you sanctioned. I might be able to argue it was due to an unforeseen effect of having Been Blued, but you can't keep 'helping' people."

Jerod put his hands on his friend's shoulders. "Coren, do you want to have Been Blued?"

Coren felt his pulse race. "Of course I do! At any cost."

"Then find someone else who does. Kelly has a sister and a stepsister. We need to find out if we should be looking at female relatives of potential mates as a source of prospective mothers."

Coren began stammering. "What, what makes you think that's likely? Why me? And why should I be the one to pick someone else?"

"Because you and I are best friends, and the women in Kelly's family may share her ability to Blue us."

Coren got up and walked around the desk. His voice returned to normal. "I see. Yes, okay, we may still be enough alike to mimic human genetic traits passed through their gene pool. The humans have yet to discover the genetic link to friendship, but our scientists spotted it before our originals were even born.

"So what do you propose, some kind of accidental meeting?"

Jerod shrugged. "I was thinking more along the lines of a setting up a nice supper in a classy restaurant. The guy you pick has to be able to keep it a secret. I don't want to inform the Coordinator just yet."

"This human has you wrapped around her finger. You never wanted to keep secrets before."

"I never had secrets *worth* keeping before." Jerod turned to leave the room.

Coren grabbed his shoulder. "Wait! What do I, uh, what do I *do?*"

Jerod smiled. "Just behave as normally as possible. Relax. Be yourself. Your *thing* will let you know if anything else is necessary." He turned, took Coren's hand and placed it over the man's heart. He beamed as he left the room.

Coren felt strangely helpless as he watched the door close. He pulled his hand away from his chest. "But who *am* I?" he asked its red ripples.

He returned to the desk and opened the top left drawer. A display screen full of data flipped up from under the blotter. An electronic console beside it lit up in the shape of a hand. He placed his own hand over it. "Computer, display all medical files on Jerod Seventeen, including all data downloads. Authorization Coren Thirteen."

A green stream of images and numbers flashed through the air before Coren's eyes. "Just as I thought," he muttered to himself. "Computer, I'm not seeing the Companion File. Does he have it?"

The word 'No' flashed in the air in front of him, overshadowing all other data.

"Download to me with a multiple use touch link." Coren gasped as a huge spark from the display screen entered his forehead. He blinked hard, and then rubbed his eyes. "Terminate this link. Return to cloaked mode."

The computer deactivated and the desk returned to being just a desk.

Coren turned to the wall and pushed against the shoulder of a nude statue. The wall opened into an unlit corridor. He walked into it. The opening closed behind him.

*   *   *   *

Darcy opened the fridge and tried to find something with a minimum of protein. It was getting harder to deny the hunger within him, and he wondered if someday he'd end up giving in. It didn't help that the meager contents of the fridge and cupboards were mostly high protein items. Picking out the last of the fruits and vegetables, he tossed them into a blender. He'd given up on taste preferences ages ago. The resulting brown liquid was definitely unpalatable, but at least it contained very little of what he was trying to avoid. He washed it down with a cold cup of coffee. Lucky for him, Jerod wasn't a neat freak who insisted on emptying the pot and washing it up for morning.

The chore gave him more time to think. A human had saved Jerod, they said. Then the stupid woman had Blued him. It seemed uncertain as to whether or not she would actually follow through with mating, as she had her own career plans and the incident seemed to have been an accident. He swore under his breath. If he hadn't caused the spotlights to fall, she might not have met Jerod. But an accident like that would cause emotions to run high, especially between genders.

Poisoning wasn't an option. The *thing* would either absorb it or cause it to pass right through a man's system. As for the human, she would now be under the constant, protective eye of Security, the computer's interactive warning system. Any attempts on her life would alert *them* to his actions. And whenever Security activated he found himself compelled to carry out the computer's subsequent instructions. He scowled over the irony of having to be head of security to get the clearance he needed to sabotage things. Perhaps it was time to take control of that aspect of his life as well.

He looked around the kitchen. It was now neat and tidy. He'd gotten all the dishes washed and put away without even thinking about it. Satisfied with his efforts, he turned, switched off the light and left the room.

*   *   *   *

Lyle's hair was cut short, his face clean-shaven. The mission had given him a nice suit to replace his old clothes, obviously something a very wealthy man had donated. The supper tonight had been a hot stew, much tastier than the pizza he used to live on.

He peered into the semi-darkness created by the streetlights. He spotted Felicity, one of the young women he'd brought into 'the trade' a few years ago. With practice, he'd gotten his new routine down pretty good. He walked up to her casually, as if meeting her was a complete surprise.

Her face was darker than when they'd met, and pockmarked from drug addiction. Her hair had once been a nice chestnut color, although now it seemed to have lost any natural sheen. Her hazel eyes were now dull and dilated to twice their normal size. They nervously darted everywhere. It was time for a change.

"Hello," he said.

She looked him up and down suspiciously. "You a nark?" she asked.

He laughed gently. "That would be a miracle, wouldn't it?"

She scowled. "Lyle? Is that you? What are you up to now?"

He rubbed her bare arm gently. It always seemed to make things go easier. "I've finally been successful. So now I want to give something back to the people who helped me get here." It was a little white lie, but it got their attention every time.

"I don't get it. What are you talking about? Have you been taking that new pill? They say it's a bad trip."

He felt the tingle in his fingertips. He watched as the red swirls formed on her arm. "Don't you worry about me. In fact, I don't think you'll worry about much any more. Your life just got better."

Her eyes rolled back in her head. The red swirls made their way through her face, clearing her complexion. She refocused. The spark was back in her eyes. "Wow. What kind of drug was that?"

"No more drugs. You don't need them anymore." He was grinning from ear to ear.

A navy blue sedan stopped beside them. A thin, cross-eyed man with glasses leaned over to talk to Lyle through the open window. "Excuse me. Is she working? I could really use some stress relief, if you know what I mean."

Lyle winked at Felicity. "Why don't you ask her?"

She leaned into the window of the car. "Let me see you left hand, okay?"

The man held it up. She took it in both of hers. Red swirls coiled under her long fingernails before spreading into his hand. "Looks like you're going home to your wife tonight, Mister. Goodbye."

He blinked back tears as his eyes straightened. He pulled off his glasses. "Of course. Thank you for your help. Goodbye."

Felicity rapped Lyle on the shoulder. "I like this. Can we do it again?"

He put his arm around her waist. "In a minute. Just act like we're a couple till that cop car goes by. He wouldn't understand."

*   *   *   *

Officer Zephyr, a trim man with a shaved head, pulled off his sunglasses and squinted at the well-dressed man on the sidewalk. He could have sworn the woman with him had been chatting up a john. But then the sedan had driven away. He wondered if the rumor about a new street preacher was true; a strange fellow now seemed to be helping 'pros' get off the street.

Not that he objected to the idea, but he was curious. Part of him worried what hidden intentions such a man might have. That's why he'd asked to switch shifts with two of his sisters. It made for a very long day and he realized he needed a coffee. He raised an eyebrow to take one last look back his cruiser's rear view mirror. He made a quick mental note of the couple's description, their location and the time before turning right at the next corner.

CHAPTER 8

▼

BREAKFAST

Kelly woke to find someone shaking her shoulder. She opened her eyes and saw a pretty brunette in a French maid's outfit.

"Sorry to wake you Miss, but it's 7 a.m., and Mr. Jerod asked me to see if you wanted to sleep in or get up."

"Seven?" Kelly sat up. "I should have been up an hour ago. Uh, thank you, Miss …?"

"Just call me Starlene. It's my stage name. I'm working as a maid to pay my own way until my big break in show business."

"I wish you luck. I think you'll do fine if it's what you really want."

"Thank you, Miss. Mr. Jerod mentioned you were an athlete. There's a pool out back."

"Wonderful. I always have a suit with me."

"The chef will make you breakfast whenever you're ready. The kitchen is to the left of the pool. If you need anything at all, just let me know."

"Thank you, but I'll be fine. Actually, it kind of makes me uncomfortable to have someone waiting on me. No offence."

"None taken. Just between us, I feel the same."

The maid left. Kelly looked about the room. It was tastefully decorated in an abstract art theme; a single large flower watercolor was the room's focal point. She hopped out of bed and stretched. She opened her suitcase, and pulled out two swimsuits. Red or blue, she wondered as she headed for the shower.

*   *   *   *

The sound of a splash brought Jerod to the window. He closed his book on lizards and looked down from the third story oriole. Kelly climbed out of the pool and headed for the diving board. What there was of her red swimsuit accentuated her curves and muscles in a most pleasing manner.

Jerod stared. The book fell to the floor. His heart raced. He felt light-headed. He turned around, gasping for breath, his face red. The door opened. Coren ran up to him.

Jerod grabbed him for support. "What's happening to me?"

Coren helped him to a chair. "It looks like you're experiencing physical arousal. You should have downloaded the Companion File the moment you'd Been Blued. Fortunately, I have a copy. Here." He touched Jerod's neck. A spark coursed through both of them.

Jerod's breathing eased. "Thank you. I wonder how human males handle that."

Coren shrugged. "We've never worried about their men. It does seem we're more incapacitated by it than they are. I suspect growing up with it makes it less overwhelming. On the other hand, human men have never had the pleasure of having Been Blued. Now, go look out the window again and tell me how you feel."

Jerod looked down at Kelly. She was pulling herself out of the pool again. This time she toweled off, picked up a fluffy robe and tied it around her waist.

"She's wonderful."

"And you?"

"I'm wonderful."

Coren rolled his eyes. "I mean, how do you feel? Back in control?"

"Completely. Wait a minute, the Companion File? Isn't it forbidden?"

"Hidden, not forbidden. It was placed in trust with the medical core when it appeared we'd lost the ability to reproduce naturally."

"So it's your fault I didn't have it?"

"Okay, it's my fault. Just remember, it's also thanks to me that we have it now. You should be able to contain yourself until Kelly decides if she's going to join us. Oh, and here's a bit of good news. I did some research on females causing us to have Been Blued."

"What did you find out?"

"There isn't much, except one way of reading our old texts suggests that our women chose their mates subconsciously and refused all others. In over two thousand years there were only two cases of a female picking a second male to Blue, and they'd both been widowed by terrible accidents. That means Kelly might not be capable of selecting a human male any more. It's you or no one. So what are you going to do next?"

"I think I'll go have some breakfast. Care to join us?"

"I'll pass. I've already eaten."

*   *   *   *

Kelly hopped onto a stool by the island counter in the kitchen. A tall blond in white clothes and a large apron was happily punching down a bowl of dough.

"Good morning, Miss Kelly. What can I get for you?" He spoke with a British accent.

"Is that a waffle iron?"

"Yes it is. The bread dough here needs to rise a few hours before I punch it down again. I just need to cover it. Then I can get some waffles going for you. But isn't that a bit heavy for an athlete? I can make you whatever you like." He flicked the switch on the waffle iron.

"It's all right. I don't have them unless I can watch them being made, which isn't often. It's just one of my little quirks."

He chuckled. "I like people who can admit their quirks. My name's Stu." He wiped his hands on the apron, shook her hand, and then sprayed the interior of the waffle iron with cooking oil.

"Stu? Like the food?"

"No. But I get that a lot. I guess it's my fault for being a professional chef." He shrugged and mixed flour with a few other ingredients in a large bowl.

"Sorry about that. Any man who can cook for me has my vote."

"Now that's something I'd like to hear more often." He winked and opened the fridge.

"Just keep cooking. Women love that." She moved her stool closer to the plates on the counter.

"I think Mr. Jerod really likes you. He was kind of, uh, glowing this morning." Stu neatly separated three egg whites and whisked them into froth.

"Really? I mean, really. So, when you say *glowing* ... "

"Oh you know. He couldn't stop grinning. And humming. And tapping his fingers. He has a great sense of rhythm. He should take up the drums or something."

"So what was he like before he started 'glowing?'"

"Kind of, I don't know, without purpose. I mean, he had his career and his friends, but he just seemed to be missing something."

"What else can you tell me about him?"

Stu looked around and lowered his voice. "He loaned me the money for university. I own an entire maid and butler service. There are eighty-two people in my employ, and I still get to do the cooking I love, all thanks to Mr. Jerod."

"Why's that such a big secret?"

"Mr. Jerod says he can't help everyone. If it gets out that he's so generous, he'd be overwhelmed by requests for donations.

"Keep that just between the two us, okay? I'd be in big trouble if he knew I'd told anyone, even you."

"It'll be our little secret. But how do I know he hasn't put you up to telling me all this? I'm not sure I can trust an actor."

"Why not?" He folded the beaten egg whites into the flour.

"How do I know he's not just acting? Actors don't exactly have a good track record with relationships."

He poured some of the batter into the heated griddle. "I guess you'll just have to rely on your instincts and take your chances like the rest of us. It's up to you to decide if the risk is worth it. Look at that lovely bit of steam."

"Hmmm. This smells so good."

Stu nudged her elbow and motioned towards the hall with his eyes.

Kelly turned around. Jerod patted the butler on the shoulder and came towards them. Kelly hopped off the stool and poured two cups of coffee from the coffee maker. She handed him one as he came in.

"Good morning, Kelly. Thank you. Did you sleep well?"

"Yes, very. The maid said it would be okay to use the pool."

"Of course. Was the water warm enough? I hate it when it's cold."

"Yes, it was perfect."

"Good morning, Stu. I hope there were enough groceries for you this morning. I don't really keep track of the shopping."

Stu chuckled. "I know. I came prepared." He opened the waffle iron with a flourish. "Waffles are ready. We have fresh peaches and whipped cream, just the way you like them."

Kelly raised an eyebrow. "How did you know that?"

"Know what?"

"That peaches and whipped cream are what I like most with waffles."

Stu nearly dropped his spatula. "I meant Mr. Jerod. That's the way he likes his waffles." He looked from one to the other. "What a weird coincidence."

Jerod was already piling peaches onto two waffle sections. He looked up. "I'm sorry, what?"

Kelly laughed. She grabbed the bowl of whipped cream and used the spoon to flick some at him. It landed on his finger. "Pay attention."

Jerod looked puzzled, as he sucked the cream off. He put his cutlery down and took the bowl from her to set it on the counter. "You have my undivided attention."

"Good. I've changed my mind." She took his hands in hers. "My answer is yes."

"Yes?"

"Yes."

"You're staying here with me?"

"For now. I mean, how could I take all that training to help people and turn down the first request for help that comes along?"

Jerod felt happy and warm all over. He pulled her to him and embraced her. Everything about her felt wonderful. "You don't know what this means to me."

She pulled away just a little. "I aim to find out. So what's a day in the life of Jerod Seventeen like?"

"Let's see. Today I have to go to rehearsal. I expect the director and the leading lady will have a nasty blowup. Then the star, that's me, will storm off the set and take his new leading lady, that's you, out to supper."

"So this is a 'take your new leading lady to work' day?"

"It will be. But are you sure you don't want to spend some time shopping or visiting with your sister?"

"I can do those things any time. How often do I get to see my leading man be a star?"

"I should warn you. The writer's a novice. Plus, my character is a hideous alien with a bad attitude."

"And he's the *hero* of the story?"

He gave her a chagrined look. "We think so. Like I said, the writer's a novice."

"Then why do the story?"

"You know, give the kid a break."

Kelly grinned. "Make a difference in his world?"

"Her world. But yes."

The butler walked in. "Message for you, Mr. Jerod. The studio called. The director's been laid up with a bad case of the flu. I'm afraid filming has been cancelled until further notice."

Jerod smiled. "Thank you, Earl. Please send the director my condolences, the usual card and gift basket."

"Very good, Mr. Jerod."

CHAPTER 9

▼

SISTERS

"So, now that you have a free afternoon, what should we do?" Kelly asked.

Jerod thought for a bit. "Did you ever manage to contact your sister?"

Kelly shook her head. "I'll try again. Maybe we could meet up."

She pulled away from him and walked to the phone in the living room.

*　　　*　　　*　　　*

Jerod folded his arms in front of him and sighed happily.

Stu put his arm on Jerod's shoulder. "What a nice lady. I hope she does join us. It'd be nice to have at least one of our own women around. I miss that."

Jerod looked up at him. "You have memories of them?"

"Of course. Oh, I'm sorry, I forgot. You were the last child born, the baby of the family, as the humans say. My original raised yours after your mum died. Maybe that's why you used to complain I treated you like a kid. I'd muss your hair, but there isn't enough of it left."

"Thanks a lot. I keep telling Coren it would be nice to have a full head of hair. Then again, it might not seem like me in the mirror. Besides, Kelly doesn't seem to mind."

"Like I was saying, it would be nice to have our own women again. Coren was thinking of having me come along on this supper you're planning."

Jerod raised his eyebrows. "Oh? You know about it?" He shrugged. "I guess you would. It's hard to keep secrets from our strongest telepath."

"Secrets? When did we start keeping secrets?"

Jerod shrugged. "It must be a female thing."

"Then I'm all for it. You're lucky you met her first, or I'd be the one kissing her."

"She's not your type. That's a kiss you'd be trying to steal for a very long time."

"Are you sure about that? She told me she likes a man who can cook."

Jerod scowled at him. "I should have you sanctioned."

"Take it easy. Look at you, what is this?" He held up Jerod's palm to reveal wildly racing red swirls. "Jealousy?"

Jerod bit his lip. "I'm sorry. Since I've Been Blued I don't know what I'm doing any more. It's a bewildering experience at times."

Stu tilted his head and touched the back of his hand to Jerod's cheek. "I'd love to be this kind of bewildered." Jerod swatted his hand away.

*   *   *   *

Kelly put the phone down and turned around. "It turns out my step-sister, Olivia, is in town visiting Katy. That's why her phone was tied up last night. When I told her about us, she insisted they both join us for supper. I'm sorry, I guess it won't be very romantic."

"Don't apologize, I'd love to meet them. If they're single, maybe I'll bring some friends along."

Kelly paused. "I think Olivia might like being introduced to Stu, if I'm not assuming too much."

"Me? What woman in her right mind would want to meet me?"

"Funny, that's sort of her attitude about men. My sister, Katy, on the other hand, she's a bit, uh, different."

Jerod and Stu looked at each other. "Coren," Jerod said.

Stu nodded. "Definitely."

"What, *Doctor* Coren? That weird physician from last night? You guys know him?"

Jerod smiled. "How do you think I got you in there so fast? Coren takes care of the entire studio, as well as his own private practice."

"Okay, then. Sound like we're all having supper. I just realized, I haven't got a thing to wear."

"I can have the maid do your laundry."

Kelly laughed. "No, I mean I *literally* don't have a thing to wear. I didn't pack any formal clothes. This was supposed to be a research trip. I guess I need to go shopping."

"I'll have Andrew bring the car around." Jerod caught the eye of the butler.

The man nodded and went out the front door.

*   *   *   *

Kelly sat at a café in a mall hallway, her two sisters opposite her, numerous shopping bags at their feet. Katy was slimmer and more muscular than either of the other women, and had long, straight brown hair. Her blue eyes twinkled in the light. Olivia had a much darker complexion, and short, curly, dark brown hair with gold highlights. Her large, brown eyes sparkled with intelligence.

"So, you really think this guy's the one, Kelly?"

"Katy, I don't know if there's just one guy out there for me, I just know that all of a sudden I want to drop everything to be with him."

"Sounds serious," Olivia's sultry voice responded. "Good thing we're here to meet him. But did he have to bring his friends? It'll be that much harder to pass judgment on him if we're distracted with our own dates."

"That's probably the idea," Kelly responded. She and Katy giggled while Olivia shook her head. Suddenly Kelly stopped laughing. "Oh. I'm sorry, Katy."

The three of them lapsed into an embarrassed silence.

Katy scowled. "I got over it. Why can't everyone else?"

Olivia tapped her arm. "Because that kind of response suggests you're still hurting." She waited for Katy to calm down. "That's better. Remember, we're there for Kelly tonight. I almost feel sorry for this poor Jerod fellow. It'll be three against one."

Kelly shrugged. "I suppose you might be able to tell something of his character from the company he keeps. His household staff seems totally devoted to him. I'm more worried about Dr. Coren. He's kind of, uh, strange."

Olivia raised an eyebrow. "Strange, how?"

"I can't put my finger on it. He seems to know things."

Katy nodded. "The man's a doctor. He has to know all sorts of things."

"No, that's not what I meant. He seems to know more than he should. He correctly guessed my hobbies as running, swimming and mountain climbing. And he seemed determined to tell me the scar tissue wasn't a problem, that medical science could help if I ever wanted to conceive."

"So?" they chorused.

"But I didn't even mention the scar tissue."

Olivia leaned back. "Then it must have been in your medical file."

Kelly frowned. "How would a hospital I've never been to get that information when the accident happened in another country?"

Olivia shrugged. "Computers?"

Katy looked at the clock across the hall, then at her own watch. "Hey, look at the time, we've only got three hours left. We should be getting back. We'll barely have time to dress and do our hair."

They looked at each other and burst out laughing.

Chapter 10

▼

Supper

Jerod, Coren and Stu wore black tuxedoes. They stood waiting at the bottom of the staircase, trying to act natural.

Jerod buttoned his left sleeve for the third time. "I see why the humans call it a monkey suit. You have to keep monkeying around with it."

Coren tugged at his tie. "Even the *thing* finds this uncomfortable."

Stu seemed relatively calm. "Don't you think we should start calling it by the right word? If these ladies choose to join us, they'll want to know exactly what it is. We only call it a *thing* to avoid human detection."

Coren tilted his head. "Good thinking. I'll send a memo to everyone to call it what it is."

Jerod handed him a cell phone.

Coren stared at it. "What's this for?"

"Pretend you're using it, and keep your voice low. That way you won't look like a crazy person talking to himself if they come down before you're finished instructing the computer."

Coren raised an eyebrow and nodded. "Very clever, Jerod. You're right, once again. It wouldn't portray me as much of a potential mate if I looked mentally unstable." He placed the phone over his ear. "Computer, memo all units to use the word 'symbiont' when referring to the life form. It's no longer to be called a 'thing' or any other euphemism. Authorization, Coren Thirteen."

Jerod nudged him and looked to the top of the stairs.

Kelly, Katy and Olivia were wearing elegant red dresses. Kelly's was cut low in the front with layered detailing. Katy's fully covered her shoulders but she was standing to show it revealed most of her back. Olivia's was sleeveless, with a slit down the leg. The three women descended, apparently pleased with the silenced awe they'd inspired.

*   *   *   *

Jerod, Kelly, Coren, Katy, Stu and Olivia waited at the entrance of the restaurant on top of the prestigious 'Banker Elite' tower. A maitre de in a black suit greeted them. "Do you have a reservation?" he queried.

Jerod stepped forward. "Jerod Seventeen, party of six."

The man used his finger to scan the listing. "Ah. *Señor* Jerod. Of course. This way, *Por Favor*."

He led them to a large round table set for six.

Coren and Stu followed Jerod's lead of pulling out their dates' chairs. Kelly, Katy and Olivia sat down. The men seated themselves.

Jerod pulled his chair a bit closer to Kelly's. She gave him a slight shake of the head. He wondered what she was trying to communicate. The Companion File offered no suggestion.

"This is a very nice restaurant," Katy said.

Jerod shrugged. "We had to come here. This is the only place in town we can get Stu to eat without critiquing the food. That's what happens when you have a professional chef with you, you can dress him up but you can't take him out."

Olivia ran her fingers down Stu's sleeve. "You look very nice. It's not fair of them to pick on you."

"Oh, I'm used to it. You know, being a professional cook doesn't keep others from being critical of you. I may put food in people's mouths, but I get blamed for everything from clumsy busboys to poorly folded napkins."

"Poor baby."

He patted her hand. "It'll be a nice change to have something other than food and diners to think about."

Olivia put her other hand over his. "I might be able to help with that." She giggled. She glanced at Katy, took on a serious look and sat up straight.

Stu wondered what he'd done wrong and glanced at Jerod.

Jerod shrugged and stole a glance at Kelly. Something was making her uncomfortable.

Coren winked at Katy. "I bet you could give a man a few things to distract him."

Katy blushed. "I could try."

Kelly cleared her throat. "Perhaps we should order."

Katy's face reddened. "Would you excuse me, I think I need some fresh air." She got up from the table, slung her handbag strap over her shoulder and headed in the direction of the glass-covered patio overlooking the city.

Coren's eyebrows went up. His mouth opened slightly. He watched her go, and then reached for his water. He nearly jumped as Jerod slapped his wrist, spilling the glass.

"Coren, you fool!"

"What?"

"Go after her!" Kelly hissed.

"Oh." Coren pushed his chair back. He tried to sound confident. "Right." He stood up and strode towards the patio, while wondering what he was supposed to do next.

Olivia and Stu looked at each other. She squeezed his hand. "Don't worry. We're still okay."

*   *   *   *

Katy gripped the railing of the patio, her knuckles white with the strain. She sighed angrily as she looked down.

"Are you okay?" Coren asked.

"I'm so sick and tired of always being seen as a victim. They act like I haven't gotten over it and never will."

"I'm a little bit in the dark here," Coren offered.

She turned around and looked into his eyes. "You really don't know, do you?"

He shrugged. "Not a clue. Do you want to tell me what it is?"

Katy felt safer than she had in a long time. She planted her fists on her hips. "I was raped when I was ten. A 'crime of opportunity,' they said, 'nothing personal.' It was very personal to me.

"I've gone through a lot of counseling, and pain, and anguish, and I've gotten past it. But I'm so sick and tired of being treated like no-one can be romantic around me, as if I'm so fragile I'll fall to pieces."

"I'm so sorry." Coren stepped forward and hugged her. She snuggled close as his hands gently touched her back.

"This is the first hug I've had from someone who didn't act like I'd fall apart."

"It could be the first of many."

Katy breathed deeply. "I think I'd like that." She pressed her lips against his neck.

Coren held her tighter. His mind was suddenly unfocused. He felt like she was holding him up. The Companion File instructed him to lean forward and bend his knees to bring his height closer to hers. His mind filled with images and memories of her life.

Katy's lips brushed his. She paused. "Are you all right? You're looking a little blue."

"It must be the lighting. I think they're having some problems with the electricity."

"Must be," she murmured. "We should probably go back to the table."

"In a minute." He kissed her, hoping the Companion File was giving him the correct instructions. Even as a doctor, he was amazed at how responsive her back and shoulders were. At length she pulled away. He straightened his back but continued to hold her.

"Another first of many?" she asked.

He smiled. "Possibly. And if you ever do need to fall apart, I want to be there to help pick up the pieces."

"Not just because you're a doctor?"

He frowned. "No. Why would that have anything to do with it?"

"You know, the Hippocratic Oath and all that."

"The what? Oh, yes, of course. The oath. I'm sorry. I guess my mind was more on the immediate biology of the moment than on the medicine."

Katy raised her eyebrows. "You are an odd one, aren't you?"

"I hear it's part of my charm."

"So what else makes up this charm of yours?"

"I'm not sure. Spend some time with me and maybe we'll both find out."

"That sounds like a challenge." She inhaled deeply, enjoying the scent of his aftershave.

"One I hope you'll accept."

"What if I'm not up to it? I don't have much experience with strange men." She looked at his tie and traced part of the pattern with her fingers.

"That's all right. I don't have much experience with wonderful women."

Surprised, she looked into his eyes. He gazed back, savoring the moment.

She blinked back tears. "I think I'm in trouble, Doctor," she whispered. "I'm falling for you and I don't think there's a cure."

"I sure hope not," he whispered back. "Just take my hand. Maybe we can find our way back to the table together."

*   *   *   *

Olivia patted Stu's hand. "If you'll excuse me, I'd like to go freshen my makeup. What about you, Kelly?"

Kelly frowned. She was staring off into space. "No, I'm good. You go ahead."

Surprised, Olivia got up. "Excuse me."

Kelly nodded, absentmindedly. Jerod and Stu half stood up. Olivia hesitated, and then left the table.

Jerod took one last look at Olivia, then resumed his chair and turned his full attention to Kelly. He glanced at Stu. "I think she's processing the last of the data Coren placed into her subconscious."

Stu frowned. "Already? She must have an incredibly strong mind for a human."

A stream of green letters and numbers formed in the space immediately in front of Kelly's eyes.

Stu leaned forward. "Can the humans see this?" he whispered.

Jerod slowly shook his head and spoke quietly. "Just us. Stay calm, no-one will notice."

Kelly's eyelids fluttered.

"She's struggling with it, it's running too fast for her. I'll have to mindlink."

Jerod placed his hand over Kelly's.

"At this speed? Is that safe?"

"No choice." The data stream widened, spreading in front of Jerod's face as well.

"That's better," Kelly responded. "There's so much data."

"Focus on absorbing the files. You can read the data inside later."

"Right. That helps. But tell me one thing. What's my role in all this?"

Stu leaned forward. "You wanted to make a difference in your world. You can make a huge difference in ours. It's your choice."

Kelly moved her hand through the data stream. "How can I say no to all this?"

A waiter across the room saw the gesture. He came over to the table. "Is there something I can get for you, *Señorita?*"

She smiled and the data stream ended. "I, uh, I thought I saw a friend across the room. Sorry, it wasn't who I thought it was." She turned to Jerod. "Are we ready to order yet? I'm starving."

He smiled. "Katy and Coren are still out on the patio. I think we can order for them. What about Olivia, what would she like?"

"Besides a husband?" Kelly gasped and put her hand over her mouth. "I'm sorry, I shouldn't have said that. We get so used to joking around with each other."

Katy thwacked the back of her neck. "That's for Olivia." She looked around as Coren pulled out her chair. "Where is she?"

"Ladies Room," Kelly answered. "It could take a while. There was a line when she went in."

The men looked bewildered.

The waiter was still looking expectantly at them. He had skillfully moved out of everyone's way at the right time. He cleared his throat. "If I may suggest, the Almond Chicken is excellent tonight."

CHAPTER 11

▼

SHOT IN THE DARK

Twilight was descending as the group came out of the restaurant. The faint scream of a siren could be heard, growing louder as they talked. About halfway down the block, they were greeted by the sound of screeching tires. A black sports car slowed as it approached. A white man with a shaved head, about twenty, in a black T-shirt and a camouflage patterned bandana, leaned out the passenger window with a pistol. He glanced around and spotted them.

"Get down!" Coren shouted, forcefully pushing everyone he could reach. The motion wasn't quite quick enough. One of several rapidly fired bullets found him. The sports car sped off.

The first police car ended its pursuit and squealed to the curb beside them. A second, then a third patrol car raced after the suspect vehicle.

"We can't wait for an ambulance," Jerod told the officer. "None of his vitals are hit, but it would be quicker to take him to Emergency in your car."

The officer looked over the well-dressed group. "You look familiar. Are you a doctor?" he asked Jerod.

"I was. I switched professions a while ago. Officer Zephyr, isn't it? We met a few times in the emergency ward."

"That's good enough for me. Let's get him into the cruiser."

Coren attempted to grab his arm. "Don't let them reconfigure me, not now ..."

"You're going to be fine," Officer Zephyr soothed, opening the back door of his car and picking up Coren's legs.

Jerod picked up Coren's arms and helped load him into the car. "I'd like to come with you, I can help minimize his blood loss on the way. The rest of our party can follow in the limo."

"Good, I'll need statements from all of you. Hop in." He turned to Stu. "Just don't break any speed limits getting there. I've never fixed a ticket and I never will."

Stu nodded. "I'm sure our limo driver doesn't want to lose his license, either. Thank you for helping our friend."

Zephyr scrutinized him for signs of insincerity. "Just doing my duty. But you're welcome."

Stu turned to the ladies. "We should get to the car and follow them to the hospital."

Kelly, Katy and Olivia were standing still, their eyes wide. Kelly spoke first. "Yes, come on, you two. Coren and Jerod will need us."

Katy's lip was trembling. "I can't lose him now, I just can't." She burst into tears.

Olivia wrapped her arms around her stepsister. "Hush, you hush now, it's time to be strong, little sister."

The effect on Katy was immediate. She stopped blubbering, wiped her eyes and stood up straight. "Let's go," she said.

They piled into the back of the limo, Katy by the passenger side window, Kelly beside her. Olivia sat between Kelly and Stu. The car started forward.

Stu leaned over to whisper in Olivia's ear. "That was amazing. How did you manage to calm her down so quickly?"

Olivia whispered her reply. "It's a sister thing. We take turns holding each other together. Either one of them would do the same for me."

Stu considered the comment. "Jerod and Coren are like that for me. I hope all six of us will be very good friends."

Olivia gave him a look that made him feel weak. "I was hoping you and I could be much more than friends. Do you have children?"

Unable to speak, he shook his head.

"Do you want them?"

He nodded.

"Good. I plan on having at least a dozen. So the sooner we get started, the better. In fact, if we were alone, we could start right away."

For a moment, Stu had forgotten there was anyone else in the car. "What about getting married?" he squeaked.

"Of course I want the father of my children to be my husband. But as long as you're willing to be a daddy, the actual marriage date isn't all that important, is it?"

Stu's Companion File popped up the response she needed to hear. He cleared his throat. "Actually, it is important, it's very important to me. If you can't wait to elope at the very least, maybe you're not the right girl for me."

Olivia burst into laughter. Stu thought he'd blown it, but instead Olivia grabbed his hands. "I just *knew* if I stuck to my principles I'd find the right man. Girls, we have a wedding to plan."

Kelly tried to smile. "That's wonderful, Olivia. But right now, we need to take care of Katy and Coren first."

Olivia calmed down. "Of course. Don't you worry, Coren will be fine, Little Sister." She reached over and squeezed Katy's hand.

Stu reached over and placed his hand on top of hers. "We'll make sure nothing happens to him. Remember, Jerod said no vitals had been hit. And he used to be a doctor. He'd never lie about a patient's condition."

Kelly looked at him. "Jerod used to be a doctor? What happened to turn him into an actor?"

"Oh you know, family pressure to be one thing, when a person wants to do something else, and then life itself throws you a whole different set of circumstances."

All three ladies nodded and looked at each other.

"I hear that," Olivia said.

"Uh, huh," and "Oh yeah," the other two responded.

*   *   *   *

Spencer and Perry, dressed as interns, were waiting as the cop car screeched to a halt at the emergency entrance. They pulled Coren out of the car and loaded him onto a stretcher.

Jerod gave them a quick run-down on Coren's condition. "No vitals hit, blood pressure is stable, but he's lost a lot of blood. He may be about to go into shock. Tell Dr. Athens he doesn't want to be reconfigured."

"Why not?" asked Perry.

"He's Been Blued."

The two young men looked at each other, big grins spreading over their faces. "Then there's hope for us all. Dr. Athens will be pleased. Don't worry, Jerod, your friend will be fine. We'll *all* be fine." They were already wheeling Coren inside, the last comments shouted over the flurry of fading sirens as three ambulances pulled away from the hospital.

Officer Zephyr looked at Jerod, his notebook and pen at the ready. "I suspect there's more going on here than I'll be able to put into my report. Now what exactly did you, and the victim, mean by 'don't let them reconfigure me,' and, 'he's Been Blued?' Remember, I have a photographic memory, so it's no use trying to snow me, Doctor Eighteen."

Jerod lifted his hands, as if to show he was unarmed. "It's actually quite simple. I'm sorry, Officer Zephyr, but I can't let you keep some of the memories in question." He held his hands almost up to the officer's face. A multicolored stream of words and images appeared between them. "Computer, delete," he pointed at specific things, "this, this, this, this and that … Also delete the memory of this interface. Leave a feeling of well-being in those spots, a sense of being totally in control. And upgrade all memories he has of my name to Seventeen instead of Eighteen."

Jerod took a moment to really look at the man now under his control. "What a fine specimen. If we were short of males, Zephyr could be acceptable. Let's see if he has any eligible sisters. Hmmm, he's got *four* of them."

Four images of pretty women popped up, two blondes, a redhead and a brunette. Jerod tilted his head, probing for more information.

"All four work in law enforcement. That could be tricky, but let's see if we can't set up a meeting with some of our guys."

He moved his hand through the data stream and pressed down on the officer's forehead to download images into his mind. He removed his hand and tapped the notepad. "That should do it. Computer, end interface."

The officer blinked and looked at his notepad, now full of his own handwriting. "It seems your statement of events is very complete. I guess you actors have to memorize things very quickly. If your friends are half this efficient, I should be out of your hair soon." He looked at Jerod's balding head. "Sorry, no offense."

"None taken. Here comes the limo now. Can we go check on Coren's progress first?"

The officer looked at the limo. "Of course. I'll go grab a coffee, maybe a sandwich in the cafeteria." He winked at Jerod. "There's a cute little nurse on the third floor who should be starting her shift in twenty minutes. That's where you'll find me."

The limo stopped and everyone except the driver got out. Kelly ran up to Jerod and hugged him. "How's Coren?"

"They started on him a little while ago. Let's go in and see what they can tell us."

*   *   *   *

Dr. Athens, a well-built man with dirty blond hair, and blue eyes couldn't keep the grin off his face. "I should be terribly jealous, but I'm just so thrilled that any of us has Been Blued. And now two in a week. Things are looking up."

Spencer and Perry had donned surgical scrubs and gloves to assist in the triage room. "We can't reconfigure him, a new symbiont may not remember having Been Blued," Spencer warned.

Dr. Athens waved his hand in the air. "Of course, of course. This body must be kept alive; you think I don't know that? Just remember one thing, gentlemen. Doctors make the worst patients. And Coren is the best doctor we've got."

"So he'll make the worst patient?" asked Perry.

"Precisely. Now, as Jerod noted, the bullet missed all vital organs. That was lucky for him, and very lucky for us. He's also bled out most of the contaminants on the bullet, so there's very little possibility of infection. In addition, the bullet completely missed his *thing*, I'm sorry, his symbiont, so it's in good shape. In fact, it's already dissolved the bullet. Bad news for forensics, good news for us. The wound should be right here." He tore Coren's shirt, starting at the hole left by the bullet.

All three of them looked at the injury. Dr. Athens sponged off the excess blood. "Clotting looks good, the wound is closing nicely. Let's get him ready for recuperation. Dress it up, make it look like we're controlling extreme bleeding. The humans would expect that." He unwrapped a syringe and filled it with a small vial from his pocket.

"Now what are you giving him?" Perry asked.

"This is a little concoction of my own making. I got tired of being yelled at by other doctors when they're recuperating, so I came up with *this*. It doesn't have a name yet, but it causes enough of a restriction in the larynx to keep a person's voice down. It's something a person can override if facing a real emergency, but most patients won't realize that." He jabbed the needle into Coren's arm and drove the plunger home.

*   *   *   *

Coren felt a presence in the room. It was morning, or possibly evening; hard to tell with twilight. In the semi-darkness he could see Katy sleeping in a chair near the window, her dress jacket covering her shoulders. He ached to touch her.

"Katy, Katy," he whispered. Strange, it seemed he couldn't talk any louder.

It had been enough. Katy stirred, and then awoke. She threw off the jacket and rushed to his side. "I'm here, Coren. I'm right here."

He reached for her face, ignoring the intravenous line dangling from his arm. "Please, Katy, kiss me."

She bent down and gently touched his lips with hers. His pulse strengthened as her touch became more demanding. He stroked her hair. She pulled away when he gently pushed against her chin.

"Thank you. I live again."

"Oh, Coren, me too. When I thought you might die, it was worse than anything else I've ever gone through."

"I'm sorry to have caused you so much pain."

She touched his lips with her fingertips. Red swirls appeared in the back of her hand, and then flowed up her arm, into her face. She inhaled deeply and smiled. "Never mind." She gently pushed him over to make room on the bed and slipped off her shoes. Picking up her skirt, she slid beside him, placing her left arm under his neck. Snuggling next to him, she put her right hand on top of the blanket, over his heart. "Let's just stay like this until morning."

Coren felt his symbiont swim beneath her hand. It nudged the female hand, detecting her affection and concern. The new symbiont was happily taking care of things.

Coren felt his own symbiont withdraw from over his heart, happy to swim about in the rest of his constitution. "Stupid thing's probably laughing to itself," he muttered.

"I'm sorry, what?"

"Katy, there's something you should know before we go any further."

She inhaled deeply again and sighed, sure signs the symbiont had been successful. "I think I already know, Sweetheart." She held up her hand to show its red swirls. "It's all right. As long as you love me, I accept everything about you. I waited for you, even before I knew about you."

"But how?"

"Women's intuition."

"Ah. The one paranormal item our scientists were never able to disprove."

Katy was already falling asleep. He kissed her forehead and watched as her eyes drooped and her head came to rest on his shoulder. He held up his own hand and watched the red spot appear.

"Thank you," he whispered. "I thought it was too soon, but you were right. You're always right." He pulled the blanket up as much as he could without disturbing Katy, his own eyes suddenly too heavy to keep open.

*   *   *   *

Dr. Athens tapped the officer on the shoulder. "Excuse me, Officer, if you could possibly tear yourself away from my nurses ..."

Zephyr's nostrils flared as he stepped back from the counter he'd been leaning on. "I beg your pardon? *Your* nurses?"

Dr. Athens scowled at him. "That's right, *my* nurses. As long as they're on duty, they're at my command. Lives depend on that."

The officer's temper abated. "Oh, I see. You meant professionally. Of course. How's the shooting victim?"

Dr. Athens took him by the elbow and looked back. The two nurses at the station quickly turned away, suddenly busy with paperwork.

"I don't like to say this, in fact I try to never use the term, but his recovery has been miraculous."

The officer took a step back. "What?"

"I said, it's a miracle. The bleeding stopped and clotted nicely, the wound is closing faster than I've ever seen and the man should be back on his feet in a matter of days.

"Now I know this creates a problem for you, but we weren't able to find the bullet."

"What?"

"It wasn't a through and through, so it must have fallen out, either at the scene or in the ambulance or between the ambulance and the hospital."

"Oh, that's just great. He didn't get here by ambulance; he came in the back of my cruiser. Bad enough it'll have to be detailed, but now I've got to search every nook and cranny first to find the damned bullet."

Dr. Athens frowned and tapped him on the shoulder. "There will be no swearing in this ward. There are children just down the hall. As a police officer, you should know better."

"Sorry, I just know it'll mess things up for the prosecution if I can't find it."
He suddenly grabbed Coren's shoulder.

"Are you all right, Officer?"

"I don't know, I feel dizzy. I've never felt like this before."

"Here, this room is empty, let me have a look at you." Dr. Athens helped him
into the nearest room and shut the door.

"This will be off the record, right? If I'm in anything but perfect health, they'll
yank my badge or worse, they'll put me at a desk."

Dr. Athens was holding the man's head in his hand, checking his eyes. He
pulled out a small flashlight out of his pocket. "Look up. Never mind about your
badge. Health is far more important than career. Close your eyes."

Officer Zephyr closed his eyes and slumped unconscious to the chair Dr. Athens had been pushing him towards.

Jerod quickly stepped inside.

"Is this your man?" Dr. Athens asked him.

"That's the one. He's such a nice looking fellow I checked for sisters. He's got
four of them."

Dr. Athens looked into the face still in his hands. "You're right. Nice looking
specimen. Let's see if everything else lines up." He pulled out a hand-sized computer from another pocket and activated it. He watched as the screen showed him
details of the officer's health.

"Good genes, intriguing personality, nice package. Coren couldn't have done
much better arranging the DNA. Oops, a slight possibility of … Never mind, I
thought I saw the precursor of Diabetes there, but I was reading the screen too
fast. You're right, Jerod, this man is as perfect as they come. Good eye, we might
not have deleted all your medical training after all. See Coren if you start having
flashbacks."

"How is Coren, anyway?"

Dr. Athens tapped a button on the handheld computer. "He's fine, and …
Aw, that's so sweet. Look at the two of them."

Jerod came closer to have a look. "Both fast asleep. And so intimate. Hey, is
that what I think it is?"

"What do you see?"

"I see a red spot that's moving."

Athens nodded. "Yes, his symbiont wasn't injured at all."

"I'm not talking about *Coren*."

"What?" Dr. Athens twisted his wrist, bringing the screen back to his own line of vision. He tilted the device to ensure it wasn't a trick of the light. "I think you're right. This is wonderful! Do you know what this means?"

Jerod lifted his hand as if to say he did, and then let it drop. "No, actually. I'm afraid that's some of the medical knowledge that's been erased."

"It *means* we've been successful. If the human women who Blue us develop their own symbionts, our future is secured."

"That's great! How do I get Kelly to develop one?"

"That depends. What kind of commitment is she looking for?"

"She wants to get married before mating."

"Then marry her. Immediately!! Doctor's orders! Katy must have felt Coren was totally committed to her or it couldn't have happened. Kelly needs to know the same about you. And see if you can't push things along with Stu and Olivia, you know how he procrastinates."

A slight groan brought their attention back to the policeman.

Dr. Athens stroked the man's forehead. A green stream of data swirled in the air between them. "I'm putting it in his head to arrange a meeting between me and his sisters."

"Athens," Jerod growled.

"All right, all right, I'll make sure at least three more of our guys are there too. Oh, I see you've begun arranging things already. You could have at least let me have first shot at them, I am a doctor, you know."

"Have you forgotten, Athens? They pick us. Or not."

"It's the second part that's been the problem for so long, isn't it? I wonder why we're suddenly back to Being Blued."

"If we knew that, we could probably solve the problem overnight. We wouldn't have to resort to doing *this* to unsuspecting humans." Jerod motioned in Zephyr's direction.

"They love it. We fix their problems and leave them with a sense of well being."

Jerod tilted his head. "Humans tend to be ungrateful. They might resent it if they knew what we've been up to."

"That's why we haven't revealed ourselves. Do you know yet what the mystery device is, the thing that weakened the spotlight supports? Coren says it's human technology."

"Yes, but he still thinks it belongs to one of our guys. It's too clean, no fingerprints, no skin cells, no body oil, nothing. 'Humans leave footprints,' remember? It would take one of us to leave anything that clean."

"I suppose. Still, it's disconcerting to think one of us might have evil intentions." Dr. Athens paled.

Jerod stared into space. "We can't claim to have eradicated all crime among ourselves. The symbiont leaves personality intact. It's possible someone doesn't want to have Been Blued."

"You'd better go. Our friend here will be coming around soon."

"What are you going to tell him?"

Dr. Athens shrugged. "The poor man has been working too hard, with all those extra shifts. He just needs some time off, maybe to reconnect with family."

Jerod cocked an eyebrow at him. "He's very fond of his sisters. You'd better watch yourself or you might discover one of his bullets in your own gut."

"Nah. He'd never dream of harming a future brother-in-law."

Jerod chuckled and grabbed the doorknob. "You keep telling yourself that. But just in case you do get yourself arrested, we've got things covered. You're now a doctor and a spy."

Dr. Athens turned back to the officer. "So, which of your sisters do you think will be the lucky lady that chooses me for her husband?"

The man's eyes opened, a blank look in them. "How should I know?"

Dr. Athens frowned at him. "Are you resisting my control?"

"Yes. Evading mind control is now a standard part of officer training at the Martianville Police Academy."

"Okay, then. Why have I been able to get this far with you?"

"I trust Jerod. He trusts you. And your intentions seem harmless enough."

Dr. Athens scowled. "Have you been exploring my thoughts?"

"You have to mentally let your guard down to connect with another mind. A few things slip through. Jerod is always careful to erase the extra data."

"Then I guess I should be just as careful."

"If you're not, I'll have dreams about you. Then I'd have to hunt you down."

"Why are you telling me this?"

"I like Jerod. I don't want him to be exposed and possibly harmed."

*   *   *   *

Spencer and Perry stared at the reconfiguration chamber. "Are you sure it's a good idea to do this without Coren?" Spencer asked.

"Piece of cake," Perry answered. "It's high time we actually did something to earn our keep. Coren never really needed us to do all that other stuff. He was just training us in case he was unavailable in an emergency. This is it, this is what we were really trained to do."

"But it's the *Coordinator*, Perry. If we mess this up, he could die. And he's already used his backup file. It would be the end for him."

"Is that the real reason you're so worried? Whatever happened to the carefree guy I used to know, the guy who'd take any risk?"

"With my own life, sure. But this isn't my life we're messing with. If the Coordinator dies, even by accident, it'll be our fault. We'd be sanctioned."

Perry crossed his arms in front of him and glared at Spencer. "We'll definitely be sanctioned if we do nothing. His body and brain are ready now. Besides, his mind is stretched pretty thin in the computer. Much more and he'll disperse, and space only knows what that would do to the mainframe."

"It might not do anything to the mainframe."

"Or it might create a whole new life form, which is what we don't want. 'No Random Species Pairings Without Full Research,' remember?"

"I doubt the Coordinator would cause a bizarre hybrid to be created," Spencer countered.

Perry gave him a withering look. "That's not the point. We've got to at least try to get him out of the computer."

The Coordinator's voice interrupted them. "You do know I can hear everything, don't you? Never mind about the risk, Spencer. Perry's right. You've got to try to get me back into a body. I can't spend much longer here. The mainframe is getting antsy."

"Antsy?"

"A joke, Spencer. The longer we leave him in there, the weirder his sense of humor becomes. Come on, let's get to work."

"Spencer, don't feel bad if I die. No one lives forever. Our technology has just made it seem like that. My only regret would be not having Been Blued. That certainly wouldn't have been your fault."

CHAPTER 12

▼

THE COORDINATOR

Jerod took a deep breath. "Ready?" he asked Kelly.

"I'm ready. But you seem terribly nervous. Are you sure this is necessary? If you have the free and democratic society you say you have, your Coordinator shouldn't try to stop us."

"Oh, I'm sure the Coordinator wouldn't dream of putting obstacles in our way. This is more a matter of respect."

He pressed the statue in the library to access the hallway hidden behind the bookcase.

Kelly peered into the darkness. "This is sort of haunted house-like."

Jerod grinned. "It adds to the whole 'aliens are us,' mystique." He flipped a switch to activate the lights. At the end of the hall, a large metal door opened into a huge conference room.

"There's no-one here," Kelly said as they entered.

A door opened across the room. A boy of thirteen, dressed in a black business suit, came in. He placed his briefcase on the table and smiled at them. "Sorry I'm late. There was a tie-up in traffic and the limo had a flat. I changed it myself, so I'm afraid my hands are a bit dirty." He shrugged, rubbed his hands together and adjusted his glasses.

Jerod bowed slightly. Surprised, Kelly did the same.

"Coordinator, I'd like you to meet Kelly Ravell."

The boy walked over and offered his hand. "A pleasure, Miss Ravell. I realize you probably weren't expecting someone so young, but I've just undergone reconfiguration. If you'll access the tenth file under 'Preservation of Life,' you'll find an overview of the process."

Kelly felt slightly overwhelmed. "I'm still adjusting to the download. It's an awful lot of information to process."

"Of course. We did spend three thousand years traveling through space. For now, it's probably just enough to know that I'm actually closer to eight hundred than thirteen."

She frowned as a bit of data popped into her mind. "Tomorrow's your birthday?"

He glanced at the floor. "I'd almost forgotten. At my age I don't usually celebrate it; too many candles on the cake, and all that. But now that you're joining us, maybe we'll all have more to celebrate."

Jerod leaned forward. "We were hoping you'd give us your blessing."

"A wedding? That'd be fantastic."

Jerod winked at Kelly. "We wanted to elope."

The Coordinator gave them a wry expression. "You could at least allow me to perform the ceremony. I am the captain of a ship, after all. There's nothing I can find in human legal precedence that excludes spaceships from that definition, in any state or country on this planet."

"So we have your permission?" Kelly asked.

He took her hands. "My dear, you bring new hope to our species. You have both my permission and my blessing.

"Now I don't want you to worry about some bizarre state of unending pregnancy. Our technology is so advanced you'll never have to carry or raise a child. As soon as you mate, we'll age your offspring to young adulthood. You can continue to pursue whatever career or vocation you like."

"But what about their childhoods? If you age them, they won't remember things like playing ball, having a pet, or friends in school."

"All the information and experience they would have gained growing up will be downloaded into their minds as part of the computer's age enhancement program. Right now, we can't afford to wait for them to grow up. We're running out of time as a species. Without women, we've had to rely on cloning. The reason I'm Coordinator Nine is because that's roughly the number of times I can still be reconfigured. If I'm cloned again, I'll be Coordinator Eight."

"But what about the problems inherent to cloning, the loss of genetic integrity in each succeeding clone?"

"Child's play, if you'll pardon the expression. Our scientists resolved those problems centuries ago. The real challenge was allowing each clone to have all the memories and life experience of his predecessors. We found that after about a hundred reconfigurations the mind simply can't hold any more. And the more you force genetics, the more physical problems tend to arise."

"Wow. Is there anything else I should know right now, so I won't seem so ignorant of our people?"

"Jerod, if you'll excuse us a moment?" The boy gave him a wink.

"Of course, Coordinator. Kelly, I'll be right outside the door."

The boy took a chair and turned it around, sitting backwards to face Kelly. She did the same.

"There is something that could come up on your honeymoon. You see, when we no longer had mates, our, uh, *things,* were reduced to minimum functioning."

Kelly felt strange, having such a young looking man explaining things to her. "What *things* are you talking about? You mean your ...?" She glanced at his pants.

He looked down, and then chuckled as he looked back up. "No. Nothing like that. Twenty-two hundred years ago we encountered an abandoned planet. The inhabitants were simply gone. Planetary records showed they thought they had exhausted all the scientific discoveries the planet had to offer. Then they moved on. Naturally, we were curious.

"We found they had enhanced their own reproductive abilities to the point where they could control every aspect of mating, right from choosing the right one to terminating a pregnancy or giving birth any time after mating. At the time it sounded so appealing.

"All we had to do was a bit of genetic tweaking and found the same science quite adaptable. The first implant was so compatible that it spread like a virus. Literally. It recreated itself in every member of our population.

"We soon discovered it was a biological symbiont. It allowed us to expand our computer capabilities and communicate with each other in a limited telepathic manner. It even helped us cure several illnesses. It worked for generations without any problems at all."

Kelly nodded. "Until?"

"Until around two thousand years later, when we made the mistake of trying to follow the course our benefactors had taken upon leaving the planet. There, on a very different and inhospitable planet, we found their decaying corpses. A virus of their own making had killed their symbionts. In trying to fight off the infec-

tion, the symbionts ended up killing their own hosts. The virus was all that survived."

"That's terrible."

"Fortunately, our scientists were able to take their research to the next level.
We found a way to negate the virus. However, it was too late for our women,
who seemed more vulnerable to it. By the time we figured out how to cure them,
all the women of childbearing age had died.

"Since then we've tried everything we could think of to prevent our own
extinction. The main thing you need to know is that we have no direct memory
of how to mate."

Kelly leaned back. "None?"

"None. In this compromised state, the symbiont does its best to remind us,
but without actual experience to draw on, all we can do is wait."

"Wait? Wait for what?"

"The expression is, 'to have Been Blued.' It's used most often in the past tense
because it's been so long since it happened to any of us. We don't know why it
happened when you kissed Jerod, or when Katy kissed Coren, because, believe
me, we've tried everything. Without having Been Blued, we simply don't mate.
The desire is there, but nothing more."

Kelly's mouth dropped open.

The Coordinator adjusted his glasses and waited. He drummed his fingers
nervously on the chair. "Please, say something."

"It's just, uh, it's just that I'd assumed I'd waited for so long to get married
that my husband would have been with other women first."

The Coordinator laughed, leaned back and folded his arms across his chest.
He shook his head. "Nope."

Kelly smiled. "So Jerod has no idea what sex is like?"

"None whatsoever. You can tell him whatever you want and he has to believe
it; not that I'd expect you to deceive him or anything. We do have laws regarding
that sort of thing. But if he's not doing something right, just tell him. All of us
are under standing orders to comply with the demands of the female who Blues
us."

"Even you?"

"Especially me. Our leadership was supposed to continue through family
lines."

He lowered his voice and looked around the empty room. "Part of the reason
they reconfigure me as a teenager is in the hopes that a very young lady will take a
liking to me."

Kelly frowned. "So you attend high school?"

"High school? What for? I have access to more knowledge than human records contain."

"Didn't it ever occur to you, that's where teenage girls are most of the time?"

The Coordinator paled. "No, it didn't. I just hung out at malls a lot, mostly in the computer stores."

"That and the suit would make you seem like a brainy geek. Girls preoccupied by fashion and makeup don't even want to be seen in the same room as a guy who looks like he's ready for the next spelling bee."

"What do you suggest?"

"First, how badly do you need those glasses?"

"They allow me to see things in multiple dimensions."

"How often do you need them might be a better question."

"Any time I wish to fully access the computer mainframe. Leading my men takes a lot of work. I oversee just about everything."

"An overworked computer geek, at that. I see I have my work cut out for me. Good thing I minored in psychology. You need help with interpersonal skills when it comes to the opposite sex."

"I've always thought we must have a few blind spots when it came to dealing with humanity. We may have originated on this planet, but we became so much more after we left, it was easy to think we'd left our own humanity behind. Maybe it's time to take some of it back."

Jerod poked his head around the door. "Am I being made to wait, or have I been jilted at the altar?"

Kelly jumped up. "I would never do that to you. But you should have told me the Coordinator was such an interesting man."

The Coordinator stood up. "I have a suggestion. Kelly, since you're joining our community, how would you feel about a traditional ceremony, Martian style? It's quick, with just a few words spoken by me."

"Martian style?"

Jerod nodded. "When we left Earth we decided to call ourselves something other than 'humans' or 'Earthlings.'"

"So you decided to call yourselves 'Martians?' Wasn't that kind of deceptive?"

"We thought the rest of humanity would be much further advanced, well out into space by now, and we wanted to prevent being mistaken as the same group of people. And we did use Mars as a base for a while. It also appealed to our sense of humor at the time."

Kelly wore a bemused expression. "All right. 'Martian style' it is."

The Coordinator grabbed Jerod's right hand and placed it in Kelly's left. He did the opposite with their other hands before wrapping his own over the resulting crisscross. "As Coordinator of our people and Captain of our course, I pronounce you married."

Kelly raised an eyebrow. "That's it?"

Jerod smiled. "Very efficient, these Martians. How does it feel to be one of us?"

Kelly gasped. "I felt something move in my arm."

Jerod rolled up her sleeve. A red spot, three inches in diameter, was growing larger. "Congratulations. You have your own symbiont."

The Coordinator looked it over. "This is an incredibly good sign."

"You could have warned me. Is it permanent?"

The Coordinator nodded. "Yes. And it should be painless. If it ever causes you the slightest discomfort, let us know immediately. It's also very cooperative. It will conceal itself under your clothes any time you wish. If you're swimming in public, it can conceal itself under the smallest swimsuit."

Jerod unrolled her sleeve. "It should make the computer interface easier to handle. These guys love data and electricity, probably the reason they took to us so amicably."

Kelly inhaled deeply. The symbiont seemed harmless, even gave her a slight sense of happiness, like seeing an old friend. It moved into the back of her hand in response to her desire to look at it. "Katy showed me hers."

Jerod and the Coordinator exchanged glances. Jerod cleared his throat. "We, uh, had sort of expected that the first woman to cause any of us to have Been Blued would also be the first to develop the symbiont."

"If it happened at all," interjected the Coordinator. "This might change things."

"What kind of things?" Kelly wasn't sure she liked the serious tone the conversation had suddenly taken.

The strident voice of the computer reinforced her concern. "Matriarch Programs reinitializing. Updates are currently in progress. Please stand by. Recognizing new Matriarch, Kelly Ravell."

"Matriarch?" Kelly gasped.

The Coordinator hopped up on a chair to look her in the eye. "Our society has traditionally been Matriarchal. With your background and training, we fully expect you to take the leading role."

"Me? Why *me?"*

He grinned. "Hesitation to take over. The first sign of a real leader."

Jerod tried to keep the smile off his face. "You'll make a wonderful Matriarch. Just be yourself."

Kelly stared at the red streaks in her hand. "I'm not sure who that is anymore."

"For one thing, you're my wife. If you don't mind, I'd like to get started on the honeymoon."

Kelly felt agreement in her newly acquired life form. She realized it was helping her stay calm. "I think I'd like that."

The Coordinator hopped off the chair. "One last thing before you leave. Jerod will now take your last name. All Earth records are already being changed. 'Seventeen' will only by acknowledged as a stage name. Very handy, some of these Earth customs."

Chapter 13

▼

The Carnival

Seated in the American Refill, Kelly looked at the new ring on her finger. The diamond was a modest size, in keeping with her wishes. It was recessed into twisting bands of tricolor gold, designed to prevent it from catching on things.

Jerod held up her hand and compared his, a larger version minus the stone. "They did a good job."

"It's amazing. They knew exactly what I wanted, without me saying a word. Is communication between our people always that easy?"

"Usually. We try not to use telepathy around the humans; it tends to make them suspicious. But just among us …" He looked into her eyes and smiled.

Kelly felt herself blushing. "Let me try." She blinked and tried to concentrate.

"Ouch." Jerod flinched.

"I'm sorry. What did I do wrong?"

"Uh, it was the way you said it. That's something you'll learn fairly quickly, the etiquette is easy to download."

"But you flinched."

"You implied my ancestors were deformed in, uh, their … Don't worry, it's just that, well, you know how humans have some sayings that sound like one thing but mean something else entirely? We have a lot of those."

Mo placed two cups of coffee on the table. "So, I hear congratulations are in order. Can we expect a new generation in the making?"

Kelly went several shades of red. "That's still something we have to discuss."

Mo looked disappointed. "I'm sorry, I just assumed …"

Jerod held up a hand. "No more assumptions, Mo. But I think we should thank you for your assistance."

Kelly looked at Mo and saw the whole sequence of events involving him. She tilted her head as she scrutinized the data. "I didn't realize how much 'help' you'd been."

Jerod sensed her discomfort. "If Mo hadn't given you a push, you might not have even met me."

"I suppose." She was suddenly aware of being the center of attention in the room. Her diplomacy training took over. She forced a smile. "Thank you, Mo."

Jerod smiled meekly. "Yes. Thank you. Look at the time, we should get going. We're meeting Stu and Olivia at three."

Grateful for the out, Kelly stood up. On an impulse, she gave Mo a peck on the cheek. Jerod held his arm for her to take. They left the café.

Jerod didn't need telepathy to tell what she was thinking. "I'm sorry, I know this must look like we've been manipulating you."

"I know, I know. We were desperate to find a way to continue. We'd even lost hope, but then suddenly our men started Being Blued. Listen to me, I'm so firmly tied into all this that now I'm using the 'royal we,' as if I've always been part of our people."

Jerod hugged her, then gently pushed her an arm's length away, his hands still on her shoulders. "It's a huge adjustment for all of us, especially for you. Look at it this way, now you can make things better for the entire planet. And I promise you, we're not here to take anything away from you. In fact, if you want to walk away from all this right now, you're free to go. Although we would have to make your symbiont dormant and erase all memory of our people from your mind. You'd feel slightly different and never be able to understand why."

Kelly looked up at him. "Are you rejecting me?"

He stroked her hair. "I could never do that. But I don't want you to feel trapped. I'd rather cease to exist than to make you miserable in any way."

Kelly looked into his eyes. Why was there a part of her that wanted to throw it all away and run and hide?

Jerod answered her thoughts with words. "It happens, sometimes. When faced with enormous decisions, fear tries to get us to retreat. It's what kept me from allowing Mo to introduce us the day we met. If he hadn't 'interfered,' we might still be without a future."

"You were actually afraid to meet me?"

"At the time I told myself it was just because I was tired of meeting new women all the time. And I might have had a slight crush on the makeup girl."

All his memories and encounters with Miss Breton popped easily into Kelly's mind. "It looks like you were just friends."

"I was hoping for something more."

"I'm glad there wasn't."

"Are you really? I mean, I know modern humans hope for fidelity while they practice promiscuity."

She smiled. The symbiont was helping her sort out her true feelings. "I do love you. And I will be the mother of our children, no matter what the cost. What do we do next?"

Jerod put his arm around her waist and they started walking down the street. "We need to push things along with Olivia and Stu. He procrastinates terribly."

Kelly laughed. "Then we'd better get started. She's the same way. Leave them alone together and nothing will happen."

"She seemed quite interested in him in the restaurant."

"Unfortunately, my step-sister is easily distracted. She's smart but gets side-tracked by details. She wants to learn everything in depth."

"And do nothing?"

"That does tend to be the result if she's not pushed."

Jerod nodded. "Stu's the same way. If I hadn't practically forced him into that cooking program, he'd still be flipping burgers at a fast food joint."

"Are we sure this is a good match? The two of them together, doing nothing?"

"If she Blues him, there's no alternative."

"There's no way to encourage or discourage that?"

"None that we know of. It either happens or it doesn't. What about among humans, how do they know if they've picked the right mate?"

Kelly shrugged. "Too often, we don't. That's one reason the divorce rate is so high, no symbiont to help us along. A few generations ago, some couples survived on little more than commitment, no matter how unhappy they were."

"I seem to remember."

She gave him a questioning look. "Oh? Oh, of course, one of the previous configurations of you. Tell me something, how many of you did I marry just now?"

"Just the one you Blued. That's why it was important to keep Coren alive after he'd been shot. The next configuration of him would have only had the memory of having Been Blued, not the actual experience. The new symbiont might not have responded to the idea of a relationship with Katy."

"She'd have been devastated."

"We'd all have felt the loss. So far there's only you and me, and Katy and Coren, and *maybe* Olivia and Stu, as potential parents for a new generation."

They stopped under a covered walkway spanning a bridge. Jerod smiled and held her close. "We could get started right here, you know."

Kelly smiled back. "Focus, Darling. The honeymoon can wait. We need to see about Olivia and Stu."

He sighed. "Duty calls?"

She leaned her head against his chest and let out a long, slow sigh. "Blame the symbiont. It wants to reproduce in its own way."

*   *   *   *

The carnival grounds were noisy, but not overly crowded. The rides in the distance seemed to keep going even with only a few people on them. The concession area was filled with stands offering hamburgers, hotdogs, cotton candy and soda. Canned circus music faded in and out of the background as the generator alternately worked and failed, paused, then struggled back to life again. An old man in green coveralls poked at garbage on the ground with a long stick, then used a gloved hand to transfer the refuse to the garbage sack slung over his shoulder.

The concession workers all wore the same yellow uniforms, regardless of what they were cooking. Olivia had eaten something called a 'corn dog,' an act that made Stu seriously wonder if they really were meant to be together.

He eyed the fluffy blue candy in the paper cone he was holding with distrust as Olivia plucked off a piece. "Don't tell me a chef has never tried cotton candy." She popped a piece into her mouth.

He rolled his eyes towards her, then focused on the mass of heated sugar. "That can't be good for you," he protested.

She giggled and tore off another piece. "It's not about being good for you, it's about enjoying the taste, the sensation, the flavor." She pressed it against his lips.

"I don't think I ..." He nearly choked as she popped the wad into his mouth.

"What do you think?"

He felt the candy melting in his mouth. Unsure whether to chew or swallow, he gulped. Moving his mouth uncertainly, he found his voice. "That really does melt, doesn't it?" He ran his tongue around his teeth. "And stick. I think I may have to go and brush."

"What about the taste?"

He shrugged. "I guess I didn't really notice the taste."

"What a shame. Try it again." She put another piece in her own mouth and pulled his head down to hers, her lips open.

The paper cone slipped from his hand. He was holding Olivia, his lips moving against hers, the sugar melting somewhere in between. He welcomed her memories as his symbiont flooded them into his mind. All too soon it ended.

She was giggling. "Look at you, it's all over your face."

He brushed at his cheeks, wondering if his face really was the same shade of blue as the candy.

She frowned. "That's odd. I've never seen food coloring wipe off like that."

He pulled her close. "Maybe it wasn't the food coloring. Want to try again, without the cotton candy?"

She searched his face. "That might be tempting fate." She tried to pull away.

He held her tighter. "Will you marry me? I mean, right now?"

She relaxed. "Was there ever any doubt?"

"Then what are we waiting for?"

She spotted Kelly and Jerod over his shoulder. "Them?"

Stu let her go and turned around. Olivia put her left arm around his waist.

Kelly and Jerod approached them. "It looks like you two don't need any encouragement after all," Kelly offered.

Olivia was looking at her right palm. "What an amazing creature!" She turned to Stu. "It's all so amazing. I don't know what to say."

Stu looked at the red swirls in her hand. He showed her his hand. "Look at this, they can move in unison." He held his hand next to hers and the symbionts matched each other's movements.

Kelly and Jerod looked at each other. "Are you two going to fool around all day, or are you going to go get married?" Jerod asked.

Olivia raised an eyebrow. "Pushy," she said.

Stu nodded. "Very pushy. You'd think we were desperate."

The two of them burst out laughing. They held hands and walked away.

Kelly looked around at the carnival. "As long as we're here, Jerod, why don't we go have some fun?"

CHAPTER 14

▼

GROWN CHILDREN

Kelly strengthened her grip and squeezed her eyes shut. She threw her head back and screamed as the roller coaster cars plunged downwards.

Jerod sat beside her, one arm around her shoulders, the other in a white knuckled grip on the bar. With one eye closed, he tilted his head and calculated their relative speed, angle of descent and distance to the next upgrade. He'd watched her enjoy the ride twice before finally agreeing to join her. He still regretted it, but tried not to show it, at least not when she was looking.

After several minutes the ride coasted to its stop. He helped her disembark.

"Was that fun or what?" she asked him.

He held her to keep her from losing her balance. "I'm afraid I still didn't get much out of it. He held up the palm of her hand. The red spot was making slow circles inside her palm. "As for you, you're making your symbiont dizzy."

She looked askance at it, still attempting to get her inner ear to behave. "What, they don't like being dizzy? Considering the way they swirl about under your skin, they should love it."

He shook his head. "Not only do they dislike the sensation, once yours has figured out which behavior led to this, it will probably try to deter you from *ever* doing it again."

She looked up. "I have a feeling there are several things I'll never do again, things I just won't have time for, now that I'm expected to take such a prominent role.

"Joining you 'Martians' has already been far more emotionally demanding than I expected. And who on Earth gets married within a week of meeting someone?"

"Do you regret it?"

"No! No, I don't, I don't know why I'm still feeling this way. I love you and I love the downloads, and even this little red thing, the symbiont, but it's all a bit overwhelming. It's a lot to deal with."

"Time to grow up?" Even before the Companion File prompted him, he knew it was a mistake. He bit his lip.

She looked deflated, and turned away from him.

He put his hand on her shoulders and turned her around. "I'm sorry. I shouldn't have said that."

She was fighting back tears. "The problem is, it's true. Part of me is so scared. What if I let you down, what if I let us all down?"

He embraced her. "The fact it worries you so much means you won't. You'll see. No matter how things turn out, you'll do your part. That's all any of us can hope to accomplish."

He tilted her chin up with his forefinger. "Is that why the last three days have been nothing but action packed entertainment?"

She nodded meekly. "You have me pegged. I'm sorry. You should have confronted me sooner."

They walked her to a bench and sat down. "I have a little confession of my own. When I first saw you in your swimsuit, something happened inside me. I became aroused. I hadn't downloaded the Companion File yet and I couldn't handle it. Ever since, I've been worried about it, terrified that when it happened again I might, uh, I might hurt you. That's the reason I haven't said anything."

"You're kidding, right?"

He felt his face redden. "No."

She stood up and offered her hand. "Come on. Let's both go do a little growing up."

*   *   *   *

Coren looked around the room. Back in his lab coat, he felt oddly at home surrounded by all the reconfiguration chambers and the rest of the computer equipment. There were times he could imagine he was merely an extension of it all.

The feeling of Katy's arms around him quickly changed his mind. She'd come up behind him, something she seemed to be making a habit of lately, something that made him not want to be part of the machinery.

"Come and look at this, Katy." He motioned towards the bank of reconfiguration chambers, their clear walls in place. Katy stepped beside him, wrapping her arms around him again. He put his arm around her shoulder. "We're about to witness the birth of a new generation."

"Kelly and Jerod's children?"

"Brought straight to us through the miracle of superior technology."

"I suppose ours will arrive in the same way?"

"Hopefully. I detect some hesitation." He looked at her probingly.

"It's just, well, with being 'slightly telepathic' and the symbionts and computers and everything, what about privacy? Is everyone going to be watching us *mate?*"

He studied her for a moment. It was a genuine concern. "We've never had to develop privacy screening. The symbiont took over that function almost two thousand years ago. All you have to do is think about it and you'll have no further telepathic contact with anyone until you want to."

"Really? So if I do this, no-one can see it?" She kissed him on the cheek.

"Not if you don't want them to." He bent down to return the kiss. A buzzer sounded. "Duty calls. Hold that thought." He held her eyes for another second before letting her go.

He walked over to a flashing panel of lights. His hands moved in a blur. Eight chambers filled with a smoky gas, and something more. Vague movements could be seen inside the chambers. He retreated from the panel. "Now, in a few minutes, the 'children' will emerge as young adults."

"But why age them?"

"Our numbers have dwindled from billions to a mere million, scattered throughout the few socially advanced cultures of this planet. There isn't time to give the next generation the luxury of a childhood, especially if we decide to return to space." He considered the look on her face. "This is our way."

She was staring at the chambers. "I was just thinking, there were several bits of my childhood I wish I could have skipped."

He wondered if she was strictly talking about the rape. "Even now you should find the symbiont taking the pain out of your memories."

She smiled. "I'd forgotten how badly I'd been hurt. It healed that, too. Too bad every victim of crime doesn't automatically get a symbiont.

"So what about our children, will they each have one?"

"One way or another. It's been so long since any of us reproduced, aside from cloning, we have no way of knowing if they'll be born with it, or if it will spread to them after they emerge. But the fact that you and your sisters developed them so quickly leads me to think they'll all be born with it."

The chambers were clearing, allowing their occupants to be seen.

"Stand back," instructed Coren.

One after another, the chamber walls swooshed into the floor. Eight young adults, five ladies and three men, stepped forward. Without a word, they turned and walked to racks of clothing on the far side of the room. Once dressed, they returned to make introductions.

"I'm Deena," said the pretty brunette. "I'm the oldest. I've inherited my dad's sense of humor and my mom's intelligence and empathy for those less fortunate." Deena turned to the short blond next to her. "This is my fraternal twin, Tom. He's shy. We're not sure how long it will take him to learn to talk."

"A speech impediment?" Coren asked. "I can easily fix that."

"No. Like I said, he's shy. I think he's just waiting for the right girl to come along."

The young man turned beet red, then paled. He cleared his throat, his voice merely a whisper. "My symbiont is making things easier, but I think I need an immediate download of the Companion File."

"All right, we'll do that right now." Coren touched the fellow's neck. A tremor went through him.

Katy spoke up. "If there are no side effects, I think we should send a general download of the Companion File to all the males, not just the ones we think might Be Blued. We don't have time to wait until they ask for it on a case by case basis."

"Agreed." Coren touched a panel and placed his palm over it. "Computer, download the Companion File to everyone still lacking it. Authorization, Coren Thirteen."

The computer buzzed an error alert.

Coren looked at Katy and smiled. "Authorization, Coren Ravell."

"You're right, that was much easier on everyone. No thrashing around."

"Thrashing around can be fun." Katy winked at him.

"Later. We have to get back to work now."

"Promise?" She rubbed the back of his neck.

"With all my heart."

A collective groan went up from the young adults. The red-haired girl crossed her arms in front of her. Her voice had the hint of a Scottish accent. "Do you mind? You didn't have to watch *your* aunts and uncles getting intimate, did you?"

Katy giggled. "Well, there was that one time."

Coren gasped. "Not in front of the *children.*"

"I guess they're human after all," Katy observed. She turned to the redhead. "What's your name, dear?"

Somewhat placated, the young woman offered her hand. "I'm Megan."

The other five stepped forward and gave their names.

"Levi," said a brunette. "After *somebody's* favorite clothing. Not mine." He rolled his eyes and stroked the sleeve of his suit.

"Terra," said the young woman with black hair. "I'm very down to Earth. For an alien, at any rate. You're so pretty, Auntie, you remind me of my mother." She touched Katy's cheek. "Can I borrow your makeup some time?"

"Uh, sure, just let me know when."

"Alan," offered the blond in the gray business suit. "I've already calculated the international stock market trend for the next two years. I think we can process a total merger or possibly even a complete buyout in five months or less."

Coren leaned over and whispered in Katy's ear. "That one bears watching."

She nodded, her eyes wide.

"Cynthia," said the last blonde. "I'm already bored, so the sooner we can get off this little planet, the happier I'll be."

The shortest, a perky brunette, scowled at her. "Honestly, you're such a prude. There's a lot to do here, a lot of fun to be had. Hi, I'm BethAnn. I hope we'll be such good friends."

Katy and Coren finished shaking hands with all of them.

Katy turned to Coren. "Now what?"

"I don't know. What would everyone like to do?"

The young people all looked at each other. "Pizza!" they chorused.

Katy smiled. "We're going to need more drivers."

Coren's eyes bugged out. "Do you know how hard it is to get one of us past the DMV requirements? They're *very* strict."

Alan rolled his eyes. "It's necessary, unless you expect us all to *skateboard* everywhere. Look, I'll hack the system and get us *each* a driver's license. We don't have time for a limited number of limos and taxis any more." Before anyone could object, he spun around and played with the computer console.

Katy pulled Coren aside. She lowered her voice. "Just how are we *paying* for all this anyway?"

He chuckled. "Don't worry, we have unlimited resources; an invention here, a trademarked product there, royalties for copyrights and film earnings, not to mention what the humans will pay for a competent doctor these days. Every one of us earns or has earned a real living wage and contributes to the entire community. After a few hundred years, without having to pay for additional training and with a few wise investments, we really do have enough resources to buy all of Wall Street. The amount of money available to us is almost incalculable. That's what happens when money isn't the most important thing, something the humans seem slow to learn."

"That might be partly because they really do need it to survive and enjoy life."

He shrugged. "I don't understand."

"Let's say you wanted to show someone a good time. Pizza, a movie, maybe a hotel, that all takes cash or credit."

"Unless you've learned to provide all those things without using cash or credit. Okay, I see your point. Speaking of pizza, we could order in."

Deena had come up behind them. "Now you're talking."

Tom nodded. "So am I. Just where does one find human females who make pizza?"

CHAPTER 15

▼

HESITATION

Coren hated confrontations like this, but he couldn't allow the situation to continue. He sat behind the desk in the library, folding and unfolding his fingers. Waiting wasn't his strong suit, and the length of this wait was making him edgy. It seemed like forever before there was a knock on the door.

"Come in!" he ordered.

Stu entered, his head hanging. Coren motioned for him to sit. He regarded his friend with impatience. Worse than waiting was seeing a man like Stu with nothing to say. He let the silence hang between them for a while.

Finally he decided on an approach. "Stu, it's been over three weeks. Olivia's heartbroken. She wanted children more than Katy and Kelly put together. There's nothing wrong with her, so it must be you. What's the problem?"

Stu gripped the arms of the leather chair, inadvertently causing a squeak. "I don't know. I don't know."

"Hell, Stu, don't make me do this, you know I hate doing this."

"I know. Just do what you have to."

Coren leaned back and turned partially sideways. "One last chance, my friend."

Stu looked up, his eyes pleading. "Help us. Help both of us."

Coren banged his fist down on the desk. *"Fine!* This will hurt. A lot. Computer, extreme scan of Stu Ravell, Authorization Coren Ravell. Search for hesitation, duplicity, impotence, attitudes, corruption of memory, viruses …"

Stu's body writhed as searing electricity enveloped him, and then jolted him onto the floor to writhe some more. Coren stayed focused on the stream of green data flashing in front of his eyes.

"Tampering, sabotage … Stand by, Computer, I said, stand by. Back up three sectors. Focus in on this." He pointed to one specific item. "That's it? For that, I had to do this to you? Computer, terminate extreme scan of Stu Ravell."

Stu's back arched. He fell limp to the floor. After several seconds he crawled back into the chair. He stared at the images. "You found something?"

Coren inhaled deeply. "I did. And it would have gone a lot easier for you if you'd been willing to talk about this."

"I guess I've just gotten used to not sharing my feelings with other men. It's this planet, it's so backwards."

Coren silenced him with a wave. "Never mind. We need to talk about this incident. When Olivia told you she wanted at least a dozen children, it caused a negative reaction deep in your subconscious. Why?"

"I guess because she expected to go through pregnancy. The idea that I'd cause her body to deform like that horrified me."

"Before the symbionts, that's how we reproduced. Humans don't have all our options, but now that she's joined us, she does. You know that."

"Mentally, yes. But I never dreamed I'd ever have the experience of having Been Blued. I'd accepted the idea of never having a lover. But then I guess I couldn't accept the idea of not being able to touch her while she was pregnant."

Coren pondered whether to delve further into explaining human biology, then wondered if he needed to. "Does Olivia *want* to be pregnant? I mean, now that she knows she doesn't have to be in order to have children?"

"I haven't talked to her about it."

Coren threw up his hands. "Now *there's* a human attitude. Why not?"

"I sensed she wanted to experience raising the children."

"You *sensed* it when she said she wanted them. Her understanding of our situation has probably changed since then. Have you taken that into account?"

He hung his head. "I guess not."

Coren smiled ever so slightly. "You've been doing a lot of guessing since we started this little talk. Too much guessing, for too long. It's time to talk to Olivia and see what she thinks." He inhaled sharply. "I'll see what Kelly says. If she agrees, and if it's what Olivia wants, we *might* be able to give some of your offspring a childhood. At least one or two of them."

Stu jumped up. "You mean we'll still *have* children?"

Coren looked up at him and tilted his head. "I don't see why not. We've eliminated all possibility of physical problems. As with human relationships, the next hurdle is usually attitude. Yours sucked."

Stu leaned forward, his knuckles on the desk. "I thought I'd be sanctioned."

Coren frowned. "Sanctioned? The only thing you're guilty of is giving in to your fear. Go on, get out of here. Your wife is waiting. You owe her the best night of her life, starting with a very frank discussion."

*   *   *   *

Coren changed into swimming trunks and grabbed a towel. Kelly would be at the pool by this time. He spotted her from behind. Being Matriarch seemed to have made her stand differently, taller, straighter, and more confident. Or it could be his own deference to her, he surmised. She was now his superior, something he found oddly intriguing.

She turned slightly as he approached. "That extreme scan looks nasty. Does it hurt the operator?"

"No, not once you learn to control it. It took me a century and two reconfigurations to completely master it. A multitasking female brain would have been able to control it with a quarter of the effort."

"Can you teach some of the children to use it?"

He thought for a bit. "I think so. I suppose it's high time to start teaching them our ways."

She turned towards him. "We have to see if we can find more women. Alan's projections on the current rate of reproduction are nothing short of dismal."

Coren bit his lip. "I wasn't sure how to bring this up, but some of the men are concerned that we're still having sons at this point."

Kelly nodded. "I've sensed that. And it's not just the shortage of females. There's a definite undercurrent of resentment, something that wasn't part of our culture until we returned to this planet. Human sexism can cut either way, but I suspect there's something else going on."

"Have you made a decision regarding our return to space?"

"Not yet. Too many of us are still in Europe and Asia. It'll be another week before we have enough for a quorum."

"You intend to put it to a vote?"

"If it comes to that. I hope it doesn't. But I won't make the decision to leave Earth without significant input and support. Our entire future depends on it."

*   *   *   *

Olivia sat on a sofa in a cozy cabin living room. Her eyes were red, unfocused on the vista of the lake visible from the picture window in front of her. Her face was drawn. The red spot on the back of her hand moved in slow, brooding loops. It had taken over telling her to get up in the morning, have breakfast, get showered, and get dressed. It still couldn't discover why they weren't happy.

The door closed. Stu came in, suddenly subdued upon seeing her. "Come on," he said as he took her hand and led her to the kitchen. He sat down on a stool facing her, bringing his face to her level. He held both her hands.

"I need you to tell me something. Do you want to get pregnant?"

A flicker of interest came into her eyes.

"*Or,* do you want our children to go straight to the laboratory? There would be fewer of them, the old fashioned way, but it's your decision."

A slow smile spread across her face. "What do *you* want?"

"I just want you. I'd like to see your body stay the wonderful shape it is now. But I will always love you, no matter what you decide, or how your body might change."

She squeezed his fingers. "Then maybe we should call the lab."

"I'm sorry."

The color was returning to her face. "What for?"

"For not simply talking to you about my feelings. For putting you through all this uncertainty."

"You mean, I *wasn't* the problem?"

He gasped. "Of course not. You could never be the problem."

She threw her arms around him. "Oh, Sweetheart, you don't know how worried I was."

He hugged her back. "Worried? Why would you be worried?"

She leaned back and ran her fingers through his hair. "It's always been my greatest fear, that after wanting children so badly I might not be able to. And when I learned years ago that Kelly couldn't, I became concerned about myself."

"But with our technology, she's been able to. We've eliminated physical weakness, most illnesses and ..."

She put her finger over his mouth. "Hush. For the rest of tonight, no more talk." Red swirls rippled through her fingertips.

*   *   *   *

Darcy looked around the computer control room. It was at thirty percent lighting, in deference to the human's current interest in energy conservation. He fished in his pocket for his tool. It wasn't there. He checked all his pockets. His symbiont triggered a memory, a small noise from below that day he'd sabotaged the spotlights. Funny, the symbiont had noticed when the tool fell to the floor, but he hadn't. He swore to himself.

Now a few of the others had found mates, even reproduced, but it did him no good. Most of the human females he'd met had shown a degree of revulsion to him. Maybe they *were* right, maybe he was too ugly to ever have Been Blued.

The thought of a new generation of the people who belittled him filled him with rage. No matter, he'd do something about it. He dismissed enough of the anger to think clearly, a little trick he'd come up with to help avoid getting caught.

He couldn't deny they were clever. The way the Coordinator merged with the mainframe when his reconfiguration triggered Darcy's virus, that was almost genius. Not quite though, the damned fool hadn't known the difference between the virus and a lack of general maintenance. Either way, it ruined his plans. He wondered whether Coren had been too slow or too clever to stop the kid. The thought of the Coordinator's brand new physical body dissolving as his mind merged with the mainframe gave Darcy a sudden flush of pleasure.

The increased blood flow triggered a muscle spasm in his leg, a sure sign he was nearly to the end of possible configurations. He waited for it to travel up his spine, through his back, his neck, and finally his brain. The resulting migraine nearly dropped him to the floor, but he sent his symbiont after the pain. It rippled through his face and neck, making everything right again. Except the spasms were getting closer, now only a few weeks apart.

What had he been thinking a moment ago? Oh, yes, sabotage to limit reproduction. He'd have to work faster, be smarter than before. The Coordinator would have done a thorough job of putting the mainframe back in order. He'd have to plant a virus to prevent further interference. He fished in his pocket for the tool again before remembering it was gone. When he was finished here he'd have to go back to the studio to look for it. All the pieces cleaned up from the accident should still be in a secure area, since *they* still investigated any accident involving one of their own.

He wondered if proceeding without the tool was wise. He sighed. The symbiont proceeded to absorb all layers of skin on his fingertips to the point where even Martian fingerprints would no longer transfer. Part of him worried about the symbiont's rumored potential for becoming cannibalistic, having tasted enough of him. He reminded himself that the idea was a myth told around campfires on foreign planets thousands of years ago. Still, it was a hard fear to let go of.

He tried to work quickly, but realized the dimmer light was obscuring his vision. Or were cataracts starting to form? He concentrated harder, the sweat beading on his brow. He finished entering his programs, then turned to go. He was almost to the door when it opened.

Coren looked him right in the eye. It occurred to Darcy that the two were about the same height, something he hadn't really noticed before.

Coren frowned at him. "Is there something I can do for you, Darcy? It's a bit late for you to be in here."

Darcy gasped, partly in pain, partly in panic. "I was looking for you. I think there might be something wrong with me."

"How are you feeling?"

"I've been having spasms again. They're only a few weeks apart now." There was no sense denying himself the best medical attention on the planet.

"I thought that would happen. You know, as you near the end of your reconfiguration potential, each new body exists for a shorter period of time. But I'm surprised this one seems to be deteriorating so quickly. Have you been exerting yourself?"

Darcy tried to laugh. "Not really, nothing you'd notice."

Coren put his hand over the man's forehead. "Something's wrong. Very wrong." He summoned his own symbiont to bond with Darcy's. It resisted, and then retreated as far as it could. "That's no good at all. Darcy, I have to reconfigure you right now."

Darcy tried to resist but couldn't find the strength. He was suddenly exhausted. Even his sheer terror gave him no strength. "No! No, you mustn't ..."

"Hush. You'll be fine in a few moments. Computer, full lighting, full power, now. Authorization, Coren Ravell. Begin reconfiguration of Darcy Three." Coren dragged Darcy to the reconfiguration chamber. He put him over the platform and eased him down as the sides began to rise.

The computer beeped a warning.

"What's the problem, Computer?" Coren asked.

"Configuration total is incorrect. Darcy subject has one reconfiguration remaining."

"Are you sure? That doesn't sound right."

"Checking. Stand by. Data confirmed. Darcy subject has one reconfiguration remaining."

"That's because he's been exerting himself?"

"Negative. All subjects currently have one reconfiguration remaining."

"What?"

"All subjects have one reconfiguration remaining."

Coren's forehead wrinkled. "How is that possible?"

"Reconfiguration parameters have been reset by Darcy Four."

"I see." Coren stared at Darcy's limp figure, now fully inside the sealed reconfiguration chamber. "I see," he repeated. "I should leave you with only one, but that's not how we do things.

"Computer, restore all computer parameters to their previous settings."

"Specify time parameters for restore point."

Coren looked at his watch. Tampering like this would have taken at least three hours. No wonder the man had collapsed, especially if he'd used his symbiont to hide his fingerprints.

"Reset to four hours previous."

"Stand by. Request will take one minute."

Coren used the time to scan Darcy with a handheld computer. "Oh. That's why my symbiont retreated from yours. You've been avoiding protein, that's not acceptable. I'd better fix that before we proceed."

He went to a table and opened a cupboard above it. He took out a vial and a needle. With a practiced hand, he filled the needle and tapped it. A tiny stream almost reached the tip. He returned and jabbed the point into the reconfiguration chamber itself. The material accepted the injection into itself, ensuring the next reconfiguration would have an initial supply of the protein.

"All programs restored to match settings of four hours previous. Reconfiguration of Darcy Three is about to commence."

"Proceed," Coren instructed.

$$* \qquad * \qquad * \qquad *$$

Kelly gasped and sat bolt upright in bed. Jerod did the same.

"What was that?" Kelly asked. A green data stream glowed in front of her. "Why has the computer been reset?"

Jerod was already wrestling his pants on. He tossed her a bathrobe. "Someone's tampered with the mainframe. Come on!"

The computer's voice resonated through the bedroom. "Matriarch Kelly, please come to the Main Computer Control."

"I'm on my way, Computer. What's happening?" She tied the bathrobe around herself.

"Darcy subject is being reconfigured. He has attempted to sabotage the mainframe."

Jerod grabbed her hand and they raced to the control room.

*   *   *   *

Coren was busy operating the computer.

"Reconfiguration protocol Omega activated," the computer announced.

"What's that?" Kelly asked.

Coren turned around. "Sorry to get you out of bed. Darcy spent the last few hours tampering with the mainframe. He's so close to the end of his reconfigurations that it left him dying when I came in. The computer refused to give him the correct number of reconfigurations, that's how I discovered what he'd done.

"I also found out he's been avoiding protein, which poisons the symbiont. He must have been quite deficient, because Omega is only activated when the next reconfiguration is about to result in a different personality."

"Standing by," the computer reminded them. "Is Omega to be activated?"

Coren and Jerod looked at Kelly. "It's your call," Jerod told her.

"Computer, this is Matriarch Kelly. Abort Omega. Continue with reconfiguration of current subject with the new personality."

She turned to Coren. "We have to find out the extent of his crimes before we proceed to sanction him."

"Agreed. Our laws hold the current configuration fully responsible for crimes any predecessor has committed. Otherwise, reconfiguration would become a way to get away with murder."

"Even if the current configuration has been altered to the point of no longer being the same individual?" Kelly asked. The computer, or possibly her own symbiont, gave her the answer. It was becoming slightly less difficult for her to tell the two apart.

"Yes," Jerod confirmed. "It might seem harsh, but we found it was better to err on the side of judgment rather than mercy. One of the biggest differences between us and the humans, I suppose."

Kelly nodded. "We can afford to be harsher. We have the symbionts to help keep us kind and honest. If Darcy had tended to the needs of his, he might have remained innocent.

"We'll have to work at remembering that when dealing with the humans."

The computer waited until the conversation seemed to be finished. "Reconfiguration complete. Aging Darcy subject to previous parameters. Instructions required for release of the subject."

Coren spoke up. "Place subject on restraint table. He faces sanctioning."

"Stand by."

A naked man resembling Darcy materialized on an examining table. His arms and legs were immediately secured with electronic restraints.

The new configuration of Darcy raised his chest and shoulders as far as the restraints would allow. He looked at them, his face penitent. "I'm sorry," he said.

"You look different" Coren commented. "Your whole physique is larger."

Darcy lay back. "It was the lack of protein. You were right; it was poisoning my symbiont and twisting my thinking. Did you know I hid its color every time you scanned me? It wasn't easy, calling up that much red blood. And it had nasty side effects. I had headaches for days afterward."

He half sat up again. "Am I handsome now?"

Kelly nodded. "As handsome as ever. And that's a woman's point of view, not one of the guys you hated so much."

He held her gaze. "Matriarch, I really am sorry. I wish I'd been a better man. I never thought I'd live to see another Matriarch. You're gorgeous. If I'd ever Been Blued, it would have had to be by someone as attractive as you."

Kelly noticed her robe had loosened, exposing more of her body than she would have liked. She adjusted it and tied the front more securely.

She approached him. "We need to know what you've done."

"Of course. I've been killing off various reconfigurations over the past five hundred years." He glanced at Coren and Jerod. "I killed you guys on four separate occasions, and once I got both of you at the same time. I was so jealous of seeing the way human females made friends with you that I killed a few of them as well.

"I sabotaged the computer on several occasions. I finally targeted the Coordinator, but I wasn't expecting him to merge with the mainframe and risk all his remaining reconfigurations. He's quite noble, you know."

Kelly looked at the door. "I wonder where he is, this reset should have summoned him as well."

Darcy laughed. "I'm sure it did. But the human taxi driver I paid to take him on a very long road trip isn't likely to bring him back any time soon."

"Wrong again, Darcy," the Coordinator croaked as he walked in the door, his suit disheveled, and a steering wheel in his hand. He was trembling, his other fist clenching and unclenching. There was blood on his knuckles. "I had to overpower him, but the taxi driver finally agreed to bring me back." He threw the steering wheel to the floor. "I can't even remember the last time I was so angry!"

"Coordinator," Darcy mused. "I'm glad you're here, in spite of how things seem. I'm sorry about the puberty thing, it just seemed like another way to mess with you at the time."

The Coordinator inhaled deeply, then shrugged. "It's temporary. I've been through far worse than you're about to go through."

Coren grabbed some supplies and began tending to the Coordinator's hands.

Jerod scowled at Darcy. "What else have you done?"

Darcy settled back. "Oh, yes. I should tell you about the virus I installed to prevent you from resetting the computer. It may behave like it's been reset, but that's only part of the sabotage. You won't be able to use it to help reproduce anymore."

He looked at Kelly. "I'm really sorry. If I'd had a conscience before doing all this ..."

"Never mind. If I interface directly with the computer, will it enable me to undo all your damage?"

Darcy thought it over. "It could. But I want to go with you, it's the only way I can protect you from several layers of brain spikes I installed."

Kelly nodded. She touched Darcy's forehead, then turned to Coren, the Coordinator and Jerod. "Wish us luck." She closed her eyes and went limp.

Coren raced over to the cupboard as Jerod grabbed Kelly. "We can do more than that. I'll give both of them a double dose of protein."

"Just hurry," Jerod said.

Coren administered two full needles to both unconscious figures.

Jerod was about to move Kelly's hand.

"Don't," Coren warned. "They still need to be physically touching for this to work."

"Can we trust Darcy to look after her in there?"

"This new Darcy, yes. Now that his symbiont has what it needs, his behavior should be as incorruptible as yours or mine. Ouch!" Coren rubbed his forehead.

"What's wrong?"

"Did you feel that?"

"I felt something. You're the doctor, you tell me what it was."

"It looks like Darcy was trying to create jealousy between us, getting me to lust for Kelly and you to lust for Katy."

Jerod's eyes popped open. "I was wondering about that. I didn't know how to bring it up."

Coren shook his head. "I'm the doctor, I should have brought it up. I'm so sorry; I would never hurt you or Kelly like that, or Katy. Especially not Katy."

"I'm sorry, too. This is disturbing, to realize we can be corrupted so easily."

The Coordinator stepped forward. "It shouldn't be so easy any more. Now we know to be on guard against this."

Jerod felt the vibrations under his bare feet. "Do you feel that?"

Coren nodded. "The computer's resetting for real this time. I thought it went too quickly before. They should be just about to return."

Kelly gasped and Jerod, still holding her, helped her regain her balance.

Darcy remained limp.

"Give him another shot of protein," Kelly instructed.

Coren did.

Darcy began to quiver. His lips were turning blue. "Did we make it?" he whispered.

Kelly stood over him. "Yes, we did. I'm afraid it cost you the rest of your lives."

"I know. And don't forget. The next few children will die. I'm sorry. I'm so sorry."

Coren began undoing the restraints.

Kelly put her hand on his arm. "It's too late. He used his last two reconfigurations to undo the damage to the mainframe. Darcy is no more."

Darcy's body began to disintegrate on the table.

Coren stared at the dust. "Sort of a self imposed sanction." He bit his lip.

Kelly hugged Jerod, tears streaming down her face. He patted her back.

The Coordinator hugged her next. "I'm sorry, Matriarch. This is a terrible loss."

Coren said nothing, his face twisted with grief.

The Coordinator pressed a button on the computer and the examining table disappeared. He turned around. "Now then, what's this about the next few children dying?"

Kelly straightened up, pulling the bathrobe tighter around her. "It took the last of Darcy's reconfigurations to repair the damage because he'd tied it into his own DNA. All of his excess energy was used to protect me from the brain spikes he'd put in place. There wasn't enough of his energy left to reset the reproductive processes of the computer. Reconfiguration programs were undamaged but the next child to be born has a twenty percent chance of surviving, the second, a forty-five percent chance and the third, seventy percent. Then the computer will return to normal functioning."

Coren turned white. "Those are terrible odds. Are you sure they're correct?"

Kelly nodded. "And that's taking into account all your resourcefulness and skill. It won't be easy to achieve even that degree of success for the next three children."

"We don't have much choice," the Coordinator stated. "We must continue to procreate, even if we lose some of the children."

Jerod hung his head. "You're going to have to be there when we break the news to Olivia and Stu."

"We'll all be there," Kelly said. She snapped her fingers, an odd look on her face. "Coren, can I see you a moment? *Alone?*"

Jerod and the Coordinator looked at each other and left the room.

Kelly waited until the door closed.

"What's this all about?" Coren asked.

"One moment. Computer, engage full privacy mode and scramble all recording programs for fifteen minutes. Authorization, Matriarch Kelly."

"Authorization acknowledged. Fifteen minute timer activated."

"Now you're scaring me," Coren said.

Kelly fixed him with a penetrating look. "As the humans say, 'you ain't seen nothing, yet.'"

*   *   *   *

Jerod and the Coordinator stood on opposite sides of the doorway.

"This is awkward," Jerod said.

"Very awkward. I wonder what they're talking about."

"Or doing."

The Coordinator crossed his arms in front of him. "I don't think they'd be doing anything bad. Do you?"

"I don't think so. I trust my wife. And I trust Coren."

"So what do you think they're up to?"

Jerod crossed his own arms. "I don't know. I don't like not knowing, but they must be doing something important. Otherwise it wouldn't be so secret."

The Coordinator nodded. "I don't like secrets. I prefer to know everything."

"No-one knows everything."

"You know what I mean. Oh, hey, Kelly told me the makeup girl has a daughter who might be about the right biological age for me."

Jerod looked startled. "Nikki? She's awfully immature. Even for a human. She dresses far younger than her real age."

"I think I'd still like to meet her. After we finally get around to my makeover."

"What makeover?"

"Kelly pointed out that my current appearance makes me look too 'nerdy.' I guess teenage girls tend not to go for the brainy type."

"Teenage girls. We barely know what adult women go for, now we have to make a study of teenage girls?"

"It couldn't hurt. In some countries on this planet, girls are having children while they're still practically babies themselves. Who are we to say that's wrong?"

"We are an advanced civilization with advanced moral ethics. You know a teenage girl is inadequately prepared to care for a child."

"With our technology she doesn't have to care for the child."

"No, with our technology the child is aged, in the case of a teen, beyond the age of the parent. What teenage girl could handle that?"

"I could have Coren age me, then look for an older woman."

"That might be a problem. We don't know the extent of damage Darcy may have caused. If we try to age you, it might backfire."

"Jerod, look at me. What you see is a man in his late hundreds stuck in the body of a child. It made sense to give me so much extra time when we had no hope of Being Blued, but now it doesn't. I want the best chance of getting a mate, at whatever age she happens to be."

"The risk, Coordinator ..."

"Is acceptable. Maybe it wasn't a few weeks ago, when we had no hope, but that's changed. Now that we have a Matriarch, I'm no longer the only leader we've got. I'm now expendable."

"I doubt the Matriarch would agree." Jerod fell silent.

The two of them stared at the floor and waited.

*   *   *   *

The computer room was once again at power conservation levels. A dim glow created faint shadows everywhere. Coren hunched over a worktable near the door. He slowly nibbled the crust of a thick sandwich while he puttered.

Without warning, the reconfiguration chamber walls slid upwards and the familiar white vapors filled it. A form began to take shape.

Coren continued to work on his sandwich. He scribbled a few words on paper.

The gases changed from opaque to clear. The process took a full fifteen minutes. The walls swooshed downward and Darcy stepped forward.

Coren turned around, seemingly unsurprised at the man's sudden appearance. "Hello, Darcy. Which configuration is this?"

Darcy smirked. "Not that it matters, you won't be alive long enough to tell anyone, but I'm Darcy One Hundred."

Coren nodded. "Of course. There was a glitch in the system when we reconfigured you the first time. We were never able to trace it, not in more than five hundred years. So we just moved on to Darcy Ninety-nine. You must have wondered what was taking so long."

"Not really. I knew your original would rather die than let a computer glitch go unfixed. I arranged that too, by the way. To help take your mind off your computer troubles."

"Oh. Thank you."

"Now, since I've already been sanctioned, I believe I'm free to go. Don't bother trying to stop me. You know you're no match for my current energy levels. That's your own fault, for making me your strongest North American so I could face Earth's dangers for you."

Coren began toying with his sandwich. "I wouldn't dream of trying to stop you." He pulled the pieces of bread apart. "Your symbiont, though, might have other ideas." He smeared the contents of the sandwich down Darcy's bare chest.

The green symbiont, ravenous for protein, caused violent ripples as it absorbed the peanut butter directly through Darcy's skin. He screamed in panic as the creature turned red.

CHAPTER 16

▼

PEANUT BUTTER AND JELLY

"Stop screaming!" Coren demanded.

Wide eyed, Darcy closed his mouth. "I'm sorry. That was terrifying, the symbiont's never done anything like that before." He rolled his tongue around his mouth. The flavor was something he couldn't recall. His tongue seemed to want to stick to the roof of his mouth. "What was that stuff?" he asked through pursed lips.

Coren looked at the two white pieces of bread in his hands. There was no trace of any filling left. "It's called peanut butter. It's an excellent source of the protein you've been avoiding. In keeping with human tradition, I added some grape jelly. How do you like it?"

Darcy was still trying to get the sensation under control. "I think … this is … the best stuff I've ever tasted. Sticky, isn't it?"

Coren nodded. "Since your symbiont seems to be sharing the sensation with you, I can assume things went according to plan." He walked back to the table, put the bread down and brought back a glass of white liquid.

"Your plan, you mean."

Coren handed him the glass. "Have some milk. It'll make the peanut butter sensation easier to swallow. Yes, I can see your point; things didn't go according to your plan. You forgot one thing, Darcy. We now have a Matriarch. Because of the symbionts, she completes our society individually and collectively. That means we're unstoppable, even by one of our own. Her symbiont accurately predicted your imminent configuration."

Darcy handed back the empty glass. "When can I have some more peanut butter?"

Coren smiled. "It doesn't always have to be peanut butter, there are many other excellent sources of protein on this planet. I guarantee you'll like almost all of them. If you're hungry, you can go to the kitchen in a few hours. We have to take care of some business, first."

Darcy looked puzzled. "Surely you don't intend to sanction me again. Our laws work in both directions. Once a man's been punished, future reconfigurations must be held innocent."

"Usually that's true. But in your case, this configuration is 'past tense.' You began this life complicit with the crimes of the past. But I'd like to know one thing before we deal with any of this."

"What's that?"

Coren crossed his arms in front of him. "We made you the strongest of our North Americans. We also made you the most virile. Didn't it ever occur to you that *you* were the most likely to have Been Blued?"

"Perhaps. But then you countered that possibility by making me unattractive."

Coren frowned. "No, you're actually quite handsome. You always were. What made you think you were ugly?"

"I read it in your thoughts. My symbiont could detect how you perceived me."

"I see. You mean you misread it. Your symbiont was green instead of red. Lack of protein gave it a filter, a twist in your perception. If you look in the mirror now, you probably won't recognize yourself, even though I haven't done a thing to change your appearance. Stay put."

Coren walked back to the table and picked up a mirror. He brought it back and held it up.

Darcy blinked. "That's me? That's my face? I'm handsome?"

Kelly walked into the room, followed by Deena, Megan, Terra, Cynthia and BethAnn. "Well, ladies, do you find Darcy handsome?"

They giggled. At Kelly's stern look, they stopped and looked serious. Each of them in turn gave the same response.

"Yes, Mother."

"Good. Now this is a man who needs a strong woman to keep him in line and to look after him. He has a history of neglecting his symbiont, and a tendency to act without regard for others. He requires supervision and an extreme amount of affection. I expect one of you to marry him."

Darcy's eyes opened wider. *"Marry me?"*

Coren winked at him. "It's been called the ultimate sanction. With your past, we can't leave you on your own anymore. Loneliness is a potential precursor of neglecting one's symbiont. It doesn't always happen, but we're not willing to take any more chances with you."

Each of the young women eyed him from head to toe. Megan smiled. "I'll take him, Mother. I want to look after him."

"All right. But you'll have to Blue him right now."

Megan walked up to Darcy and gave Coren a gentle push as she went past. Nervous, Darcy stood totally still as she pressed against him. She tilted his face down to hers with delicate hands. "Look into my eyes."

Darcy felt weak. His symbiont informed him that from now on he'd only be able to do what his wife allowed. He'd never felt happier. He bent his head down to kiss her. He felt his arms reach around her, his back and legs lift her from the floor, his feet spin them both around. He wondered if he'd pass out from ecstasy. And he felt something rising in his cheeks. He'd Been Blued.

Kelly turned to her other daughters. "Are you witnesses that your sister has Blued this man?"

"Yes, Matriarch," they chorused.

"And you, Dr. Coren?"

"Yes, Matriarch. I'll remain here to tend to their children."

They all looked at the happy couple.

"Time to leave, girls." She turned back to Coren after they'd left. "She knows. They all knew and they were all willing to take the risk. Perhaps this would have been easier if we'd prevented him from being reconfigured."

"It's only right, Matriarch. 'Hoist by his own petard,' as the humans say. The death of two of his children might help us recover the good in the man. Besides, one day we might have to explain all this to the humans. How would they react if we let him die without a chance of redemption?"

"You do realize you'll have to come up with a new occupation for him, something that keeps him out of upper echelons?"

Coren shrugged. "This is almost a new individual. This is what the original Darcy could have been if he'd taken care of his symbiont. We don't know this man yet. We have some work to do before assigning him his."

He stroked her face with the back of his hand. "Don't worry, Matriarch. You've done the best you could by him, been fairer than any of the rest of us would have been without you. You need to rest now, doctor's orders. I'll stay here and see things through."

*   *   *   *

Doctor Athens carried a black valise in his left hand. His right hand held a cell phone. He ended the call as he left the hospital and crossed the parking lot. His car, a black four-door sedan, was sitting in a shaded part of the parking lot. He wondered about the police cruiser parked behind it. They usually parked in the emergency lot.

A tall, brunette policewoman was standing just behind his car. "Dr. Athens?" she queried as he approached.

His pulse quickened. "Yes. How can I help you?"

"Are you also known as Charles Marr?"

"No. What's this all about?"

"Please place your case on the trunk of your car and open it."

"I can't do that. My files are private and confidential."

"I don't want to read them, I just want to be sure there's nothing harmful in there."

Dr. Athens swallowed hard. He carefully placed the valise flat on his trunk and slowly unzipped it.

The officer gave the top paper a quick look. "I don't recognize that language. How would you feel about coming down to the station?"

"I'd rather not."

She cuffed his right wrist, and then reached for his right. "Yeah, well, it was largely a rhetorical question. Spread your legs, please."

Dr. Athens waited for her to finish the pat down. He forced a smile. "What would you like to do next?"

She opened the back door of her cruiser. "Get in."

He was nearly seated when he thought he noticed a small red swirl on the back of her left hand.

*   *   *   *

Officer Zephyr looked up from his desk with a frown. His sister, a fellow officer, was bringing in someone familiar. He got up and went over to her desk as she sat down opposite her prisoner.

"Liz, what are you doing? This is Dr. Athens, from Martianville Memorial."

She handed him a paper as she began entering data into her computer. "Are we sure he's really a doctor?"

He looked at the paper. "A warrant for Charlie Marr? Okay, so he looks a little bit like Dr. Athens, but it can't possibly be the same man." He looked down at Dr. Athens. "Can it?"

Dr. Athens shook his head. "No. I've never gone by any other name than Athens."

Liz Zephyr raised an eyebrow. "What's your first name? The hospital doesn't even have it on file."

He shrugged. "It's not a name you could pronounce. As you saw from my papers, English isn't my first language. This isn't my country of origin."

"Immigration doesn't list your first name either. What is it you're trying to hide?"

His face turned red. "It's a matter of security. But it's nothing I can tell you. You'll have to take my word that it's nothing illegal."

"My sister doesn't go around arresting people on a whim, Dr. Athens. I'm afraid you're going to have to tell us, regardless of what level of security you think you have."

Dr. Athens leaned back as far as the handcuffs allowed. "The warrant for Charles Marr is a device to alert my superiors to my possible detection. Right now all your computer screens should be showing a restricted access alert."

He gave Officer Liz an apologetic look. "I'm sorry, but *your* files from the last two weeks are currently being erased. Oh, and you now have a week of paid vacation, which is supposed to be spent being debriefed by me."

She looked at her computer. The message 'Access Denied' flashed in neon lettering just before her screen went black.

A large black man in a suit stormed over to her desk. "Liz, what the Hell did you think you were doing, trying to bypass national security like that? I'm under orders to place *you* in the custody of Agent Athens, also known as Dr. Athens, for one week.

"*Agent* Athens?" she sputtered. "I'm sorry, Captain. I didn't know, I was just trying to break a case."

He looked down at Dr. Athens. "You're free to go, Doctor. This time, try to bring my officer back without a scrambled brain. We had to give Alec an extra week off by the time you were done messing with him."

Dr. Athens chuckled. "I didn't do anything like that to him. It sounds like he put one over on you. Good thing he's been transferred." He winked at Liz. "But I'll try to bring this one back in one piece."

∗   ∗   ∗   ∗

Liz Zephyr eyed Dr. Athens from across the table. She'd worn her little black dress, and was surprised when he'd placed his dress jacket over her shoulders when he picked her up. She handed it back to him. "I wasn't cold, it wasn't necessary for you to give me your jacket."

"It's not that, my jacket happens to be bulletproof. Being with me puts you in a bit of danger." He tried to touch her face.

She swatted his hand. "It does not."

He leaned towards her. "How did you know?"

She frowned. The red swirl appeared in her left hand.

He gently stroked the discoloration. "How long have you had *this?*"

She pulled her hand back. "It started after I tried to talk to this new street preacher, Lyle. There's a rumor that he's been getting prostitutes off the street, but no one ever sees them again. Supposedly, they go home, back to whatever life they had before. I tried to ask him about what really happens to them, and he just laughed and shook my hand." She held it up and scrutinized it. "Do you know what it is?"

He smiled. "It's nothing harmful."

"Then what is it?"

He leaned back and sipped his coffee.

She leaned towards him. "Are you going to tell me or not? Is it connected to all the secrecy surrounding you?"

"If you were that worried about it, why didn't you arrest Lyle? You arrested me quickly enough."

"That was different, I thought there was a warrant out for you."

He gave a tiny laugh. "You don't lie well, Officer Liz. I'm sorry, but I refuse to be just another conquest to you."

Her eyes narrowed. "What do you mean?"

"You've got everybody else fooled, don't you? Even your brother thinks he still has to protect you and guard your 'innocence.' Why don't you tell him you've got more than a few notches on your handcuffs?"

She started to get up. "How dare you?"

"Sit down. I'm looking for a mate, not heartbreak. As a doctor, I can tell you a thing or two about 'free love.' It's usually pretty expensive in emotional terms and health care costs."

She sat down and glared at him. "I suppose *you've* always treated women with the utmost of respect."

"Actually, I have. My family demands it. If you want to be a part of it, you'll have to be ready to make a significant commitment."

"What makes you think I want to be part of your family?"

He held up her hand to show the red swirls. "This thing does." He held his hand next to hers to show the same red swirls. "Welcome to the family."

She blushed as his face turned blue.

CHAPTER 17

▼

PRESIDENTIAL PROJECTION

The podium of the hotel conference room was draped with the Presidential insignia. Coren stood absolutely still, holding his hands behind his back. The President of the United State of America walked in, flanked by two men in black suits and several bodyguards.

Coren noted the man's graying hair, the slight paunch in his belly and the protruding roundness of his knuckles. Tendencies towards diabetes and arthritis, he noted to himself, staring into the overly bright blue eyes. At least the fellow didn't try to cover his bald patches with a comb-over.

The President offered his hand. Coren shook it, noting the excessively firm grip. The man was used to getting his own way.

"Pleased to meet you, Mr. President."

"Likewise. Sorry about the search, but after the recent terrorism, we've been a lot more careful. You understand."

"Of course. Believe me, there are far worse things than a body cavity search."

The President motioned towards the only table in the room, a four by six foot rectangle. "Let's sit down and talk. Can we get you anything, coffee, tea, or whatever it is you aliens drink?"

"No, I'm good. But thank you." Coren sat down and the President took a chair on the opposite side of the table.

"You have your own set of laws?" the President asked.

Coren leaned back, his arms folded across his chest. "Of course. As does every sovereign nation on this planet. As you might imagine, we expect a higher moral standard from our people, partly because we are capable of better self-control. No offense intended."

"So you do consider your people to be superior to those of us who have never left this planet?"

"There's no question of our superior technology. We had space flight capabilities thousands of years ago. We each carry a symbiont that allows us to have higher intelligence without the corresponding surge in ego that usually accompanies it in humans. Our morality has developed to address the questions of ethics regarding all our applications of science, with the capability to predict new discoveries and enact relevant laws quickly. Each of us is expected to take full responsibility for the actions that our freedoms engender. We have protocols regarding interspecies communication and politics. In almost every area our society far surpasses that of yours."

"Can you tell me more about this, uh, symbiont?"

Coren held his hand palm up, and swirls of red coalesced into a single, irregular shape. "It likes to swim about the fluid in the body. It's very benign, willing to hide anywhere if the host doesn't want it visible to others. The only time it's obvious, literally 'in your face,' without the host's knowledge is when we're sound asleep. So far all the women who have joined us have developed one. It seems to spread through interpersonal contact. We should have studied it more, but there seemed to be no need once we determined it was harmless."

"I hope you won't take offence, but I have to ask the question. Are you here to conquer Earth or the United States?"

The secret service men and presidential bodyguards instinctively tensed up.

Coren looked baffled. "Why would you think that?"

"If you're not here to conquer us, why come back at all?"

Coren unfolded his arms and placed his hands on the table. He leaned forward and inhaled sharply. "We were hoping that since your world population consists of far more females than males, we might find enough willing to join us, so that we could …" He waved one hand in the air. "You know, continue."

The President's eyes narrowed. "You're after our women?"

The secret service agents exchanged tiny smiles.

"Just the ones who are willing. You see, some time ago, a deadly virus killed all our females. We found a cure, but unfortunately, it was too little, too late. By the time we figured out that they needed a higher dosage of the vaccine, the damage in the few women that were left was irreversible."

"None of your people are infected now?"

"Don't worry. The disease was completely eradicated. We sterilized the planet it developed on, an easy decision since there was nothing else left alive."

"I guess I was really asking if Earth is in danger."

"That's a logical question. We've been back for over three hundred years. In all that time we've been nothing but helpful to you. If you need documentation, we can supply specific incidents where we gave your scientists a push in the right direction, and prevented large scale disasters on your international political stage."

"You mean you've been interfering with human affairs."

"I suppose that might be one way to look at it. Here's another. Is it interference to arrest a criminal in the act of committing a crime, or to save a busload of people from plunging off a cliff? We tried to never interfere with primitive human politics unless necessary for some greater good. Why do you think there hasn't been more warfare in recent history? Why do you think Canada still exists?"

"Fair enough. I suppose you can provide specific incidents for our experts to investigate.

"But why only reveal yourselves to us now, since you claim to have been back on Earth for a few centuries?"

"Because something has come up. We were convinced that we were going to become extinct since it seemed human females weren't interested in us. We'd already resorted to 'reconfiguring' the population we had. You think of it as cloning, but our procedures are far better. We thought we would be as much benefit to humanity as we could, then quietly die off.

"That expectation changed a few months ago when the first human female chose to mate with one of our men. First, she and her two sisters joined us, then several sisters from another human family. Suddenly we had hope, after generations of seeing our population decline."

"So what's the problem?"

"There are nearly a million of us who still haven't got a mate. We'd like to speed things up, but we need to figure out why we had a breakthrough in the first place."

The President shook his head. "I'm missing something here. How exactly do you expect us to help you, when you haven't figured out what it is that you need?"

"Mister President, we were hoping a *male* human perspective might make the difference."

"It seems to me that what you need is a female human perspective, and you've already got that if you've found human women who were willing to join you."

Coren interlaced his fingers. "And so far, they have no idea either, except that they've pointed out that women are only half of the human equation."

The President stood up. "Doctor Coren, I think I've gone as far as I can go in this matter. As far as human women are concerned, my answer is 'no.'"

Coren looked up at him. "I beg your pardon?"

"As leader of the most powerful democratic nation on Earth, I'm saying 'no' to you on behalf of the women on this planet."

Coren stood up. "Mr. President, I'd like to respectfully point out that it's not your decision. It's theirs. Try to prevent them from having this choice and you're as guilty of sexism as less enlightened nations where they're forced into marriages they don't want or prevented from marrying men they love."

"What's love got to do with it?"

Coren inhaled sharply. "From what we can tell, more than we ever suspected."

The President leaned forward, his knuckles on the table, his face inches away from Coren's. "Here's what I can tell you, Doctor, if you really are a doctor, continue to pursue the women on this planet and we will be at war."

Coren jumped back. *"War? Are you crazy?"*

"I'm human."

"I guess that answers that question. Seriously, Mr. President, what do you think you'd be defending yourselves against? Our people have been nothing but beneficial to this planet."

"No offense, it's just 'primitive human politics.'" He turned to go, then looked back. "But there is one question I'd like the answer to. Why did your people leave Earth in the first place?"

Coren crossed his arms in front of him. "It was the only way to save it."

"Explain that."

"The records are somewhat fragmented, but in essence, Earth was facing an alien invasion. They weren't interested in 'undeveloped, unsophisticated' societies like ancient Egypt or Greece, so we used our technology to distract them from the rest of mankind. There was a war in space, several light years beyond this solar system, which we won. Once we got that far out into space, we liked it so much we just kept going."

"Would you have ever come back if you hadn't needed help?"

Coren shrugged. "I don't know. Leadership isn't really my strong point."

"You got that right." The President exchanged a look with one of the men in black suits. The man pulled out a small gun and shot Coren.

*   *   *   *

"Computer, pause program." Kelly looked away from the data stream and over at Coren, her eyes wide. "I don't care for this simulation's ending at all."

"Nor do I," Coren said. "I've never been shot more than once a century." He turned to Jerod. "Are you sure that's how the current president would act?"

Jerod was looking almost as surprised as the rest of them. "I guess so. This one's hard to peg down. He's either a very Democratic Republican or a very Republican Democrat. He ran as an independent. He builds as much confusion as consensus, even among his own humans. Just when I think I've decided I like him, he goes and does something crazy again, like shooting you."

"Jerod, he didn't shoot me. It was just a simulation."

A twinkle danced in Jerod's eye as he pretended to check Coren over. "Are you sure? You might be right, I don't see any new bullet holes or blood."

Kelly looked at the two of them, then back at the data stream. "Settle down, you two. Computer, resume simulation."

They looked up.

The President was bending over Coren's body. "Infect the women on this planet, will you?" He motioned to one of his bodyguards. The man handed him a gun. He fired the entire clip into Coren's body.

"Let's go," he ordered. "Now we know how to hunt down the rest of them."

The simulation clicked off, leaving them staring upwards.

"That's the limit of the parameters I entered," Jerod said. "I hope it helps you make your decision."

Kelly frowned. "What's the degree of probability for all events in that simulation, assuming we do contact the President?"

Alan stepped forward. "I was able to bring the accuracy of the probability factor up to ninety-three percent, an increase from seventy-nine percent over previous projections."

Kelly cocked an eyebrow at him. "You must remember, humans are wildly unpredictable, especially when dealing with the unexpected."

"'Past behavior is the best predictor of future behavior.' I learned that from you, Mother."

"But you must also remember that personality is both the most changing and unchanging thing about a person."

He nodded. "I did take that into account when I did the upgrade."

Kelly started pacing. "Was it my imagination, or did the President say something about an infection?"

The computer snapped the simulation back on, frozen at the moment when the President was bent over Coren's body. It played the scenario again.

"Infect the women of this planet, will you?"

The real Coren took a step forward. "Computer, hypothesize on the comment, 'infect the women of this planet.' Specifically, what are the odds of all Earth females developing the symbiont? Authorization, Coren Ravell."

The images disappeared, replaced by a stream of quickly computing numbers. After a minute the numbers stopped and hung suspended in the air. The computer voice responded to the question. "Odds of human females developing the symbiont estimated at ninety-eight percent."

Coren looked at Kelly. "And without further interaction with our people?"

"Odds remain at ninety-eight percent."

Kelly looked at him, then at Jerod. "Computer, what are the odds of Earth *males* developing the symbiont?"

The numbers began moving again. Suddenly they stopped, and then diverged. "There are two possibilities," the voice said. "Zero or infinity. Specify further parameters to continue."

"I think I might know what it's asking," Jerod offered. "Computer, first set of parameters: no further contact with human males. Second set of parameters: limited contact with human males. Third set of parameters: both genders in unlimited contact with human males. Authorization, Jerod Ravell."

The voice answered almost immediately. "First set of parameters: without further contact, human males will never develop the symbiont. Second set of parameters: limited contact with human males, results unpredictable. Third set of parameters: both genders in contact with human males, ninety-nine percent probability all human males will develop the symbiont."

Kelly shook her head. "We're nowhere near ready to leave this planet, are we?"

The Coordinator stepped forward. "Actually, we can leave at any time. The ships and all their components and equipment have been kept in perfect running order. We can leave the planet today, if that's your order."

Coren shook his head. "That won't stop the spread of the symbiont. If enough women developed them for the President in the simulation to know about it, and the time frame is only three months from now, it's already too late to contain it. We can't stop the symbionts from spreading to the women of this planet. And unless we were to take them all with us, it's too late to limit their contact with human males. The humans will develop the symbiont."

The Coordinator tugged on Kelly's sleeve. "You need to take steps to avoid a global panic. Humans get scared when they don't know what's going on."

She nodded. "I know. The question is, how do we tell them? The simulation was designed to tell us what would happen if we revealed ourselves to the President in sort of a 'take us to your leader' scenario. We saw what happened there."

Coren snapped his fingers. "Wait a minute. I remember researching some of the humans' viral outbreaks. There was something a few decades back that we might be able to make use of."

Jerod groaned. "This smacks of full computer interface requiring more than one person."

Coren clapped him on the shoulder. "Ah, the benefits of the buddy system. Let's go, interface buddy. Come with us, Alan, you'll also be of use. We've got work to do."

The three men left the room.

The Coordinator leaned against Kelly's arm. "You know, I really hate being a teen. Unless I find a girlfriend soon, I'm going to have Coren age me."

Kelly put her arm around his shoulder. "This really does feel like thirteen to you, doesn't it?"

"Yeah. I can fly the most sophisticated spaceships in the galaxy, but they won't let me drive a car." He rubbed his face. "At least the symbiont ensures I don't get acne, even if Darcy did make me go through puberty. Again."

"If it's any consolation, I sort of know how you feel. Puberty is no picnic for girls, either."

"You went through puberty? Oh, right, I guess you would have. When we finally start giving our children real childhoods, I guess they will, too."

"Coordinator, I've been meaning to ask you a few questions. This seems like as good a time as any."

"Fire away."

"Don't you have a name?"

He laughed. "I used to. That was such a long time ago, I barely remember it. Come to think of it, I doubt I can even pronounce it now. It was in our third language, something we've all but lost. We speak Earth's languages now. Which reminds me, I'm on the verge of breaking the encryption in one of the old medical files. Any time you can spare with the computer would help. It might tell us something more about our symbionts."

"How is that possible?"

"One would hope, the aliens who first developed them knew more about them. What's your next question?"

Kelly nudged him. "How'd it go with Nikki?"

His face turned red. "Not well. She tried to throw a lizard at me. It fought back, giving her a nasty nip. Then the poor thing ran up to me and jumped into my arms. It kept hissing at her until her mom scooped it up and put it in its cage. I don't think I'll be seeing any of them again."

"If you do, you might want to introduce yourself as your own older brother. If Coren ages you, it won't make sense that you're suddenly older."

He grinned at her. "You're awfully smart."

"For a human," they both said at once, before bursting into laughter.

*   *   *   *

Megan stared at the memorial, her eyes red from crying. Darcy stood behind her, his hands on her shoulders. They were both wearing black pantsuits.

Darcy slid his hands down her arms. "If only I'd taken care of my symbiont from the start, this wouldn't have happened. I'm so sorry. Please, please, talk to me. It's been two weeks and I don't know how much longer I can stand the silence." He held each of her hands, hoping his symbiont would find hers quickly. Red swirls formed in his left hand. It intrigued him that she was also left-handed. He felt the warm sensation of her symbiont touching his through their skin. Grief and consolation registered and flowed through both.

Megan cleared her throat. "I'm sorry. I knew this was inevitable, but I've never had to deal with anything like it." She pulled his hand to her mouth and kissed it. "We should focus on taking care of the rest of our girls. We'll make sure they never forget their sisters."

"Rene and Gail. At least the computer has a record of their personalities."

Megan leaned back against him and sighed. "Wait a minute." She turned around and faced him. "Wait a minute, that's right. The computer does have a record of their personalities, and a record of their DNA. I wonder if we can use that."

His eyes lit up. "Maybe we could use reconfiguration technology to recreate them."

She hugged him. "I knew I married the right man. I always believed in you, you know, ever since Mother told me about you. Even when ..." Her voice broke off as she choked back more tears.

He held her tight. "Then I must thank the Matriarch for our happiness." He rubbed her back. "Are you hungry? I could go for a whole jar of peanut butter."

"You and your peanut butter." She stroked his cheek. "If you're not careful, you'll turn into a big nut," she teased.

He shrugged. "You mean a legume. There are worse fates."

They returned to the group of six young ladies standing at the bottom of the rise. Megan grabbed the hands of the tallest one. "Girls, your father has come up with a wonderful idea. We might be able to recreate your sisters. They may not be exactly the same as they might have been, but it's worth a try."

They all gave Darcy coy looks of admiration. He grinned as they surrounded him, hugged him, and knocked him to the ground.

*   *   *   *

Coren waited for Jerod in the library. "About time you got here," he greeted him.

Jerod bit his lip. "Do you think they'll be alright?"

Coren shrugged. "Knowing Darcy, he'll come up with some crazy suggestion for restoring his daughters."

Jerod sat down, yawned and stretched in the chair. "Why not?"

"What do you mean, why not?"

"You're the doctor, you tell me. Why not use the reconfiguration technology to restore them? Space knows we could use more females. And Darcy seems almost incapable of having sons."

Coren sighed in exasperation. "For the same reason we couldn't save the previous Darcy. You know the technology requires some spark of life itself to work. We have to get to the person before death in order to make the energy transfer. In your case, we were just lucky we had a live backup file to use."

Jerod frowned. "I don't remember a backup file."

"You wouldn't, would you? When the backup file is successfully implemented, the reconfiguration uses all of it, and then some."

"Do you mean to tell me there's a piece of my memory missing?"

"Worse. You're remembering more than you should. When I was shot, the stress on you triggered a partial recall of your medical training."

"How did that happen? Those files should have completely purged."

"It might be partly due to having Been Blued. The symbionts are behaving differently than before. We weren't expecting that."

"Is that going to be a problem for us? And what about the humans?"

"So far, it looks like the main difference for humans is an improvement in telepathic ability. The negative aspect seems to only affect us, the inability to be reconfigured."

"That's right. I remember now, we only succeeded with reconfiguration technology after there were no more females. In that partially dormant state, the symbionts finally allowed the technology to work. So that was the 'bug' we never figured out, the symbiont itself."

"And in that state of mind, we just accepted it, we never worried about finding an explanation."

Jerod fingered the row of books in the bookcase nearest him. "Do you think our mental state has changed since so many of us have Been Blued? Are we different than we used to be?

Coren briefly scanned the titles of the books that had caught his friend's subconscious attention. "Maybe. The Matriarch and our other women have certainly added a new perspective to our society. But I doubt books on human psychology will help us with our own. I'd prefer to rely on our own computer records. Besides, we have a history the humans don't share, the experience of our space travel."

"It's a bit of a fiction, isn't it?"

Coren snorted. "I beg your pardon?"

Jerod turned back to him. "What I mean is, our originals and their succeeding reconfigurations had those experiences, and the genetic memory of them has been passed on to us. Take me for example. My original invented the last bit of space technology three years ago, and I remember that. But this body I inhabit is less than four months old, in spite of appearances. Yours is just over a year old. When it comes to actual experience, we can't count on it. When Katy Blued you just before you were shot, you were scared stiff that you'd have to be reconfigured and the next Coren wouldn't carry over enough of the experience to support the relationship."

Coren scowled. "I hoped that if I was reconfigured and lost too much of the experience, she'd Blue me again. But you're right, it might not have happened." He sighed. "It's all speculation at this point. Even more worrisome at the time was the fact that I was only the second one to have Been Blued."

Jerod turned to face him. "How many of our men have Been Blued so far?"

Coren brightened. "Nearly two thirds. It looks like we won't become extinct after all." He grabbed Jerod's hand and pumped it vigorously. "Congratulations, Jerod Seventeen. You were successful as an actor, where you failed as a doctor."

Uncertain of what to do next, Jerod gave him a hug.

Kelly opened the door. She cleared her throat noisily. "Am I interrupting something? You guys do know we have women for this sort of thing now, right?" A twinkle danced in her eye.

Jerod strode over to her and embraced her tightly. "I'm sorry, Matriarch. Is this better?"

"Much."

Coren shook his head, smiling. "We were just discussing the possibility of recovering Darcy and Megan's daughters. It might not be successful, but with your permission, we can try something new."

"Don't tell me what it is. I want to see if my symbiont has developed enough to receive non-verbal information. Kelly placed the back of her hand over Jerod's cheek. His symbiont responded to her touch immediately. She frowned and looked at Coren. "Do you really think that will work?"

He bit his lip. "With his talent for abstracts, Alan would be better at projecting the odds of success. I hate to refuse them any possibility at this point."

"But what it would require is a tremendous sacrifice for the donors. What if no-one is willing to take the risk?"

Jerod inhaled sharply. "Here I am, in the dark again. What *risk* are we talking about?"

Kelly's eyes were large. "We'd need two men who haven't Been Blued yet to donate their live backup files. They'd run the risk of dying before having Been Blued, without the possibility of ever being reconfigured if they died unexpectedly."

Coren snapped his fingers. "Unless they were to become fully human. If we removed all their Martian upgrades, it might be possible for them to mate without having Been Blued. That was our problem, not the humans.' The trouble is, they'd have to decide everything before donating their backups. Once that's done, there's little more even I can do to change the DNA."

"Miracle worker that you are," Kelly teased.

"Thank you, Matriarch. That means a lot coming from your august person.

"So how do we look for donors? Do we send a general call or just ask those who haven't yet Been Blued?"

Kelly nodded. "Both. We explain it to everyone, but make it clear that only those who haven't Been Blued can donate. That way everyone knows what's going on and if we get the donors everyone knows what a sacrifice they're making."

The door opened. Darcy and Megan stepped inside. Megan came over and grabbed Kelly's hands. "Mother, Darcy has a wonderful idea."

Kelly nodded. "I know. We're already taking steps to see what can be done."

Darcy looked around the room. Funny, the way the people he knew so well had changed. They all looked happier, friendlier, and more attractive. He had difficulty accepting that he was the one who had changed. But all through the centuries, they had never lied to him; even his earlier versions had admitted that. How could these people be untruthful now?

The smile on his face was almost painful. "You're going to help us?" was all he could manage.

Now the Matriarch herself was actually giving him a hug. It felt so good, but different from when his wife hugged him. It was different from when his daughters hugged him. He'd had no idea there were so many variations in expressions of affection. He hugged her back, and she didn't pull away. He was suddenly aware that other arms were now encircling both of them. He peeked with one eye to see Jerod and Coren had joined in. Across the room, Megan was smiling, amused at his bewilderment and pleasure. One simple sensation overwhelmed him. Life was good.

CHAPTER 18

▼

BACKLASH

Coren paced in front of the desk in the library. Jerod leaned his backside against it, his arms crossed. Both men were frowning.

"You must have some sort of medical theory," Jerod offered.

Coren stopped pacing. "There's only one thing I can think of. It must be all your fault."

Jerod straightened up. *"My fault?* How do you figure that?"

"You were the first to have Been Blued. And you went ahead and took things into your own hands with that pimp."

"I still don't see how that makes things *my* fault."

"Remember what we learned about the humans, how some people are immune to certain diseases, and those same people might be carriers of the virus they're immune to?"

"Yes. So?"

"So, in essence, the pimp must have either been immune to the symbiont or it was immune to him."

"You mean he's become a carrier, spreading the symbiont to human males while unable to develop one himself?"

"Females, not males. Think back, Jerod, what did you tell Lyle to do?"

Jerod smiled. "I told him to return the girls he'd kidnapped to their parents unharmed, then he was to turn himself in, get treatment, and start helping prostitutes get off the street."

Coren shook his head. "Whatever possessed you to do that?"

"It was the other girl."

"What other girl?"

"The girl he was pimping that night. She hated what she was doing and she seemed so tired and helpless that I just lost it. I sent her home too, before dealing with him."

Coren stopped pacing and blinked. "You touched her skin?"

Jerod nodded. "I downloaded the command to return home, along with anti-toxin to clean her system from the drugs and eradicate the addiction."

"So *she* would have been the first human female to develop the symbiont, then most likely the two girls the pimp took back to their parents. That explains why the symbionts have spread so fast. Initial symbiosis occurred much earlier than we realized."

He sighed and rubbed his forehead. "Jerod, you have a nasty habit of leaving out important details."

Jerod nodded. "You're right. It's all my fault." He laughed. "And they thought I was *repressed.*"

Coren sat on the edge of the desk next to him. "Oh well, I suppose it would have happened sooner or later, if it was going to happen at all. At least we've got the people in place to limit interference with the symbiont."

"Interference? You know, if I was still a doctor, I might have some idea what you were talking about more than just half the time."

Coren tilted his head. "If the human medical profession was to panic, begin treating the spread of the symbiont like a disease instead of the benign creature it is, it's conceivable they could trigger a recurrence of the disease we had to cure."

"But we did cure it. Didn't we?"

"Back then, yes. But space only knows what twist of genetics contemporary human scientists might add to such an effort. The question might become, can we cure it again?"

"And how many women would die before we could?"

"Or men? We can't say for certain that human tampering wouldn't affect males more this time. We just can't afford to allow the humans to overanalyze the situation."

"What do you suggest?"

"We'll introduce a vaccination story. As long as the humans see the symbiont's presence as an effective way to stop Ebola hemorrhagic fever, they'll readily accept it."

"Does the symbiont actually stop Ebola?"

"It has it for breakfast."

Jerod looked puzzled.

"It's an old Earth expression. The symbiont responds to Ebola exposure by rendering it completely harmless before the patient's cells can be irreversibly damaged. They might have a bad nosebleed, but that's about it."

A knock on the door interrupted them.

Jerod looked at Coren. "Were you expecting company?"

Coren looked just as puzzled. "No. Not at this hour. It's not one of our people."

The knock came again, louder and more insistent.

Coren shrugged. "Open it."

Jerod opened the door. He stared blankly at the four people.

The President of the United States of America stared back at him. "I know you're aliens, but you're living as American citizens. You could at least invite the leader of your own country inside."

"Mr. President? Of course, please come in. I'm sorry, I didn't mean to be disrespectful, but we weren't expecting you."

The President entered the room, followed by two men and a woman, all in black business suits. He crossed the room and took a seat behind the desk. He held up his hand to reveal red swirls.

"That's all right. I wasn't expecting *this*."

Coren and Jerod exchanged looks of alarm. Jerod retreated to the sofa. The woman in black sat down beside him and crossed her legs and arms. She glared at him through dark sunglasses. Red swirls raced through her face and neck.

The two men in black suits stood on either side of the President. Their faces also showed red swirls.

Coren sat down in the chair opposite the desk. "How did this happen?"

"My goddaughter and her best friend were kidnapped a few months ago. Her parents barely had time to contact the police when the kidnapper brought them back to her parents, unharmed. In fact, the only difference we could see were these strange red swirls in their faces when they slept. They woke up talking nonsense about aliens who weren't really aliens. When their parents, and then my wife and myself developed the same discoloration, we had to believe them.

"I will admit, I've never felt better since all this happened, but this administration wants to know what the Hell is going on."

Coren leaned towards him. "It's a long story."

The President put his elbows on the desk and leaned towards Coren. "My schedule's been cleared for the next week. I had little choice, since my brain has been more or less abducted by your computer. So, tell me everything. I'm particularly interested in your recent simulation." He turned towards Jerod. "Although I'm surprised that you could think I might have your friend here shot in cold blood."

Jerod looked away from the hostile woman beside him. "I, uh, I went with the best information available at the time. You're a hard man to predict, Mr. President. And we had no idea those girls had any connection to you, or that they'd developed the symbiont."

"A symbiont? Is that what it is? That explains a lot. So it's permanent?"

Coren nodded. "That seems to be everyone's first question. To answer the next one, it's totally benign as long as you eat protein. Most people will subconsciously be prompted to consume what the symbiont needs, even on a vegetarian diet."

"What all does it *do?*"

"It allows a degree of telepathy between those who have one, it enables direct computer interface if the computer's sophisticated enough and it gives us control over reproduction. It also tends to heal injuries and cure diseases. The only limitation we've found is that our men cannot mate without having Been Blued."

"What's that?"

"A woman chooses her mate and shows him affection to the degree that his symbiont turns his face blue. It usually happens during a kiss, which is kind of convenient because it hides what's happening. People on this planet usually close their eyes when they kiss."

The President nodded slowly. "I felt that blue thing happen with my wife. She thought I was having a coronary. But things have never been so good in the bedroom."

He looked around the room at the bemused faces and cleared his throat. "So, I guess maybe I should ask you to take me to your leader."

Kelly opened the door and stepped inside. "No need, Mr. President."

Everyone in the room stood up. Kelly smiled. "Please, be seated.

"Mr. President, I was aware of your presence from the moment your symbiont accessed our systems. As a sign of friendship and good faith, I've let you have free reign within our database. However, you're getting dangerously close to overloading your own brain, and I'd like to request your immediate withdrawal from the system."

The President returned her smile. "Of course, Matriarch. You may have to assist me, I'm afraid I've been just stumbling around."

She crossed the room and took his head in her hands. "I know. I've been picking you up whenever you 'tripped.' It's a bit like learning to walk, isn't it?"

She let go of him.

The President rolled his eyes back and refocused. "Phew. Thank you. I was beginning to feel the strain. Like you said, it was like learning to walk."

Coren spoke next. "Wait a minute. If you accessed the mainframe, why are you asking us all these questions?"

The President leaned back, looking more relaxed. "Just double checking. This all seems too good to be true. A symbiont that removes the tendency to harm others and cures most diseases, the knowledge that there is life on other planets, a gigantic database that can answer most of mankind's questions, and a society largely devoid of anything bad. You can see how I'd be skeptical."

Kelly bent her head slightly and rolled her eyes up at him. "And I'm sure you can see why we must not reveal ourselves until the symbiont has spread to nearly all of this planet's inhabitants. There would be international alarm, perhaps to the point of some fool starting a cataclysm."

He tilted his head. "I agree. That's the main reason I'm here. I wish to present this country and myself as friends to your community. We want to pursue good faith between us. But as President of the most powerful nation on Earth, I do have to ask one question."

"What's that?"

He gave her a sheepish grin. "Do I still get to be president?"

Everyone laughed, except for Kelly. She nodded.

"We have no desire to take over the politics of this planet. However, once the symbiont has spread throughout mankind, you may find world politics taking on a new personality. The symbiont has little interest in promoting the most strident interests of some of this planet's people. Like all symbionts, it follows its own agenda; eat, rest, and reproduce. It seems to perceive anything more than that as icing on the cake.

"It will only allow its hosts to fight when there's a just cause, and to be honest, it seems to have a better idea of what that is than a lot of people do."

"I've been wondering if our troops should pull out of all the countries we're in."

"You are the President. But if I may offer a suggestion, why not wait for the symbionts to spread into those areas, and then decide? You may find the fighting stops of its own accord."

The President inhaled deeply. "This really is going to affect the whole world, isn't it?"

"It's the dawning of a new day, Mr. President."

He stood up. "I'm glad I was here to help usher it in. I'd like to assign one of my best people to act as a liaison between you and the White House. Anything you need just let her know. Sheila?"

The woman who had been sitting beside Jerod stood up and held out her hand. Her voice was friendly but resolute. "I'm Sheila West. Pleased to meet you, Matriarch. I'm happy to be working on behalf of both our worlds."

Kelly took her hand. "Actually, Earth is our world, too. We left thousands of years ago, but never claimed another planet as our own. There just wasn't any need, as our ships were relatively self-sufficient. But please, call me Kelly."

"Of course. I'll be staying on, living among you, if that's all right."

Kelly winked at her. "It could be risky. We still have a lot of men looking for a mate."

Sheila cocked an eyebrow and took off her sunglasses. Her intense blue eyes sparkled in the light. "I'm willing to take that chance."

The President chuckled and whispered something to Coren. He smiled, but quickly managed to adopt a neutral expression.

"Is there a place we can meet tomorrow? All the chiefs of staff have developed the symbiont and they have a lot of questions."

Jerod nodded. "There's a café called The American Refill, near our movie studio. I'll give your drivers the directions. I see they have the symbiont as well."

The President's eyebrows rose. "Really? They didn't before we got here."

Coren smiled. "Once the symbiont starts spreading, it goes quickly. We may not have to worry about a public panic beyond …"

He thought for a moment. "Three or four months."

The President inhaled deeply. "Still enough time for terrorists and the like to do some damage. I'd go to yellow alert, but that might bring about the panic we're trying to avoid."

"Unless there was a different reason for going to yellow alert," Jerod suggested.

The President came over and shook his hand. "I like you, Jerod. What's your role here?"

Jerod blinked. "My *role,* Sir?"

"Your occupation, your assignment, or whatever it is your people call it."

He laughed. "I used to be a doctor, but now I'm just a computer consultant with a sideline as an actor. My assignment was to continue working on finding some way for our men to have Been Blued. I guess I was successful, since I married our new Matriarch, but the problem is, we still don't know why."

"Why, what?"

"Why we now have our men Being Blued, and therefore suddenly able to mate, when we've had to rely on cloning for centuries."

The President looked at Kelly. "She's on the verge of finding out. It was something I saw in the databanks, you're working on translating something?"

Kelly shook her head sharply. "Just finished. You know how if you let something simmer in the back of your brain, sometimes the answer pops up? The translation matrix fell into place for me while I was guiding your mind out of the system."

Coren looked excited. "You know the answer?"

"I almost wish I didn't. It turns out that any interference with the symbiont causes it to revert to an earlier stage of its life cycle, sort of a semi-dormancy. What we thought was a disease ages ago was nothing more than the result of the symbionts' developers trying to augment them. They can remain semi-dormant for a very, very long time. The only thing that fully wakes them is when they subconsciously perceive no further threat. Even the 'cure' we came up was perceived as a mild threat, in spite of preserving both species."

Jerod came and put his arm around her shoulder. "Your desire to use your life to make the world a better place must have been what awakened mine."

Kelly leaned against him. "You mean, in five hundred years you never found anyone else as altruistic?"

"Maybe it was your faith. A lot of people on this planet merely use theirs as a means to some other end, but you were inspired to do wonderful things."

She nodded. "Faith as a vehicle to hurt others is wrong in anyone's theology. You do realize this changes our science regarding the symbionts. They must have at least a basic moral sense in order to have an aversion to what we consider evil."

The President headed for the door. "I'll leave theorization in your hands. Unless there's something else I need to know right now, I'd like to get some sleep before tomorrow's meeting." The two bodyguards followed him out the door as everyone else wished him a good night.

Kelly turned to Sheila. "I'll show you to your room."

Sheila gave her a tight-lipped smile. "Could we make a side trip through your kitchen? The President often forgets to make time for meals."

Kelly glanced at Jerod and Coren. "Of course. You two go get some sleep."

Kelly led Sheila towards the kitchen.

"So, how did you become leader of these aliens, Matriarch?"

Kelly laughed. "I was as human as you a few months ago. But that was before I fell in love with Jerod. I almost walked away without giving the relationship a chance. I just wanted to change the world for the better, start a few charitable organizations, that sort of thing."

"What made you stay?"

"I did. I decided to take a chance on love once I found out Jerod had helped someone else become successful."

"When did you find out about all this?" Sheila waved her hand around in the air.

"It wasn't all at once, they were very careful to give me enough time to process the information. The more I learned, the more everything stopped being strange and began making sense. I guess it was a good fit with my original goals. With the symbiont spreading, mankind is becoming better. How has your life changed since you developed the symbiont?"

"It's too early to tell."

"No, my dear, little white lies simply won't work anymore. Try to reserve your subterfuge for the humans, the ones who haven't joined us yet. Anyone with a symbiont can spot deception immediately. Yours tells me that you're expecting recent developments to work to your advantage."

A clatter of silverware and the sound of drawer being closed greeted them. A man in black dress slacks and a white shirt bent in front of the fridge, his broad back to them. He turned around and stood up. He was holding a couple of slices of pizza on a plate and two bottles of water.

Kelly pulled a chair up to the counter and motioned for Sheila to do the same. "Andrew Eleven, this is Sheila West. She'll be staying with us for a while."

Andrew popped the pizza into the microwave before joining them. His green eyes flashed a piercing look. Sheila found it hard to concentrate on the rest of his evenly chiseled features.

He gave her a probing look. "Did the President really think we needed a spy here, Miss West?"

"Andrew!"

Sheila met Andrew's gaze as best she could. "It's all right, Matriarch. I should have known it wouldn't be possible to hide that from another symbiont."

Andrew turned as the microwave beeped. He opened it and gave Sheila one of the pizza slices. "You've been looking for a way to get to the top. How do you feel about being here?"

She chewed a bite before answering. "I think I like it. It's a bit early to tell." She fixed her eyes on a tile on the counter. "I doubt I'll 'Blue' anyone."

Kelly tilted her head, a question in her eyes. Andrew winked at her. He swallowed and put the rest of his slice back on the plate.

"On rare occasion it's the man who Blues the woman." He put a hand on Sheila's forearm.

She looked up. She was suddenly unable to look away from him. Andrew gently traced the features of her face with the back of his other hand. "Interesting. An almost photographic memory and a high IQ. Bit of a propensity to jump to conclusions, but a willingness to apologize quickly enough. I think she'll do." He turned to Kelly. "That is, with the Matriarch's permission?"

Kelly shrugged, a slight smile on her face. "She's the one you need to ask."

He turned back to Sheila. "I think she's too smitten to speak."

Kelly raised her eyebrow. "Well, you should do something. She's quit breathing."

Sheila's cheeks were turning blue.

Andrew grabbed her face and put his mouth over hers. He parted her lips with his own and blew gently. She responded with a start and pulled him closer. The blue shades in her face spread onto his. Memories and images passed between their minds.

"A double Bluing. That doesn't happen very often," Kelly muttered to herself. She turned to go, then paused. She shrugged, came back, and put one hand on each of their shoulders. "By Martian law, I pronounce you married."

Sheila pulled back. "Married?" she gasped. "Already?"

Andrew nodded. "We don't tolerate long engagements, especially when we're so short on children. Doesn't this please you?"

She opened her mouth, and then closed it again. She moved closer. "Of course it does. But you might want to give a girl some warning next time, this was awfully fast."

"This is our way. And we only choose one mate, so you can just forget about that 'sampling' you were planning on."

Sheila felt all the color drain from her face. "A girl just wants to have fun," she stammered.

"Fun? How can you call it that when you regretted it so much?"

Sheila's face turned red. "Now wait just a minute. How is that any of your business?"

"Your symbiont wanted me to know. You can learn a lot from it, if you'll shut up long enough to listen."

Kelly yawned. "I'll leave the two of you to argue. I'm going to bed." She left the room.

Sheila blinked. "How did you know about, uh, I mean …"

Andrew waited, enjoying her discomfort.

She took a deep breath. "I'm sorry. Now that we're married, I can't even imagine being with someone else. It's like all my desires to run wild have been tamed."

Andrew cocked an eyebrow. *"All* your desires?" Before she could think of an answer he gave her a gentle kiss. He frowned, opened his eyes and backed away. "You know, I think this pizza is lacking something. You go ahead and eat. I'm going to a real restaurant, one that uses fresh vegetables, instead of frozen."

He threw on his jacket and left her alone in the kitchen.

Sheila wondered if she'd been had. The symbiont was telling her everything was working out the way it should, but it didn't even try to resolve her confusion. She realized she was still hungry, so she ate her slice of pizza, then his. She yawned. Without any real plan of where to go, she got up and found her way to a bedroom.

Once inside, she realized it was *his* bedroom. So the symbiont had recognized the marriage as legitimate, and led her here. Fine, but there was no way she was taking off her clothes or getting into his bed. Deciding it was better for him to find her sleeping in an inconvenient position, where it was harder for him to get at her, she stretched out on the recliner in the far corner. She got up, took the top blanket off the bed and returned to the recliner. Let him find his own blanket, she thought. She'd scream bloody murder if he tried to take this one.

*   *   *   *

Andrew chewed another bite of pizza. Mo brought a fresh cup of coffee and sat down opposite him. "You look strangely unhappy for a newlywed."

"Strange is definitely the right word. My wife's emotionally damaged. I have to help her, but I don't know how."

"Fascinating. I had no idea these humans could be so fragile. What do you plan to do?"

"Support her, be there for her, and offer myself to her."

"And what about your needs?" Mo looked concerned.

Andrew smiled grimly. "Helping my wife has just become my biggest need."

"Sounds like you'll need some time off. I'll ask Mandeep to cover for you."

Andrew yawned. "Thank you. I should get back. She's waiting for me. Sort of."

*   *   *   *

Andrew came into the room as quietly as he could. He saw Sheila half asleep on the recliner. He tilted his head. He left the room and returned with a fresh outfit for her. He placed it on the chest of drawers. He crossed to the far side of the room and began undressing. His symbiont informed him of Sheila's conflicting desires to remain distant yet become intimate. What to do? He decided to leave it to her discretion. Naked, he stretched out on the bed facing away from her and fell asleep.

Sheila had heard him come in. She pretended to be asleep while she watched him undress. She acknowledged a slightly perverted pleasure from the deception, and then remembered the telepathic abilities of the symbionts. He probably knew she was pretending to be asleep while peeking out from under the blanket. But he did nothing about it. She wondered just how long he could be the perfect gentleman under these circumstances.

CHAPTER 19

▼

TELLING THE WORLD

The American Refill barely held the President, his chiefs of staff, the bodyguards, secret service men and women, as well as everyone Jerod and Coren could think of having present.

Mo had spent the night bringing in tables from the patio and trying to get extra chairs. Fortunately, Kelly had reminded him to have extra coffee on hand. Mandeep had arranged for extra food and worried it still wouldn't be enough.

The President looked around for Sheila. On seeing her across the room, he knew she'd failed in her first objective, to stay detached. Her angry expression was gone, replaced by something akin to contentment. He'd never seen the outfit she was wearing, a grey suit with a pink blouse, complimented with a large pink brooch. He couldn't remember the last time she'd worn anything but black. She caught his look, smiled and shrugged.

The café host seemed determined to fall all over him. The man had barely served coffee to everyone in the room before he was back, asking if the President would like another waffle, more coffee, eggs, anything … He was surprisingly quick for someone who looked so old. Another benefit of the symbiont, the President wondered?

The tone inside the café was friendlier and more relaxed than any other meeting the President had held. The buzz of conversation and new friends in the making proceeded for over an hour. The President found himself wishing he'd brought the First Lady.

The chatter stopped when Kelly walked in. Silence descended as she took a seat beside him. "Thank you for coming, Mr. President. Would you like to call this meeting to order?"

He smiled and tried to think of something to say. Funny, he was never short on words before. "All right. I guess I'm calling this meeting to order. Since this is the first meeting between our two governments, there's no old business to discuss."

A roar of laughter interrupted him. Kelly smiled and waited for it to die down. "Before we go any further, I'd like to clarify something. We have leadership, as well as laws and responsibilities. While we don't think of ourselves as having a government by the human definition, we're willing to accept the word for the sake of expediency. It is, at the very least, a form of government."

He nodded. "All right then. Should we appoint a secretary to record the minutes?"

"It's your choice. We have no need, since the symbionts ensure complete records of all such proceedings in our database. But we'd encourage your administration to create its own records for the sake of accessibility, if nothing else."

"Accessibility? By whom?"

"Mankind, of course. Just because the world is inheriting the symbionts doesn't mean we're going to throw open all our science and research to you. It would be disaster."

The President frowned. "Oh really?"

Kelly gave him a reproachful look. "Would you give all your administration's secrets to the world on a platter? Or to people who have been away from Earth so long they seem like aliens?"

He smiled. "I see your point. As long as there are people in the world who don't want to live in peace, it's not wise to give them an undue advantage."

"Exactly. Who did you have in mind for your secretary?"

The President craned his neck to see where the man he wanted was sitting. Before he could call his name, the husky blond rose and came towards them.

"Was it me you wanted, Mr. President?"

"Yes, Phillip." The President turned to Kelly. "Do you ever get used to this?"

She nodded. "Eventually."

The man nudged the bodyguard sitting next to the President. "This is my seat now, Malcolm."

The bodyguard rose and stood behind the President. Phillip sat down and pulled out a small handheld device. "I think my personal digital assistant may have to be upgraded for next time, Mr. President. For now I'll use shorthand."

Kelly reached over and placed Phillip's hand over the screen of the device. "Your symbiont will record things for you if you keep your hand in this position. It'll treat the PDA as a memory stick and interface with it as you wish afterwards. No typing or stylus required."

Phillip tilted his head and grinned. "Thank you, Matriarch. That makes things much easier."

"And that brings us to the first order of business. How do we tell the world about the symbiont without creating a panic?" The President looked around the table.

Coren caught his eye. "We've been doing some research on recent epidemics. We'd like to introduce the symbiont as an vaccine to all known strains of the Ebola virus."

"But what about when people really do encounter the Ebola virus?"

"We've already tested that. The symbiont kills all subtypes of the virus. The patient may have a severe nosebleed, but no permanent damage is done. The patient suffers no permanent harm."

"You've already ...? It would take months for our administration just to approve the funding."

Kelly grinned. "Our leadership doesn't face the same constraints as yours. You may find that in time your government won't find so many constraints necessary. For now, it's best for everyone to continue with the status quo. Any upset could trigger the panic we're trying to avoid."

"Agreed. But it's going to take time for us to get used to doing things your way."

"You don't need to do things 'our way.' Just do what's right for you, what's right for mankind."

"Of course. I'm sorry if I seem jumpy, it's just that I'm used to being in control. This," he motioned around the room, "doesn't feel like me being in control."

"Think of it as similar to being in the mainframe. I'm just here to help you when you trip."

"But it was still your computer system."

"It's still your country and your administration."

Phillip looked at his hand. "I believe that last exchange should be stricken from the record."

Coren spoke up again. "I'd like to make a motion, that we use the World Health Organization to announce the rapidly spreading vaccine to the Ebola virus, with assurances that the resulting red swirls are harmless and indicate that the vaccine is active."

"So noted," the President announced. "All in favor?"

The united response was unanimous.

"Opposed?"

Silence greeted the question.

"Motion carried. Now, I'd like to know whether or not you have people in place to make the announcement."

Coren pulled out his WHO membership card. "I may not have the photogenic face of our friend, Jerod, but I do know a few things about medicine. I'm ready for any questions human doctors or the media might come up with."

The President looked at the card. "Just how many human organizations are your people involved in?"

Coren thought for a bit. "Let's see, uh, most of the good ones. We avoid ones that promote discrimination or abuse, but anything that's good for mankind tends to be good for us too."

"So you have people on the UN Council, for example?"

Kelly placed a hand on his arm. "You're starting to sound a bit paranoid again, Mr. President. You know that's not necessary. If you need assurances, I'm afraid you'll have to learn to look within."

He nodded. "The symbiont." He looked at the swirls in his hand. "It knows you as well as it knows me."

Kelly's mouth fell open. "I guess it does. That's a saying none of us has heard in over three hundred years."

*　　　*　　　*　　　*

Jerod came into the library carrying huge bags of popcorn. "Yet another human tradition containing food," he said. The computer view screen had been turned to act as a TV, and several rows of couches had been brought in.

The President and selected members of his team were seated in the front row. Jerod handed them some of the popcorn, then joined Kelly in the second row. The President turned back to speak to them.

"Are you sure you two don't want to join me? I could boot a couple of these bodyguards to cheaper seating."

"We wouldn't hear of it, Mr. President. Besides, the Coordinator's already in the front row."

The President looked at the end of the couch. *"That's* the Coordinator? What happened?" He turned back to the young man. "You were a kid the last time I saw you."

The Coordinator ran a hand through his short, dark brown hair and gave them a smirk. He appeared about twenty. "Coren aged me. Then the Matriarch gave me a makeover. I've been working out. And a certain young lady who just turned nineteen still hasn't had the nerve to tell her parents about us. They're going to be scandalized, but then they'll probably be relieved to learn we got married before the children came." He looked towards the last row of couches. Five young adults smiled back at him.

He turned his attention back to the President. A frilled lizard seemed to come from nowhere to perch on the Coordinator's shoulder. He raised an eyebrow to coincide with the creature's tongue flick.

"Those are *your* children?" the President gasped. "How is that possible?"

"With our technology, and the shortage of time we're facing, we age the next generation to young adulthood."

"Amazing."

Jerod tapped him on the shoulder and pointed at the screen. "It's time."

The computer snapped on to receive the news broadcast. A blonde with long, curly hair in a conservative blue blouse was announcing current events. An insert that showed news video accompanied her. Her voice was strong but pleasant.

"At 10 a.m. this morning, the international cult watcher organization, Break Free Now, reported the annual mass marriage ceremony of the Markstone Sect was immediately followed by the unexpected mass annulment of most of its participants. Break Free Now is at a loss to explain this unprecedented occurrence. Markstone Sect authorities declined to comment, although a few of the wedding participants claimed it was a simple case of changing their minds.

"And an important development on the international medical front today. Dr. Coren Ravell joins us on the World Health Organization's emergency broadcast system. Now I should point out that use of the emergency broadcast system doesn't necessarily mean bad news. Isn't that right, Doctor Ravell?"

The insert had changed to a video feed of Coren. He wore a white lab coat and was standing in front of a long table full of test tubes and microscopes.

Coren smiled. "That's right, Molly. In fact, we have wonderful news. I don't know if you recall the Ebola virus outbreaks a few decades ago, but we've been working hard to create an vaccine."

"Could you give us a bit of background information regarding the Ebola virus? In layman's terms, of course."

"Certainly. Ebola hemorrhagic fever is a severe fever that causes death in most of its victims. Some patients suffer internal and external bleeding. Other symptoms may include a rash or red eyes. It's highly contagious; it passes itself on to new victims through infected body fluids or contaminated objects."

"That sounds horrible."

"It is nasty. The good news is that we've created a vaccine. It renders the Ebola virus virtually harmless. In the worst cases, the victim suffers a severe nosebleed. But even so, no permanent damage is done by the virus."

"That's incredible. It almost sounds too good to be true."

"It's true, Molly."

"What about side effects? Something so powerful must have some appreciable side effects."

"Actually, we did have to make the vaccine airborne to be completely effective. And there's one more thing." He held up his hand to reveal the red swirls. "The red color you see in my hand is proof that the vaccine is working. It spreads quickly from person to person."

"Does it cause any discomfort?"

"None whatsoever. We have studied it in depth, and aside from a slight increase in feelings of well being, we've found no side effects at all."

"Did you have to tamper with the human genome to develop this vaccine?"

"Fortunately, no. We were able to come up with the vaccine without altering human genetics at all. Now, that's all that I can say without giving away some very important scientific trade secrets. Copyrights and patents, you understand."

"Of course. Is there anything else you can tell us about this new vaccine?"

"Just that the World Health Organization wishes to reassure the general public that this vaccine is beneficial. People tend to fear what they don't understand, so we wanted to be proactive in spreading the knowledge. We recommend that those who don't yet have the vaccine should spend time in the presence of people who do."

"Is there any way to speed up receiving the vaccine?"

"No. It must spread naturally or it won't be effective. This is not something you can get from your family doctor; it just doesn't work that way. Now, we are fortunate, in that there are currently no reported outbreaks of the Ebola virus. This makes us confident that the vaccine will have time to spread to most people throughout the world before another outbreak can occur."

"Dr. Ravell, how many lives do you think this will save?"

"In the event of a sudden, uncontrolled outbreak, the virus we're talking about is so aggressive that an extremely conservative estimate would be in the range of thirty million."

"That's a lot of lives that might have otherwise been lost."

"Yes it is, Molly. You can see just how important it is to let the vaccine do its work."

"Once someone has the vaccine, and the, uh, red swirls, is there anything else he or she should do?"

"Not a thing. Molly, the World Health Organization considers this vaccine so important that it has accepted funding from several private corporations that wish to remain anonymous. All costs of the development and initial distribution of the vaccine have been covered."

"Wow. That's almost as incredible as the vaccine itself."

"And we're out of time. I've been talking with Dr. Coren Ravell, of the World Health Organization. Next on this channel …"

The view screen clicked off.

The Coordinator twisted his back against the arm of the couch to look at them. The lizard on his shoulder easily shifted to keep its perch. "What do you think?"

The President was pursing his lips together. "I wish I'd had you guys working on my campaign. I would have had an appreciable margin of victory, not just gotten in by the skin of my teeth."

CHAPTER 20

▼

DOUBLE AGENT

Sheila hesitated, and then knocked on the bedroom door.

Kelly opened it and took her hand. "Poor thing, you're in terrible distress. Come in."

Sheila stood still. Kelly touched her cheek. Red swirls rose in her hand and Sheila's face. The distraught woman's tears flowed freely. Kelly led her to a chair, sat her down and faced another one opposite her. She sat down, offered a tissue and waited for the sobbing to stop.

"Now then, since your symbiont is so new, I'm not getting much from it. Tell me what this is about."

Sheila found her voice was more confident than she expected. "I thought marriage would be quickly followed by a honeymoon. Andrew hasn't come near me since we met. We don't even sleep in the bed together."

Kelly leaned back in her chair. "I see. You were expecting something different. You've overlooked one thing. Andrew's been giving you what you need, not what you expect."

Sheila looked baffled. "What do you mean?"

"You came to us with so much anger and pain that any romantic attempt on your husband's part wouldn't be well received. Instead, Andrew has been giving you acceptance and support, the two things no man has ever given you before."

"The President always supported me."

"That's not entirely true, is it? He never accepted your anger. He wanted you to change before he'd give you the assignments you really wanted. Being a spy among us was your idea; one he only agreed to because so many others thought it was a good idea.

"For your part, you haven't accepted Andrew for who he is. You've been waiting for him to act like every other man you've known. That's the one thing he's incapable of. All he can do is give you what you need. He can't force himself on you."

Sheila wrapped her arms around herself. "So it's not because he doesn't want me?"

"It's because there are parts of yourself you're having difficulty accepting. Andrew will help you with that."

"How?"

"That's something the two of you will have to work out together."

Sheila started to get up.

"There's one thing you should know," Kelly offered. "It's not too late for an annulment."

Sheila smiled. "I don't think that will be necessary."

$$* \qquad * \qquad * \qquad *$$

Andrew parked the limo in the garage for the night. It was his last night before a well-earned week off. He was disappointed that being married hadn't seemed to change anything, but it had been his personal opinion that humans weren't ready to join them after all. Thoughts of how Kelly and her sisters had fully integrated intruded on him, a stubborn reminder that things could change. It was a possibility he hoped for.

He peered into the dark kitchen as he walked by. Strange how a room that saw so much of life could seem so empty with no one in it. He was tempted to have a late night snack, but the symbiont resisted. He sighed and loosened his tie.

He was surprised to see Sheila actually on the bed, in a red negligee, no less. He wondered why she wasn't trying to sleep in her clothes on the recliner, like every night before. Maybe it hurt her back.

She was reading a book. She put it down when he walked in. It appeared to be the old diary he kept a few hundred years ago. She must have been going through his drawers to find it. He wondered if she had learned Spanish before reading the book or if the symbiont was translating it for her.

He took off his jacket and placed it over the back of a chair. "I have a week off starting tomorrow," he said. "If you'd like, we can spend it together. Or apart. Whatever you want."

She gave him a curious look.

He stopped unbuttoning his shirt. "Am I making you nervous?"

"Not exactly. But I haven't been fair to you. I'm sorry. I've had a lot of bad experiences with men."

Andrew nodded slowly. "I felt that. You know, I'd rather die than cause you pain. Funny thing, this human affection." He resumed undressing.

Sheila watched with growing interest. "So, what did you have planned for all that free time next week?"

"I was hoping to get to know my wife better, maybe make her a little less nervous around me." He tried to avoid her eyes.

"You could just throw her to the ground and have your way with her."

He looked up. His face, neck and most of his chest turned red. The symbiont was no help at all in deciphering her expression. He quickly turned his gaze to the floor, and then realized that was too much in keeping with her suggestion. He met her eyes as best he could. His voice was so quiet she strained to hear him.

"I can't." He cautiously got onto the bed and leaned back. "All I can do is ask her to take what she needs. Until those needs are met, I'm helpless."

Sheila felt her symbiont stir. There was something else. "And?" she prompted.

He remained silent.

She tried a different track. "Uh, so how many women have you *been* with?"

He gave a nervous laugh. "Counting you? None."

"None? At your age? How is that possible?"

He rolled onto his side and looked at her, his weight on his elbow, his fist propping up his head. "Our men don't mate until a female chooses to mate with them. It's a side effect of the symbiont. Or possibly its main purpose, I don't know. As for my age, I'm over five hundred, if you don't count how many times I've been reconfigured. I try not to. So if you think I've been patient, you're right. And wrong. A man can't override the symbiont and until it senses willingness in a female, there's no mating to be had.

"Now, since you seem unfamiliar with our version of 'the facts of life,' I may as well tell you. Every male of our species is under orders to comply with the mating demands of any willing human female. Since you are the woman who chose me, whatever you want, I have no choice but to do as you ask."

"But do you want to?"

"Of course I want to, desperately! What kind of a question is that?"

She brushed her lips over his. "A stupid one. Forgive me?"

"Yes," he mumbled. "I have no choice."

✳   ✳   ✳   ✳

Coren knocked on Andrew's bedroom door. Receiving no answer, he paced for a bit. "Computer, override this door lock, Medical Authorization, Coren Ravell."

The door slid open. He shook his head on seeing the two unconscious figures under the sheets. "Computer, close door, seal this room and flood it with Emergency Compound Twenty-four."

A gray gas poured in from ceiling vents above the bed. Coren sat down in the recliner, crossed his legs and waited for his patients to awaken. A steady stream of green data in front of his line of vision kept him occupied.

Sensing the couple's impending return to consciousness, he dismissed the data stream. Three hours had passed, and the gas was nearly gone.

Groggy, Andrew sat up. He shook his head, and then spotted Coren. He shook Sheila's arm. "Wake up, we have company."

She yawned, rolled over and tried to go back to sleep. He rolled her back by the shoulder. She blinked and looked at him. "Good morning."

"That's all you can say for yourself?" Coren demanded.

Sheila gasped, jerked upright and pulled the blankets in front of her. "What are you doing here?"

Coren crossed his arms, a wry look on his face. "I'm bringing the two of you out of stasis. It happens sometimes when there's been a double Bluing." He raised an eyebrow in Andrew's direction. "Especially when the male has resisted the Companion File download."

"I swear, I was driving through a tunnel when it came through. It interrupted the transmission. I didn't think it was that important, I never thought a female would pick me."

Sheila put a hand on his arm. "Sweetheart, what are you talking about?"

He looked at her, then back at Coren. "Maybe you should explain it to her."

Coren stood up and began pacing. "Physical arousal has always been difficult for our males. So a long time ago, a very intelligent Matriarch wrote the Companion File to work in conjunction with the symbionts to give us a degree of dignity and self-control. Without a full download of the file, it's a wonder you two didn't injure each other. I checked, while I was waiting for you to wake up. You're both fine. A little bruised in places, but that's healing. I completed the download while you were in stasis, so you shouldn't have any further problems. If you do, call me." He turned to leave.

Andrew looked at Sheila. "Wait. How long were we in stasis?"

Coren turned back. "Let me put it this way. You only have four days of vacation left.

"Computer, unseal this room, and remove all trace of the gas." He opened the door and walked out, closing it behind him.

Andrew started to get up.

"Where are you going?" Sheila asked.

"You heard the man, I've only got four days of vacation left. We should get dressed."

She tugged on his arm. "After a bit. I seem to remember something about you being under orders." Red swirls were circled through her fingertips. He smiled at the ones streaking around his arm where she held it.

*   *   *   *

"I've never seen anyone actually climb a coconut tree before." Sheila watched the young man drop several coconuts to the ground before shinnying back down the tree trunk. She wondered how the fellow managed to keep his shorts from shredding.

Andrew shrugged, his arm around her shoulder. "Please don't ask me to do that. I drive. I don't climb trees."

She laughed as she took the coconut offered by the young man. "Thank you."

"I can do this, though." Andrew pulled a small tool from the pocket of his shorts. With one quick movement he stabbed three holes, one big enough for pouring the milk out. "Close your eyes, tilt your head back and open your mouth."

He poured the thin white liquid into her mouth.

She swallowed. "That was amazing. You didn't spill a drop."

"Steady hands. I've driven some of the most important people on this planet around. Sometimes I've had to save their lives when some idiot gets road rage."

She looked into his eyes. "You be careful out there."

"Don't worry, I have a feeling this planet's about to become a whole lot safer for everyone. On little islands like this, the symbiont has spread so quickly that no one's the least bit self-conscious about it. Look around."

Sheila scanned the beach. Dark skinned natives and pale tourists alike exhibited red swirls in constant movement through their bodies, hidden only where swimsuits or t-shirts covered the route of the symbiont. No one was afraid, and everyone seemed to be enjoying the sun.

"These symbionts will make the world a better place, won't they?"

"We think so. Look, the muggers who used to prey on unwary tourists, now they're just having fun." He pointed to a group of young adults playing soccer along the beach. Their ball strayed in his direction. With a firm kick, he sent it back to its owners, resulting in friendly waves and smiles.

"Wait, those guys were all pickpockets? Not that it was a good thing, but how will they make a living now?"

"That's up to them. They'll just naturally gravitate towards what they enjoy doing. Some of these young people, this is how they'll find out they're Olympic material. Others will return to fishing, boat building or tourism. I think some of them have real musical talent. See that child whittling on a conch shell? She's going to be something spectacular, instead of another devastated rape victim. In fact, the possibility of her being raped on this island has dropped from almost a certainty to being highly unlikely. The world's children are already much safer."

"And the starving countries of the world?"

"We're taking steps there. As soon as the leadership of those countries develop symbionts we'll release massive food shipments, especially high protein food. In fact, that's something you can help us with."

"Me? How?"

He rubbed her arm. "Did you ever think of becoming a double agent?"

She giggled. "Back when I was so angry, I sometimes thought about it. Maybe the President was right to not give me too much responsibility."

Andrew turned to face her directly. "No. He was wrong. You knew it, and that was part of what caused your anger to build. You knew the difference between being angry at what your uncle did to you years ago and being angry at being held back in your career. It wasn't until the President continued to hold you back that the anger became almost unmanageable."

She gave him the most defenseless look he'd ever seen. "I'm not sure all my anger is gone. Kelly said you'd be able to help me."

Andrew hugged her tightly and closed his eyes. "Just trust me. Let it go."

Sheila hugged him back, her head on his chest, her eyes closed. She felt safe, as if nothing in the world could ever hurt her again. At length, she released her grip. She opened her eyes and was surprised to see the entire beach population gathered around them in a giant circle. Everyone's eyes were closed. Taller people were at the back, shorter ones were in front. Children were sitting on the ground. A few babies were lying in front of the children. They were all silent.

"Andrew," she whispered. "What's going on?"

"This is our way," he whispered back, his eyes still closed. "We look after each other."

"It's a lesson in human empathy," she whispered.

"It's what humanity should look like."

From the back, people began to open their eyes and move away. In a few moments the children were also gone. A few adults gathered the infants and left.

Still in Andrew's embrace, Sheila looked up at him. "That was incredible. There was no organization or announcement."

"Just a common feeling of well being. It's an overwhelming draw for us. A few humans are born with it; they're the ones animals are inexplicably drawn to. The animals on this planet feel a similar kind of attraction to them, although they're often put off by bad people. I guess there will be fewer 'bad people' as time goes by."

"Maybe world peace will become a reality."

"That might be a stretch, even for the symbionts. But I think we should have you working to get your government to agree to the food relief."

"I finally get to be a double agent?" She grinned.

"Why not? As long as I still get to drive."

She gave him an impish grin. "I think that can be arranged."

*   *   *   *

"Admiral, you'd better come have a look at this." A muscular young man with a shaved head, in loose fitting khakis and a headset was sitting at a computer console. His blue eyes showed grave concern. A tiny green blip lit up the screen at regular intervals.

Another man who looked like an older version of him came over. "What's the problem, Calvin?"

Calvin pointed to the screen.

"I see. How long until the humans detect the signal?"

"Let's see…." Calvin grabbed a chart and a calculator. "Piggybacking our signal onto human technology has tripled our probe's reach, so allowing for projected advances in human technology …" He stabbed at the calculator while glancing back and forth at the chart. "About three years."

"That's not much time. I'll inform the Matriarch immediately."

Calvin's eyes were wide. "Admiral Bryan, do you think we'll be at war?"

The Admiral patted his shoulder. "Maybe. But this time we won't be fighting them alone. The humans have been surprisingly receptive to the symbiont. They'll join us, if only as a matter of common survival."

His eyes narrowed as he looked at Calvin's tense face. He touched the young man's cheek with the back of his hand. Red swirls circled his touch. "Don't worry. Your children will be just fine."

Calvin closed his eyes. "Thank you, Sir."

"Right, then. You'd better return to the Martianville Air Force base."

"Aye, Sir."

The Admiral gave him a wink and left.

Calvin patted the console in front of him before grabbing his jacket. "Think the Martian spaceships can get along without me for a few days, Old Girl? Fend off the aliens all on their own?"

"Yes, Calvin," a pleasant female computer voice responded. "The necessary equipment and personnel are in place on all Martian ships."

*   *   *   *

The Admiral had changed into his white uniform and carried his hat in his hand. He went straight to the kitchen, where his symbiont sensed the Matriarch. She was wearing a housecoat over her bathing suit, looking relaxed. She stiffened at the sight of him.

"Admiral. I'm sorry I haven't had time to inspect the ships yet."

"Sorry to interrupt, Matriarch. As you've probably guessed, I have terrible news."

She nodded, poured herself a cup of coffee and sat down. "They're coming back, aren't they? How long?" She motioned towards another chair.

He removed his hat, poured himself a cup of coffee and sat down opposite her. "Two, maybe three decades before they arrive. We estimate three years before human technology detects them."

"I've been thinking about that. Alan mentioned that our fundamental assumptions about human technology have to be discarded. Now that humans have the symbiont, they'll become smarter, and more aware of our existence. The resulting combination should speed up their rate of technological advancement, and possibly our own."

He swallowed, digesting the information with the liquid. "I see. So we can effectively toss all our equations out the window."

"The ones regarding human development, at any rate. Let's just hope the aliens haven't returned to a sophisticated home planet and developed or stolen technological advances we can't predict." She drank deeply.

"Leaving us Martians caught in the middle again?" He gave her a droll smile.

She laughed, and then became serious. "Did we ever find out if their tests on humans succeeded? They were somewhat confused about human anatomy, but sometimes blundering and stupidity succeed where brilliance fails."

"Ah, their hybrid projects. I never did see the final report, that was *Darcy's* responsibility." He furrowed his eyebrows. "With the spread of the symbiont, I suspect we'll know soon enough. You should keep alert for anyone who seems to pass on the symbiont without developing it."

Kelly's eyes popped open wide. "Lyle! We have to find him, immediately!"

"Who's Lyle?"

Kelly placed her right hand over his left cheek. "Mindlink with me, Admiral." A green data stream flashed in the space between them. The Admiral's eyes took it all, from the encounter between Lyle and Jerod at the hospital to Liz Zephyr's story about the street preacher.

He jumped to his feet. "I'll get right on it. All units will be informed."

Kelly was half way to the living room. "Jerod!" she called out. "Where are you?"

Jerod came running. "What's wrong?"

"We need to find Lyle immediately. Contact Dr. Athens. His wife's in law enforcement. She should be able to help us."

*   *   *   *

Mandeep and Mo were sitting at the café, a nearly empty pot of coffee between them. "It's not what I had in mind for contributing to the next the generation," Mandeep said.

"But it would be a contribution, nonetheless. What do you think the chances are that we'll ever find mates? I know most of the others have, but I mean you and me?"

Mandeep chewed on his lip. "We look too much like we're from their Middle East, I think. Maybe if we had Coren change our faces, North American women would be more attracted to us. They're friendly, but it doesn't seem to be enough."

"I don't want to look like anyone else," Mo said. "It just wouldn't be me in the mirror every morning." He sighed. "Being tall, dark and handsome doesn't seem to do the trick for us."

Mandeep stared at the coffee pot. "Rene and Gail. If it worked, they'd sort of be like our daughters."

Mo shrugged. "Maybe. Darcy's pretty possessive of his family. I guess that's why he's so desperate to see if anything can be done for them. You know, it's hard to believe he was evil for so long, that he did so much damage before he was discovered. And now that he's taking care of his symbiont, he's just a big teddy bear."

Mandeep nodded. "This is the real man, the one he would have always been if his symbiont hadn't been deprived of protein. If he's like this, his daughters can't help but become solid citizens."

"Yes, but keep in mind, they'd also be the granddaughters of the Matriarch. A lot of their nature will come from her. Darcy can't take all the credit." Mo finished his coffee.

"For the Matriarch's sake, I could make the sacrifice."

Mo held up his empty cup. "So could I. For the Matriarch, then."

They tapped their mugs together. With a frown, Mo inspected the one Mandeep was holding. "Did you just chip your cup?"

*   *   *   *

Darcy's arm encircled his wife's shoulders. "This is it," he said.

Megan said nothing. She leaned against his side, biting her lower lip. They watched Coren activate the computer program.

Two reconfiguration chambers slid into place. Coren gave them a sidelong glance as he manipulated the controls. He didn't dare use the extra energy required for the computer's voice recognition program. Like any dangerous new procedure, this one made him nervous. He wondered if this was similar to the way the fictional Doctor Frankenstein felt when trying to bring his creature to life. What if it failed? What if it worked?

Failure would mean the final dashing of hope for an already distraught family. It would also mean incredible disappointment for the two men who cared enough to donate their potential for a future. And according to Martian law, this kind of failure would prohibit further experimentation with this application of technology.

But if it worked a whole new branch of science would be created. Hope could be provided in a few otherwise hopeless situations. At least for a time, until they were out of men who hadn't Been Blued. And two people, women who were lost to them, would be restored. A family would be made whole. Yes, he decided, it was a risk worth taking, in spite of his initial hesitation. He smiled as he entered the final instructions for the computer.

In a matter of minutes, Rene and Gail emerged from the chambers. The two young women were darker skinned than their parents, with short, jet black hair and large, dark brown eyes. They stepped forward and went to the racks of clothing. They got dressed and returned to Darcy and Megan. They both spoke in sultry tones as they comforted their parents.

Coren fought back the tears forming in his eyes. He breathed deeply, as his symbiont swirled freely throughout his face and neck. Soon he found himself surrounded by the grateful family. He let his own tears flow.

CHAPTER 21

▼

HYBRID PROBLEMS

Lyle sighed. Life had improved since the encounter with the strange man at the hospital several months ago, but something still wasn't right. He'd been trying to figure out what was bothering him. The memories he'd lost to years of drug abuse were gradually being restored, something he couldn't explain but felt he shouldn't push his luck with. There was still something he needed to make restitution for, something that might make everything fall into place.

He stirred his coffee, his newest, and now his only addiction. The waiter brought him the peanut butter and jelly sandwich he ordered. The old man gave him a quizzical look as he ate.

"We don't have many people asking for PB and J sandwiches. Anything else I can get you?"

Lyle looked up at him. "Can you sit for a while?"

Mo looked around. There were no other customers at the moment. He took a chair. "All right. For a while. Now, what's on your mind?"

"I'm not sure. I think I need ... I think I need to buy a puppy."

"A puppy? What makes you think that?"

"I don't know, exactly. I get these impressions of things I should do, without knowing why. Usually I go and do them, and things seem to work out good."

"So what do you think you're supposed to do with the puppy?"

"I think I'm supposed to give it to someone. I don't know who, yet."

Mo tilted his head and furrowed his eyebrows. The young man showed signs of contact with a symbiont but hadn't developed one. Obviously the fellow's previous lifestyle had been ugly and destructive. The symbionts wouldn't have liked that, but they'd still had some influence on him. Maybe it was just a matter of cleaning him up before his own symbiont could form.

Mo tried to make telepathic contact. It was no use; this mind was somehow impervious to his probing. At a loss for what to do next, Mo resorted to his humanity. "What kind of puppy?" he asked.

Lyle brightened. "A cute gray miniature poodle with curly fur." His face fell. "Oh, no. Oh my god, no." He buried his face in his hands.

Mo put a hand on his shoulder. "What's wrong?"

Lyle looked up, his face wet with tears. "I shot their little dog. They were just having fun, playing in a pool, and I shot their little dog. I can't believe I did that."

"Lyle Jenkins?"

He turned to the voice behind him. "Yes, Officer?"

The brunette policewoman placed a hand on his shoulder. "I'm placing you under arrest for outstanding warrants and the careless discharge of a firearm. Please stand up slowly and place your arms behind your back."

"Of course, Officer." Lyle obeyed the instructions. "Looks like I have to go, Mo." He turned to the officer. "There's a ten dollar bill in my wallet if you'd pay the man for me. I don't need to be charged with an eat and run crime on top of everything else."

Mo shook his head. "That's not necessary. His sandwich and coffee are on the house."

"Wouldn't hear of it," she responded, taking out Lyle's wallet and handing Mo the money. She winked at the old man, as a small red streak encircled her eye, and then disappeared.

Mo tucked the money in his apron. "Thank you, Officer Zephyr. Please let me know if I can help in any way."

*   *   *   *

Lyle stared at the policeman sitting in the front passenger seat. "You look vaguely familiar."

Jerod turned towards him and removed his hat and sunglasses. "Do I?"

Lyle's memory of the night at the hospital surfaced. "Hey, you're the guy who fixed Hallie and me. I've been wanting to thank you."

"Don't thank me yet. Do you remember your parents?"

"I was an orphan. Never knew who my parents were."

"No, you're an alien hybrid your species left behind to infiltrate Earth."

Lyle's mouth fell open. "You're serious, aren't you?"

"Dead serious."

Lyle looked at the woman officer sitting in the driver's seat. Red swirls were present in her neck. Similar ones were running through the hand Jerod had placed on the headrest. Lyle swallowed hard. "I'm in more trouble than I thought. What should I do?"

Jerod's eyebrows went up. He hadn't expected the humanity to overwhelm the alien nature. He cleared his throat. "We'll take you to our chief geneticist. He should be able to help you."

"Good. I don't want to be a monster. Since you straightened me out, I've helped sixty-three prostitutes get off the street. Tonight I realized I need to buy a puppy to replace the dog I shot when I kidnapped two little girls. I hope they're okay."

"They're fine." It was all Jerod could think of to say. He nodded to his temporary partner. She started the cruiser and drove off.

✳   ✳   ✳   ✳

Coren paced in the lab. The information Jerod was sending him telepathically was somewhat disturbing. The hybrid had been taken without difficulty. It had seemed willing, even relieved, to submit to their authority. It wasn't acting like any of the hybrids they'd had experience with. It was showing remorse for wrongs it had committed, and seemed to be looking to them for some kind of help. How could he kill such a creature? Or trust it enough to allow it to live? And could he help it, if it was deemed to be a creature of conscience?

Had it summoned its progenitors from deep space? Was that why they were returning to Earth after having been soundly defeated? Or, as far-fetched as it seemed, had they finally learned to compromise and live in peace?

He shook his head. Too many questions without answers. He turned and took the coffee cup Katy offered. Funny, he hadn't noticed her enter but had still been aware of her imminent actions.

"You're thinking too hard," she scolded. "That's why you didn't notice me come in."

He swallowed half the cup before handing it back to her. "We have a *big* problem."

She shrugged. "So check the hybrid for alien DNA and replace anything you find with the human equivalent. You're not even worried about his 'human rights' but he's been behaving as a real person to this point. He doesn't want to be evil, and the thought of being an alien must scare him to death. That fear was probably what started him on the path of crime in the first place. He probably thought if he was as bad a person as he could be, at least he'd prove he was human, not alien."

"You're saying he was always aware of being an alien hybrid?" Coren found the idea disturbing.

"On some level. He knew he was different, but didn't dare to think that might be the reason. You saw the relief in his mind when Jerod explained bringing him here to you."

"I wonder if I could help him. We've always just killed hybrids in the past, since they were little more than killing machines."

"You might not want to tell him *that* right away."

Coren frowned. "If he really is human, the truth won't destroy him. Besides, it's not my decision to make. The Matriarch's authority is absolute on matters like this. The hybrid's life is in her hands, not mine. If we show him mercy, it's entirely her doing."

"Kelly won't be back from Europe for a few days. What'll you do with him until then?"

"Follow protocol. Restrain and pacify him."

CHAPTER 22

▼

HYBRID SOLUTIONS

Jerod felt the strange sensation of being woken up by his symbiont. He tried to wipe the sleep out of his eyes before sitting up. There was someone else in the room.

"Mr. President?"

The President was sitting on the edge of the bed. Jerod looked around for the Secret Service men. "They're in the limo. They weren't happy about it, but at least my symbiont was successful in assuring theirs I wouldn't be in any danger."

"Sorry to wake you up like this, but something's come to my attention and I need answers."

Jerod covered a yawn. "What is it?"

"This *individual* you have in custody, Lyle Jenkins. You claim he's an alien hybrid?"

"That's right. Good thing we found him, too. Space only knows what damage he might have done."

The President stood up and started pacing. "I'm afraid we have a problem. As far as I know, he's an American citizen who's been apprehended and held without trial or counsel. He's innocent until proven guilty in a court of law."

Jerod blinked. The symbiont raced through his brain, erasing all trace of sleepiness. "Mr. President, this alien hybrid offered no resistance or objection when we apprehended it according to our laws. It didn't even *try* to claim to be human, and it certainly didn't insist on the rights of an American citizen."

"What would you have done if he did?"

"I don't know. I suppose we would have contacted you."

"Uh, huh. You should have contacted me anyway. I'd like to see him once you're dressed."

*   *   *   *

Jerod stopped in front of the door to the computer room. "I know your symbiont's already informed you about the hybrid's current state, but you still might want to prepare yourself for a shock." He led the President inside.

One of the reconfiguration chambers was in place, filled with a transparent blue haze. Lyle was suspended as if draped over an unseen bar inside.

"What have you done to him?" the President whispered.

Coren joined them. "It's in stasis. Poor thing hasn't slept in over a year. The illegal drugs kept it from resting; a common means the aliens use to fight fatigue. They think sleep makes for weakness, so they try to avoid it. They're not only mean, they tend to be intoxicated and sleep deprived."

"What makes you so sure he's an alien hybrid? He looks human to me."

Coren tilted his head. "You think so? Computer, open the mouth of the hybrid subject."

Lyle's mouth gaped open to reveal ghastly fangs and a forked tongue inside a blue mouth.

Coren spoke with the enthusiasm of a kid with a new toy. "See the discoloration in the mouth? The hybrid's blood circulates in a whole different way. It makes six complete trips through the body *before* oxygenation. At any given moment, there's less than thirty percent of oxygenated blood in its system. Want to see its real skin color?"

The President shook his head. "No. I think I'd lose my supper. And don't even think about showing me his scales." He shook his head. "But I can't get past the fact that his human rights have been violated."

Coren blinked. "It's not exactly human, Mr. President. I don't know what else we can do to verify that for you."

Jerod put his hand the President's shoulder. "In the interest of cooperation with your administration, I suggest you appoint one of your own people as council for the hybrid. That way you can see it's fairly treated by your own standards. And if we discover Lyle is more human than alien, your laws will be respected regarding him. But you may want to keep in mind; at this point he's an illegal alien by definition of both our governments. He was born in space, not the USA."

"I don't know whether to laugh or not. But your proposal is acceptable."

Coren shrugged. "Do you want to tell him or should I?"

"Tell me what?"

Jerod gave him a twisted half smile. "Mr. President, this is the man who kidnapped your goddaughter and her friend with the intent of turning them into prostitutes."

"What? How do you know that?"

"Just before we apprehended him, he was talking to Mo about replacing the poodle he shot to trick them into getting into the van."

The President gasped. "Talk about taking the wind out of one's sails. And to think I was just berating you for not giving him a fair shake."

"Justice is blind, Mr. President. Fortunately, mercy is not. It was Jerod's initial interference with Lyle that caused him to return the girls unharmed. I hope that answers your fears about how fairly we'll treat this hybrid. For now, we'll err on the side of our own justice and safety."

"What will you do with him?"

Coren flicked his head up and Lyle's mouth closed. "First, we'll get it rested up. It requires a few more days in stasis before its genetic memory can be accessed. Then it may remember enough to speak for itself. There is a chance we might be able to make a human out of him. But we need more information, which the computer can acquire while he's in stasis."

The computer started beeping. The President nearly jumped. "What's that?"

Coren frowned. "I'm not sure. Computer, what's the problem?"

"Subject is exhibiting intolerance of dietary infusion."

"Can it be corrected?"

"Affirmative. Switching to high protein formula indicated by changes in subject's physiology. Subject is responding."

Coren and Jerod looked at each other. The President looked at both of them. "What does this mean?"

Coren stepped up to the chamber and put his hands on its outer walls. "Fascinating. They do their best thinking during their sleep cycle. Normally they shun protein as much as possible. This one may have figured out that it can't develop a symbiont on a normal hybrid diet. It must want to become human very badly."

The President turned to Jerod. "What can you tell me about his alien side? What kind of people are they?"

"Remember the Roswell incidents; several reports of anal probing and the like? The aliens don't have a solid grasp of human anatomy. They tried their best to correlate their body configuration with that of a human. They mistook the human rectum for a mouth. One of the easiest things a doctor can do is ask a patient to open his mouth and say 'ah.'"

"You're joking."

"These aliens are no laughing matter. They wanted to learn as much about humans as they could in order to eradicate them."

"But, why? What did we ever do to them?"

"We denied them this planet. Twice. The first time, it got our people out into space. That was several thousand years ago. We returned in time to thwart their second attempt. I assume it's been too long for them to actually remember what they knew about humans back then. We planted a virus in their ships' computers to slowly corrupt their data, so the humans they found were nothing like what they expected. That must have been a surprise."

"What do they call themselves?"

Coren came over to them. "They don't have a name for themselves. They don't refer to themselves at all. If you want to know what they're like, just remember that the word 'alien' means 'not like us.' We can show you what they look like and break down their anatomy for you, but it seems their collective and individual personalities all agree on one thing; destructiveness. The only way we'll know if there might be hope for Lyle is if he doesn't kill us when he wakes up."

"You mean we're in danger as long as he's in the same room?"

Jerod snorted. "No, we're in danger as long as he's on the same planet. We've already taken the Coordinator and his family to a place of relative safety, all things considered, and I'd suggest you do the same for yourself and your staff."

"What about the Matriarch?"

"She's coordinating our people overseas. It's a real morale booster for them to meet her in person. She'll be returning here in a few days. If there's anything left to return to. If not, it'll be up to her to destroy him."

"Why would you take such a risk? You seem like such responsible people most of the time."

"Because of what you'd call a 'faint hope clause.' We keep hoping there's a chance we can find one of them who isn't a monster. Lyle might turn out to be the bridge of communication between humans and the hostile aliens. That's why we haven't eradicated his alien DNA. If he loses too much of it, he won't be able to communicate with them."

Coren had started pushing buttons on the computer console. "I wonder how much of his own DNA he'll change. We've allowed him some leeway to turn himself into who he really wants to become. In the past three hours he's accessed most of his human genes and altered thirty percent of the alien DNA. I have an idea, but it's risky."

The President peered over his shoulder, pretending to read the foreign symbols on the terminal in front of them. "What is it?"

"If the three of us place our hands in the same spot on the chamber at the same time, and will our symbionts to effect a transference, we might enable him to develop his own symbiont. His protein levels are now high enough to support one."

Jerod peered over his other shoulder. "They should be. Look at how much protein he's absorbed. He'll either develop a symbiont or obesity."

"Or it could be a trick to lull us into a false sense of security," Coren suggested.

The President rubbed his forehead. Red swirls followed the tracing of his fingers. "All right. I'm in. Let's see if we can help him."

The three of them approached the chamber. Lyle's face seemed to relax. They put their hands on the chamber and focused their concentration. Red swirls appeared in their fingertips.

His eyes still closed, Lyle placed his hands against the inside of the chamber, in the same spot as theirs. His hands turned the same shade of red as their symbionts. The red streaks traveled up his arms and flowed through his face. His hair changed to a light blond, and the telltale pockmarks of extended drug use disappeared from his face. He mouthed the words, 'thank you,' from human looking teeth and lips.

The computer started beeping, and then announced, "Subject will awaken in five minutes."

"Computer, what about his alien sleep cycle?" Coren asked.

"Alien sleep cycle is no longer required for this subject. Physiology is ninety-two percent human. Symbionts are acting within normal parameters."

Coren squinted. "Symbionts? Computer, how many symbionts does the subject have?"

"Three. Now four. Now five. Now six. Subject has a total of six symbionts."

"Computer, that's *not* normal."

"Normal is relative. Six symbionts are currently required for the complete health and stability of this individual."

Jerod shrugged. "Stability is good. Isn't it?"

Coren looked at the two of them. "That depends. Even with eight percent of an alien physiology, he might still be dangerous. 'Stability' might just turn out to be evil genius in his case."

The President was staring at Lyle. "I don't think he means to harm us. I think he just wants a chance to make restitution, like he was doing before you apprehended him."

Lyle's eyes opened. He gazed at the President and nodded meekly.

"It could be a trick," Coren whispered.

"I don't think so," Jerod responded. "I'm willing to accept custody of Lyle if you think he's ready for release."

"Okay, then," Coren responded. He tapped the console and the walls of the chamber slid downward.

Lyle stood up straight. "I haven't been this hungry since I quit the drugs. Can we go eat now?"

The President smiled. "I think I know a place."

CHAPTER 23

▼

FEEDING FRENZY

Mo barely recognized the young man walking in with Jerod, Coren and the President. He looked a little bit like Lyle. The fellow came right up to him and gave him a bear hug.

"You're the best friend I ever had, Mo. Thanks for listening to me before. And for feeding me."

Mo gasped. "You have *six* symbionts? How'd you manage that?"

Lyle backed off. "I guess that's what it takes to keep the alien part of me in line. But they require a lot of protein. Is there any of that chicken pot pie left?"

Mo clapped his hands together. "Of course. I just finished baking a dozen more. They're still hot." Beaming, he hurried to the kitchen.

Some of the Secret Service men pulled a few of the tables together. Everyone sat down.

"It seems you've made a friend here," the President noted.

"Mo's been a friend to almost everyone he meets. It's people like him who give people like me some hope."

Mo brought a huge tray filled with steaming chicken potpies to the table. Lyle was halfway through the first one in seconds. Without a word, Mo returned with plates and cutlery. He picked up the now empty pie tin and came back again with another tray of pies.

Coren watched with fascination. "Do you think you'll always need this much food or will your metabolism slow down after a while?"

Mo brought pitchers of water and drinking glasses. Lyle took a long swig of water. "I think it will slow down after a few days. The aliens can go for months without a decent meal, but they never had symbionts swimming through their bodies." He neatly cut up one of the pies and placed a piece on a plate. "Sorry for my lack of manners. I do know how to use cutlery, but Mo's such a good cook and I was so hungry."

Mo was now standing behind him. "Would you like some coffee? I could just leave the pot."

Lyle nodded. "That'd be great. Thank you." He deftly shifted plates and utensils in front of everyone else. "Surely, you're not going to make me eat all this food by myself."

Coren shook his head. "Of course not. But if you don't mind, we'll monitor you for a while. We've never had an alien among us who wants to eat something other than us before."

"Ah, but those aliens never tasted chicken. Funny, you'd think with all those farms they attacked …"

The secret service men snapped to attention. Coren, Jerod and the President exchanged glances.

"How did you know about that?" the President asked.

Lyle looked up, surprised at the tension in the room. "Oh. I'm sorry. It seems I have a certain degree of genetic memory." He paused, nearly breaking into tears. "Those poor people. I'm so sorry. And what we did to the cattle …"

His face brightened. "Say, what does beef taste like?"

Mo placed a plate of cheeseburgers in front of him. "I noticed you never ordered meat before, so when you came in changed tonight, I thought I'd better be prepared."

Lyle dug into one. Through bites of burger and sips of coffee, he managed to speak. "So tasty. Mo, you are definitely the next one we kidnap."

The room fell silent, with all eyes on Lyle. He looked around, a twinkle in his eye. "Gotcha!" He swallowed and burst out laughing.

Jerod spoke up. "It might be a bit too soon for jokes like that."

"Forgive me. I didn't mean to offend you."

Coren reached for his fork. "I think we should all have something. This has been a stressful evening. Eat up. Doctor's orders."

*   *   *   *

Rene and Gail entered the café. Mo dropped the cloth on the table he was wiping and greeted them with enthusiasm. "I'm so glad we were able to help you ladies."

Rene smiled coyly at him. "We talked it over and decided there might be something we can do for you."

"And Mandeep," Gail added.

Mandeep came out of the back. "I thought I heard my name being mentioned." He stopped and stared at the two women.

Gail crossed the room and hugged him. "Thank you. I wouldn't exist if it wasn't for you."

Mandeep looked at Mo, his eyes wide, his arms hanging limply by his sides. "What should I do?" he whispered.

Mo ignored him as Rene gave him a long, deep kiss. Mandeep noted the blue coloring on his friend's face just before Gail's lips found his.

Lyle started to come out of the kitchen, then turned around and blocked Jerod with his arm. "So, with six symbionts, does that mean I'll get to have six wives?"

Coren scowled at him. "I hope not. I have enough patients to tend to."

Lyle grinned. "With what's going on out there, you'd better get ready for some more."

Jerod peered around one of the swinging doors. "Rene and Gail. They've just Blued Mo and Mandeep."

Coren's frown deepened. "Is that ethical?"

Lyle smirked. "Now, he worries about ethics."

Jerod shrugged. "It'll have to be. Once a man's Been Blued, there's no fixing it."

"How does one go about getting himself 'Blued?' I know I used to be a pimp, but I've never actually, uh, you know …"

Coren cocked an eyebrow at him. "Mated? Are you serious?"

"I was never *human* before. I might have looked like one, but it was all appearance, no substance. My symbionts have been informing me of what I've been missing." He looked between the swinging doors. "The aliens would be willing to give up everything they are for what humans take advantage of so easily." He turned back to Jerod. "It seems to mean a lot more if it's given freely, without somebody paying for it."

Jerod smiled. "It might seem that way, but without commitment, it often leads to pain and suffering."

Lyle let it sink in. "I think I'm starting to understand." He closed his eyes and fell to the floor.

Coren rushed over to him. He knelt down and scanned him with his handheld computer. "I wish I knew what this meant. He's lost a symbiont."

"What do mean, he's *lost* a symbiont? How can that happen?" Jerod's voice was almost hysterical as he dropped to his knees beside Lyle.

"The computer says he only has *five* symbionts now, not six. And there's something else."

"What?"

"I don't know. I'm trying to figure out what it means. His physiology is altering itself. Wait, I think I know what's happening. He's erasing more of the alien DNA. His protein levels are off the chart. What the Hell?"

"I doubt Hell has anything to do with it. Keep an eye on his symbiont count." Jerod held Lyle's face. Fading pink swirls rippled through his hands.

"He's down to *four,* now *three,* now *two.* Now he has just *one.* "

"Just like the rest of us," Jerod sighed. "Any alien DNA left in him?"

"Not a trace. He won't be able to communicate with the aliens for us."

Jerod stood up. "Maybe that's just as well. He has to *live* with *us.* As long as he had alien DNA we couldn't fully trust him."

Coren got up. "Maybe this is the answer. If Lyle can become human after being a hybrid, maybe the aliens can too. There aren't that many genetic differences between our species. Maybe the symbionts can form the bridge to span them."

Lyle sat up. "What happened to me?"

Coren helped him to his feet. "You're human now, practically one of us."

"Yeah? And my wife? How do I go about finding her?"

Jerod and Coren smiled.

"Uh, it's not that simple," Jerod offered. "Usually she finds you. None of us were expecting to have Been Blued."

"Yeah, but it's happening all over the place now, isn't it? Now that the symbionts are fully awake, we're irresistible, right? Wasn't that the point of coming back to Earth, for love and family?"

"He's got us there, Coren," Jerod teased. "How does our science respond to that?"

Coren scowled. "With a big dose of skepticism. There's no way to predict love."

Jerod tilted his head. "I think I might have an idea."

CHAPTER 24

▼

OLD FRIENDS

Lyle was finishing his second burger. He'd barely touched the fries on his plate. Having one symbiont instead of six had really put a dent in his appetite. He drank the last of his coffee. It had been another delicious meal, but he was feeling lonely. Rene was taking up most of Mo's time now and the café's new host wasn't as attentive to him. He cheered up a little when Jerod walked in and sat down, all smiles.

"Hey," Lyle said between swallows.

"I think maybe you should be taught some table manners, Mr. Jenkins."

Lyle stopped eating and frowned. In all his life, the only person to have ever called him 'mister' was the parole officer assigned to him when he was eight. Surely the symbiont would have informed Jerod of the bad connotation.

"I don't understand."

Jerod glanced over Lyle's shoulder. He realized someone had walked up behind him while Jerod had kept him distracted. He turned and looked at the blonde standing beside him. She wore a fitted blouse and a black skirt. Silver bangles dangled on her left arm.

She was vaguely familiar. One fist on her hip, she raised an eyebrow. He recognized the gesture. "Hallie?" he gasped.

He jumped to his feet and grabbed her shoulders. "Is it really you?" He patted her arms and looked her over. "Are you okay? How's your head, I'm so sorry I hurt you. I didn't mean it, I didn't mean any of it."

The tilt of her head made him shut up. "Forget it, Lyle. I wasn't sure if I really wanted to see you again, but I'm glad you're okay. Jerod told me everything. I'm glad those girls are okay, too."

Lyle slumped in his chair. "I can hardly believe what we nearly did to them. I'm going to buy them another poodle to replace the one I shot. I've been so hungry since they apprehended me, I nearly forgot."

"Why don't we go look for one together? I feel partly responsible."

He looked up at her. "Really?" He looked at Jerod. "Can we?"

Jerod considered the question. "Your judgment is still pending. Anywhere you go until then, I go with you."

Hallie looked at him. "His judgment? Apparently you *didn't* tell me everything."

"Under Martian law, Lyle is still a potentially hostile alien. That means he's in my custody until the Matriarch decides his fate. But making restitution for past wrongs can only speak in his favor. I'll drive you to the animal shelter."

"Think of him as a really old chaperone," Lyle offered.

Jerod raised an eyebrow. "Old? Next thing I know, you'll be calling me repressed again."

"That mouth of yours always did get you into trouble, Lyle. When we get there, you'd better let us do the talking."

*   *   *   *

The noise of yapping and barking greeted them upon opening the car doors at the dog shelter. Lyle remained in the back seat of the car after Jerod and Hallie got out. "What's wrong, Lyle?" Hallie asked.

"Flashbacks. I was bitten by a large dog when I was seven."

Jerod pulled him out by the arm. "Let the symbiont deal with those memories. It makes things much easier."

Lyle stood up. "Wow, it sure does. I'm not afraid now. And the dogs have stopped barking."

Jerod nodded. "The animals on this planet are almost compatible enough to develop the symbionts. Not quite, but close enough to make them friendly to us. Any animal sounds you hear now will either be friendly or vocalized in warning of some threat."

They stepped inside the door with the *open* sign on it. A calico laying in a basket on the counter yawned, licked a paw and got up to greet them. It purred as Jerod rubbed its chin.

"Where's the receptionist?" Hallie wondered.

A plump, middle-aged woman entered the room from a side door. Her white smock bore various colors of stains. A baseball cap covered her bald head. She looked them over while rubbing her bare, red forearms. "It's the cats. The girl who looks after them is sick today. Me, it's allergies. I usually just look after the dogs. Strangest thing, though, them all suddenly being nice and quiet like this."

Jerod inspected the rash on her arm. "Do you put anything on this?" he asked. The red swirls in his fingers caused red streaks to form along the irritated skin. The rash began to fade.

"Not usually. I just try to avoid the kitties. Guess I don't have to now. Thanks to you." She gave him a little smile. "So the cancer won't be coming back either?"

He shook his head. "Not ever. Just tell your doctor you feel fine."

Red swirls ran through her face. "I see you'll be needing a poodle puppy. I think I have a few you might be interested in. They're the standards, not the miniatures, but they're easy to train. Wait here."

Hallie was smiling. "I didn't think there was anybody left who didn't have a symbiont."

"One less person now," Lyle said.

The woman came back with two puppies in a box. "Here we are. These two haven't been named yet, but their shots are all up to date. Why don't you take both of them?"

"We might have to bring one back," Jerod cautioned.

"That's all right. I have a feeling you'll find them both a good home." She lowered her voice. "I wasn't supposed to tell you, but their mum sees a good future for these two if you take them both. Poodles can sense these things, you know."

Lyle frowned. "You're kidding."

The woman removed her cap to reveal quickly growing red hair. "I could read the minds of dogs long before the symbiont. Now they're even more clear to me."

Jerod patted Lyle on the shoulder. "Concentrate." He winked at the woman. "Can't you hear the dogs' thoughts?"

Hallie half-closed her eyes. "One's scared to be here, three others are trying to comfort him, and the mother poodle just hopes all her little ones will find good humans to love."

Lyle squeezed his eyes shut. "I can't hear them. I can't hear anything. All the symbiont tells me is …" He opened his eyes and swatted Jerod. "You're all making fun of me!"

Jerod and the shelter woman laughed. Hallie giggled. "Yes, but it took three of us to do it. We wouldn't have been able to if it was any one of us by ourselves."

Lyle looked into the box. "Can you believe what they just did to me?"

Both dogs covered his face with puppy kisses.

*   *   *   *

Amber and Alison worked on a castle in their sandbox. They ignored the four men in black suits and dark sunglasses surrounding them. They failed to notice when all four men turned towards the back gate. The simultaneous clicks of four guns being cocked was the sound that made them look up.

Jerod stepped through the gate first. The men in black relaxed their stance and put the guns away. They glanced at each other as Lyle came into the yard carrying the box. Hallie followed with a box containing kibble and various other dog care items.

The first man glanced into the boxes, and then smiled. He and all but one of his men resumed their guarding positions.

Lyle crouched a short distance away from the girls and put the box down gently. "Hello, girls. I owe you an apology."

Amber and Alison eyed him warily. "What's an apoplexy?" Amber asked.

"I think he said 'apology,'" Alison stated. "It means he says he's sorry."

Lyle nodded as he reached into the box. "Right. And I have something to make up for what I did. That's if your parents will let you keep these guys."

He put the poodles on the ground. They ran to the girls.

Amber hugged the one that came to her. Alison lifted the other one into the air. Both girls were squealing with delight.

"I'm naming mine Kiko Two," Amber said.

"I'm naming mine Curly," Alison responded.

Jerod crossed his arms in front of him. "I don't think there'll be any problem. Do you, Hallie? Hallie?"

Hallie was staring into the eyes of the largest man in black. He took off his sunglasses and pulled out his earpiece. The box of dog care supplies sat on the ground between them. Lyle's mouth dropped open. He started to move towards them. Jerod blocked him with a hand. "Time we were getting back," he said. "Nice seeing you again, girls, Hallie. Come on, Lyle."

Lyle continued to stare at Hallie as Jerod pulled him out of the yard by the arm.

*   *   *   *

"I don't get it, I thought Hallie was my future wife," Lyle protested as he put on his seatbelt.

"She was part of your old life, Lyle. Don't forget, you weren't exactly human back then. You merely used her for your own profit."

He sighed. "I suppose I did. But still, now that I am human, I guess I just assumed she would be mine."

"Really? Why?"

"Hallie was the only girl to take me seriously. All the others just laughed. She was nice to me. That's why I ..."

Jerod started the car. "That's why you what?"

"Nothing." He looked out the window. "I just, well, I guess I was wrong."

Jerod shrugged as he eased the car into gear. "Even with the symbionts, nobody's right all the time."

Lyle looked back at him with animosity. "You got that right." He pulled his sleeves over his wrists to conceal the formation of dark green scales.

*   *   *   *

Jerod couldn't shake the strange feeling that kept him from thinking clearly. He had brought Lyle back to the main computer control room but couldn't remember why. He pushed the door open and looked in with glazed eyes. "Coren, I think there's something wrong with me."

Lyle let go of the back of his neck, pulling his wrist talon out of Jerod's spine. Jerod fell to the floor. Blood trickled from the injury.

Coren looked up from the clipboard he was holding, his eyes wide with alarm.

Darcy's smile faded as he took in Jerod's limp form. "I thought you said his alien DNA had been eradicated," he whispered.

"It was. Totally. I don't understand this at all."

Lyle smirked at them. "It's true. I am human. But I found the symbionts' weakness. I'm almost surprised you didn't catch on, with all your 'smarts,' Doctor. Reducing the number of symbionts in my system to one, that should have been your first clue. But like most humans, you only saw what you wanted to see. And like any human, I reverted to my true nature when I realized I couldn't have what I wanted. I suppose Hallie's already married to that other guy. Martian law, and all that."

Coren tilted his head. "So you say the symbionts have a weakness. We'd love to know what that is."

Lyle stormed towards him and grabbed his shoulders. With surprising strength, he lifted Coren into the air and threw him to the floor. "This isn't about you, it's about *me!*" he roared.

Darcy stepped in front of him. "That's enough of that!" He grabbed Lyle's arms and yanked out the talons growing from his wrists. Blood gushed from the wounds.

Lyle howled in pain, as he fell to his knees.

Kelly entered the room and stepped over Jerod. She gave Darcy a nod. He picked Lyle up and carried him to a reconfiguration chamber. The walls slid into place.

"Computer, execute extreme scan of subject in chamber. Analyze its current genetic profile. Record, and then purge any non-human or non-symbiont DNA present. Reduce subject to its resulting life form."

Coren shook his head and struggled to get up. Darcy helped him to his feet.

Kelly glared at him. "Why was the hybrid removed from the chamber ahead of schedule?" she demanded.

"My apologies, Matriarch. We witnessed his development of six symbionts and he tried very hard to change all of his alien DNA to human. Even the President asked us to consider his human rights. At first he thought Lyle was an American citizen."

Kelly continued to glare at him. "I'm surprised at you. Have you forgotten what we learned fifteen hundred years ago?"

Coren felt his strength returning, although Kelly's stare unnerved him. "That DNA is only the physical part of an individual. The nature of the individual cannot be so easily set aside."

"*And,* the fact that some species hide their DNA within the strands of others. What you did only erased some of the camouflage layers of DNA."

"Lyle was right. We only saw what we wanted to see."

Kelly looked at the figure writhing in the chamber. "Never mind. He did a convincing job of playing human. I might have even been fooled."

Coren shook his head. "No, Matriarch, we were the fools. And it still might cost Jerod his life."

Her look softened. "Do the best you can. I'll deal with our *guest.*"

Darcy picked Jerod up and brought him to another reconfiguration platform. Coren sighed deeply and began pushing buttons.

CHAPTER 25

▼

REHAB

The President, flanked by four men in black suits, entered the computer control room. Kelly stood with her arms crossed in front of her, a grave look on her face. "Mr. President, I'm afraid I have some bad news for you. I thought you should see this for yourself and I wanted you to be adequately protected in case anything else goes wrong. That's why I ordered the bodyguards to accompany you."

The President stared at the chamber Lyle was in. "I apologize, Matriarch, for trying to intervene on this alien's behalf. At first I thought you were detaining an American citizen without representation. You can see how I couldn't allow that."

"The explanation is unnecessary. But thank you. We're going to need to trust each other if Earth is to have a future. In light of that, I think it may be just about time to tell the world we're here. And I give you my personal promise that we're only here for the good of all humans. Most of the world now has the symbiont, and you've seen how dramatically the world political stage has changed. Wars have been reduced to skirmishes, without sacrificing human rights. Extremists have become moderates, at least in behavior. People still disagree, but usually without the desire to harm those with different opinions. Sexism is history, as are most other illogical prejudices."

The President nodded. "All it took was symbiosis with an alien life form."

"At least it's a benign alien life form. Unlike what once made up part of this individual."

The President looked at Lyle's unconscious form inside the chamber. "He looks the same as the last time I saw him. How could he have reverted to alien DNA?"

"He didn't. He reverted to alien personality traits. With a symbiont inside him, a single personal disappointment was enough to trigger vestigial cell memory. He started to become what he used to be before his true identity was hidden within layers of alien and human DNA."

"I don't understand. You're saying Lyle isn't a hybrid, but some other kind of alien?"

"It appears his species found a way to disguise his true nature from the hostile aliens we'll be facing. It was probably an attempt to save his life."

"Can you help him?"

Kelly planted her fists on her hips. "You're something else, you know that? When you found out Lyle was a kidnapper and a pimp, you wanted to execute him on the spot. Now that he's committed even worse crimes, you want us to help him?"

The President stepped back. "I know he's committed crimes against humanity. But if you can help him become human in a way that prevents him from reverting to his alien side, we may have a powerful weapon against other aliens. Besides, he was like a baby left on Earth's doorstep. It wasn't his fault that we didn't know how to look after him properly."

Kelly turned to look back at Lyle. "All right. But if he's going to live with humans, he'll have to grow up as a human. We'll restore him to his true nature later on."

"What are you going to do?"

"Lyle met Hallie when he was nine. Something about her triggered some alien instinct, so he aged himself and became her pimp. I'm going to return him to that age. Minus all alien DNA and memories, of course. It'll be up to you to find him a home."

"Will it be safe for human parents to look after him?"

"Yes. I'm instructing his symbiont to self-destruct at the first indication of violent tendencies. You must not inform his foster parents of this, since they might decide to try and counter it. That could return him to being a dangerous individual."

"Agreed. You've done more than I could have hoped, Matriarch. On behalf of the entire planet, I want to thank you for your mercy and your vigilance. How's Jerod doing?"

Tears streaked down Kelly's face. "We'll know in a few weeks. The damage to his nervous system was too severe to predict a recovery rate. And if he loses his symbiont he'll die."

The President hugged her. "I'm so sorry. It was all my fault. If there's anything I can do, if there's anything this country can do …"

She pulled away from him. "It wasn't your fault. None of us blame you. Jerod knew, better than anyone, the risks he was taking when he assumed custody of Lyle.

"But Mr. President, you have to prepare the world for an alien attack. They'll be here within a matter of decades. I've been working with the more responsible leaders in Europe, Asia and the Middle East. We may be able to bring the developing world up to speed in the time we have, but it will be a challenge."

"Don't worry, Matriarch. This time your people won't have to defend Earth alone and in secret. The whole world will be behind you."

*　　　*　　　*　　　*

Jerod opened his eyes. He seemed to be lying down. Everything he could see was white. There was no visible distinction between ceiling, walls or floor. He shook his head in an effort to clear it. The resulting contact with something hard underneath sent searing pain down the length of his spine, back up again and throughout his brain. He groaned and tried to remember what happened. The only thought that came to mind was that he was in a white room in one of the ships.

White Room. Why would he be in a white room? They were only used in extreme cases of medical emergency, and then only when one's symbiont was in danger. He held up his hand and squinted at it. It seemed to take forever for his eyes to focus, but finally he saw little red streaks swimming in his skin. He breathed a sigh of relief.

He hadn't seen or heard anyone enter the room but now there was a pretty woman standing over him. "Hello. Do I know you?"

Kelly picked up his hand and held it. "You don't remember who I am?"

Jerod closed his eyes. There was something pleasantly familiar about her, but he couldn't access all the right memories. "You're the Matriarch?" he asked, his eyes filled with admiration.

"Yes, that's right. If you remember that much, the rest will come in time. How do you feel?"

"Hungry. Thirsty. And a bit lonely. As if something's been taken away from me. I don't understand, I still have my symbiont. What happened to me?"

"You've had a terrible shock. An alien used a talon with a nerve spike to penetrate your spinal column. It seems to have absorbed some of your personality."

"That explains the pain."

"Use your symbiont to heal the damage. Do you remember how to do that?"

"No. Can you help me?"

Kelly put one hand behind his neck. The red in her palm was met by red streaks where she touched him.

Jerod felt the voids in his memories filling in. He reached up to touch her face. "You should sanction me, Sweetheart. I put so many lives at risk."

"What could I do to you that would be worse than the pain you've been enduring for the past three weeks?"

"Three weeks? I've lost that much time?"

"Yes, we have. Jerod, being your wife means a whole lot more than if I'd married a human. I feel everything your symbiont feels. My concern now is how much you'll remember when we're not near each other."

"What makes you think I'll forget?"

"You have every day for the last three weeks. This only seems like the first time I've visited you, but I've been here every single day. You've gotten stronger and you can finally access your own symbiont. But it's been a struggle for both of us."

He sat up and hugged her. "I'm sorry. I never meant to cause you pain."

"It's enough that you remember some of the time for now. Do you feel strong enough to come home?"

"Yes. Of course."

"Are you sure? Last time we only made it to the door."

"This time I'm not hallucinating about Lyle. Am I?"

"Not if you can remember enough to ask the question."

*   *   *   *

Jerod looked out the window of the limo. "'The Fill?' I thought we were going home."

Kelly got out and waited for him to join her. "This is part of our home. We own half the town, remember?"

Mo came out to greet them. He grabbed Jerod and hugged him. "Jerod! It's so good to see you again!"

Jerod blinked, his arms limp at his sides. "Who are you, again?"

Mo backed off, a distraught look on his face.

Jerod punched his shoulder. "Gotcha!"

Mo shook him by the shoulders. "Don't do that! I'm an old man. I nearly had a heart attack when they told me Lyle had attacked you."

"I'm sorry, Mo. It's good to see you, too. What's on the menu today?"

Mo smiled. "Anything you want."

*　　　*　　　*　　　*

Alison and Amber were barely visible as they walked their full-grown poodles towards the park. Large men in black suits surrounded them without hindering their progress. The two girls changed their pace at will, sometimes walking, sometimes skipping. The men kept up with brisk steps.

A father was pushing a blond boy on a swing. The child pointed to the men and asked his dad a question. The man shrugged.

Alison and Amber came towards the swings. The men in suits encircled the boy and his dad. The boy tilted his head and grinned at the girls and the dogs. The poodles ran up and licked his face. One of the men spoke to the boy's dad. He nodded.

Alison grinned. "I'm Alison. This is Amber. These are our poodles, Kiko Two and Curly. What's your name?"

The boy grinned back. "I'm Lyle. My last name used to be Jenkins, but I have parents now, so it's been changed to Andrews. I like having parents. Will you be my friends? I don't know anybody here yet."

The girls nodded. "Can you keep a secret?" Alison asked as she rubbed the toe of her shoe in the sand.

Lyle nodded. "Sure."

Alison whispered in his ear.

"Aliens?" he said. "Wow! Are we gonna fight them?"

Amber nodded. "The whole world is. We're gonna win!"

"That's 'cause we're the good guys!" Lyle said. "The good guys always win! Hey, let's go play on the slides!"

978-0-595-44843-2
0-595-44843-7

Printed in the United States
93553LV00003B/34-102/A

9 780595 448432